Readers love
SJD PETERSON

BAMF

"I loved that this book kept me guessing the entire time I was reading. I never knew what would happen or how the characters would react."

—Love Bytes

"I started this book when I went to bed one evening… At 5:15 the next morning, having never put it down all night, I finished the book. This is one book you REALLY can't put down!"

—Happily Ever After (*USA Today*)

"Big thumbs up and YES, to this book; another winner for SJD Peterson!"

—My Fiction Nook

Splintered

"This was an exciting, thrilling, sexy, book, and an intense ride… The author penned an intricate murder mystery, with a killer I wasn't expecting."

—Rainbow Book Reviews

"…it's definitely worthy of four stars. I'm going to look for more SJD Peterson books."

—On Top Down Under Book Reviews

Tuck & Cover

"The story was fun and sexy with enough depth in both of their struggles to come to terms with their sexuality within the confines of the military to be interesting."

—Live Your Life, Buy the Book

By SJD Peterson

BAMF
Beyond Duty
Leon
Masters & Boyd
A Night Never Forgotten
Plan B
Rival Within
Splintered
Tuck & Cover

GUARDS OF FOLSOM
Riveted
Pup
Tag Team
Pony
Roped

WHISPERING PINES RANCH
Lorcan's Desire
Quinn's Need
Ty's Obsession
Conner's Courage
Jess's Journey

Published by DREAMSPINNER PRESS
http://www.dreamspinnerpress.com

Rival
Within

SJD PETERSON

Dreamspinner Press

Published by
DREAMSPINNER PRESS

5032 Capital Circle SW, Suite 2, PMB# 279, Tallahassee, FL 32305-7886 USA
http://www.dreamspinnerpress.com/

This is a work of fiction. Names, characters, places, and incidents either are the product of author imagination or are used fictitiously, and any resemblance to actual persons, living or dead, business establishments, events, or locales is entirely coincidental.

Rival Within
© 2014 SJD Peterson.

Cover Art
© 2014 Anna Sikorska.
Cover content is for illustrative purposes only and any person depicted on the cover is a model.

ISBN: 978-1-63216-424-7
Digital ISBN: 978-1-63216-425-4
Library of Congress Control Number: 2014945928
First Edition December 2014

Printed in the United States of America
∞
This paper meets the requirements of
ANSI/NISO Z39.48-1992 (Permanence of Paper).

To all those who have struggled to find their place in this world. This book is for you.

"When you come out of the storm, you won't be the same person who walked in.

That's what this storm is all about."

~Haruki Murakami~

Chapter 1

Ramer, Tennessee April 5, 1952

BIG BLUE eyes full of sadness and innocence stared up at Officer Thomas Webber, eyes reminiscent of a time before the harsh realities of the world had left their marks, scarring them. The same untainted eyes that had once stared back at Tom in reflection now belonged to his son.

"Why can't I stay with you, Pa?" Tommy cried.

Tom pressed his palm against his son's cheek and brushed away a tear with his thumb. "I need you to stay with your ma. You'll need to be a big boy now and look after her for me."

"But I don't wanna go! Please! I wanna stay with you." Tommy continued to cry, the tears streaming down his reddened face.

The sounds of Tommy's distress, his damp cheeks, and pitiful pleas caused Tom's chest to clench painfully. His son, barely into his fifth year of life, wasn't old enough to understand the dangers of the coming storm. There was no way in hell Tom would put his boy in danger. Thomas Junior was his pride, his heart, his true happiness.

Marna, Tom's wife of seven years, tried her best to comfort the boy, running a soothing hand down Tommy's back and speaking in low, reassuring tones. Tommy shrugged off her touch, refusing to have anything to do with her. The child wanted his father and would not be placated. Marna was a good mother, a good wife, and a fine woman. Tom pushed away the all too familiar guilt as he watched the struggle before him. Marna took second fiddle to her son in her husband's heart and also to her husband in her son's heart. She deserved better. Marna deserved a real husband, a loving one, and a loyal son. Instead….

No, he wasn't going to think of such things now. He'd done what was expected of him, what was right by her. He'd provided a good home, plenty of food on the table, and a strong hand to lead the boy. It wasn't perfect—marriage often wasn't—but she could have done much worse for herself than a man who provided for her yet didn't love her. At least that's what Tom repeatedly told himself.

"Boy," Tom scolded harshly and hated himself for it. "Listen to your ma. It's too dangerous for you to stay behind. Now give me a hug and do as I say."

Tommy tried to stifle his sobbing, tried to do as he was told by covering his mouth with his hand, but his grief came out as muffled hiccups, the tears impossible to stop on demand. Tom's heart broke for his little guy. He was such a good boy.

"Y-y-yes, Pa," he finally managed.

"Be brave for me." Tom ruffled his son's unruly curls.

"Yes, Pa," Tommy whispered and hugged Tom's waist tightly.

Tom held his son and looked to his wife, who met Tom's gaze expectantly as she so often did, no doubt waiting for the same kind of affection and tenderness Tom bestowed upon his son. Simple emotions, deserved ones, and yet, try as he might, Tom couldn't muster true affection and tenderness for his wife.

"I spoke with your dad. He'll pick you up at the train station, so no worries," Tom told his wife. "I'll ring once the storm has passed."

As Tom had seen too many times to count, Marna's eyes filled with tears born of disappointment, but they did not fall. She nodded and, like the dutiful wife she was, took their son's hand and led him to the train.

Some days Tom truly hated himself. As he turned away without so much as a wave for his family, he knew today was one of those days.

TOM STARED out the rain-streaked windshield as lightning burst and crackled in the black sky. The brilliant flash lit the stark trees, the naked branches on either side of the lonely country road like withered fingers and claws grasping for the light, railing against the oncoming storm. Tom shivered.

Pushing down the uneasy feeling, Tom zipped his yellow rain slicker, pulled the hood over his head, and stepped out of the car. The county was under a severe thunderstorm warning, and the possibility of a tornado was high. It had been raining for hours; an early warming trend had melted winter's snow and left the streams and rivers overflowing. This newest weather pattern caused them to swell further and wash out bridges and roads. Tom considered the black sedan with no license plate before him with a critical eye. He noticed the dent on the right side of the bumper, the crack along the back windshield, and the discoloration of rust along the edge of the trunk. He took in the minute details, all the while wondering what the hell this yahoo was doing out here on a night like this. He figured it came down to being lost, a fool, or up to no good.

Cautiously Tom made his way along the vehicle. A prickling sensation caused the hair on the back of his neck to stand on end, and he reached through the slit in his raincoat and unsnapped the strap securing his service revolver. His hand hovered close to the butt of the gun. Using his other hand, he trained the beam of light from his flashlight into the car and swept it across the interior, then on the lone occupant.

"Evening, Officer." The stranger's voice was deep and whiskey smooth with a hint of a northern accent.

Not from around these parts. Tom wouldn't have forgotten that seductive voice or the face that went with it. The man's cheekbones were prominent on his thin face; dark brows and liquid brown eyes glistened in the light. His dark brown pompadour was slicked back—not a hair out of place—the slight scruff on his jaw and chin giving him a roguish appearance. A thin scar ran from his temple down his cheek, curving at the tip of his full upper lip, curling it into a sly grin. Tom brushed his thumb over the butt of his gun as another warning of caution furled in his gut.

Dangerous flashed in Tom's mind.

"Not the best of nights to be out," Tom drawled.

"No, sir. Highway's been shut down about a mile back," the stranger said with a slight nod toward the direction from which he came. "I was forced to take a little detour."

"Won't be makin' it through Ramer tonight. Bridge is washed out. You'd best be turnin' around and headin' back the way you came."

"Damn." The stranger rubbed a hand across his chin.

Tom studied the man carefully, his gut telling him to take the stranger into custody, but with the power out, phone lines down, and floodwaters rising, the last thing Tom wanted was to have to deal with a prisoner. Tom hesitated for a moment, trying to get a read on him, but it was difficult with the permanent smirk and his demeanor: calm, almost nonchalant. All Tom had was gut instinct. He stared for a second longer before deciding the best thing to do was get the stranger's name and cut him loose. He'd do some inquiring after the storm broke.

"Can I see some identification?" Tom asked politely.

"Well now, there is the first problem," the stranger muttered with a shrug. "I'm afraid I've misplaced my wallet."

Lightning cracked open the sky in an impressive display of light and power, and a loud boom of thunder shook the ground. The man before him didn't flinch or react in the slightest.

Tom stroked the butt of his gun again when his unease grew, a nervous habit, but he forced himself to stay calm. "Anything with your name and address on it will suffice. Car ownership—"

As the stranger reached toward the passenger side of the car, Tom's beam of light glinted off steel gray beneath the stranger's brown leather jacket.

Tom shifted his stance and pulled his gun. "Hands where I can see them. Do it. Do it now!"

The stranger lifted his hands slowly and turned his head back toward Tom. "Hey, hey, easy there, Officer. Was just going to grab the info you asked for," he said with a wink.

The son of a bitch was smiling and winking. He didn't appear to be rattled in the least that one slight squeeze, a twitch of a finger, and a bullet would explode between his eyes. Tom ignored the spark of irritation the man's blasé attitude ignited, instead finding that cold place within himself when it dawned on him this man was no stranger to the gun. Tom's focus narrowed as his finger ghosted over the trigger.

"With your left hand, reach out and open the door," Tom called and took another step back. As soon as the suspect complied, Tom added, "Now, keeping your hands where I can see them, step out of the car."

"It's raining," the stranger complained. "I might melt."

In small town Ramer, population one thousand three hundred and sixty-nine as of last week when one of the locals popped out twin boys, they had little crime. The worst Tom had seen in his ten years as an officer was a drunken brawl down at the little dive bar on the outskirts of town and two summers ago when a couple local teens went around vandalizing cars and stealing tires. He'd pulled his gun before, but had never actually pointed it at another human being. He was proud and yet shocked his hand was steady, considering that the danger radiating off this stranger had him nervous, agitated, and to be quite honest, more than a little scared.

"Step out of the car now or I will put a fucking bullet in you," Tom barked as a clap of thunder boomed, seeming to give his words even more power.

Once again the stranger gave no outward appearance that the noise, the pissed-off cop, or the situation in general bothered him in the slightest. He did eye the gun briefly before he shrugged one shoulder and did as he was instructed.

"Face the car and lace your fingers behind your head."

Tom unzipped his raincoat, slid the flashlight through the loop on his belt, and grabbed the cuffs. With the gun sited on the back of the man's head, Tom attached the cuff to one wrist, tightening it before he returned his gun to its holster. He grabbed the man's other wrist at the pressure point and wrenched it down.

"Oh, baby, I like it rough," the man purred.

Tom gritted his teeth as he secured the jokester's other wrist, then grabbed the back of his jacket, curling his fingers in the soft leather and pulling him back roughly. "Let's see how you like it over the trunk of the car, smart guy."

"Mmm, like it rough too, do you?"

Tom refused to respond to the taunt. He shoved the bastard toward the back of the car and forced him to bend. Actually, Tom had a sneaking suspicion *force* was a relative term. He felt the hard muscles beneath his hand, and had the man not gone passive, Tom would have had a difficult time manhandling him. Tom kicked the stranger's feet apart, but didn't release his hold on the jacket. Tom couldn't shake the feeling that he had his hands wrapped around a deadly animal who was merely playing with its prey—a belief hammered home as Tom patted down the muscular calves and thighs.

The wind gusted and the heavy downpour forced the suspect to close his eyes as he lay across his car, cheek against the trunk, but his smile never faltered. Something about the man, perhaps the danger, the arrogance, or maybe his calm, unhinged Tom, and he found himself wanting to slap that smug smile off the bastard's face and leave him cuffed and bleeding in the ditch. Tom hated to lose control—he couldn't afford to lose control, *ever*. One look, one curl of lip, had Tom fighting to keep himself composed.

Tom slipped a hand beneath the leather jacket and groaned when he came in contact—not with the gun he had suspected—but what felt like a flask. He snatched it out, and it was in fact an ornate steel-gray flask. He threw it aside angrily. Tom found nothing else on the man other than a Zippo and half a pack of Lucky Strikes.

Without another word, Tom grabbed the scruff of the man's neck, pulled him upright, and pushed him toward the cruiser. "Have a seat," he growled as he opened the back door.

"Is there a problem, Officer?" the man asked innocently as he slid into the backseat.

Tom slammed the door and stomped back to the sedan, cursing the entire way. He should be sitting at his desk, feet propped up, with a glass of Old Crow in his hand as he rode out the storm, but no. He was out in the rain, dealing with a smart-mouthed stranger with thick, bulging muscles and a perpetual smirk.

A quick search of the sedan left Tom scratching his head. It was empty, not so much as a candy wrapper on the floor. He snatched the keys from the ignition, rolled up the window and locked the doors, then checked the trunk. He found a small green duffel bag containing clothes and a single-action Colt, but again, nothing that would help identify the stranger. He took the duffel and slammed the trunk. The wind increased and the rain changed to hail that stung Tom's cheeks.

Time to go batten down the hatches.

Tom threw the bag into the passenger seat as he slid into the cruiser. "How is it you have no identification?" he asked the stranger, looking at him in the rearview mirror.

"I told you I m—"

"Misplaced your wallet," Tom finished for him disbelievingly. "Unfortunately, or fortunately—whichever way you choose to look at it— Mother Nature is forcing me to take you in."

"I'll have to thank her, I'm sure." The seductive lilt in the stranger's voice went straight to Tom's crotch. The tingling sensation irritated him for reasons he refused to think about at the moment. Grudgingly, Tom pulled out onto the road.

Tom had been born and raised in Ramer. He'd learned to drive on this very road, had been patrolling it nearly every day for the last ten years, and still as he got them going down the road, he had a hell of a time keeping his bearings. With gale-force winds, heavy rain, and flooding, it took twenty white-knuckled minutes to drive the mile stretch back to the station. The instant he had the car in park and cut the engine, Tom blew out a relieved sigh. He pried his fingers from the steering wheel and scrubbed them across his face.

"I'm impressed."

Tom jerked when he heard the stranger's voice; he'd forgotten he had a passenger, the road and weather demanding his full attention. Tom looked to the silhouette behind him in the mirror; it was too dark to see the man's eyes, but Tom could feel them boring into him. He had to clamp down on the shiver that threatened. He ripped his gaze away, grabbed the duffel, and stepped out of the car. Tom stood with his hand poised on the back door handle, the wind whipping, rain stinging his cheeks, but he ignored them. He needed a moment to calm himself. He rolled his shoulders and huffed out a breath before opening the door.

"Let's go," he demanded as he grabbed the man by the bicep and tugged him from the car.

Strands of the stranger's hair covered his eyes as the rain streamed down his face. Anger flashed across his features, his brow dipping into a deep scowl; he pursed his lips but caught himself quickly, and the smug smile once again reemerged as Tom manhandled him. It was the first crack in the guy's calm façade. Tom didn't give the ire a second thought as he was beyond irritated himself. He was pissed off at the whole situation, especially as it brought all the forbidden desires he had buried long ago back to the surface. Why now? Why did they have to come back and haunt him?

With the wind now blowing nearly sideways, Tom fought to keep his feet on the rain-soaked walkway and his hand securely on his prisoner. Tom had sent his partner and the only other officer in Ramer, Frank Compton, home to his wife and kids hours ago. There had been no reason for them both to be at the station, and Tom knew had he not sent Frank on his way, he'd have had to listen to him fret and fuss until Tom considered shooting him. Now as he pushed the cuffed man through the door of the dark and deserted station, Tom wished Frank were there. He wasn't afraid of what the stranger would do to him—although he supposed he should be—but instead, Tom was afraid of what he would do to the stranger.

Tom slammed the door behind them, then spun the stranger around and shoved him against the door. "Don't fucking move," Tom growled against the man's ear.

"You know, Officer," he said in a singsong voice. "You really have to learn to relax a little. Why are you so upset with me? I've done nothing but lose my wallet."

"Because you—" Tom snapped his mouth shut and closed his eyes against the dizzying wave of nausea. Yet even with the unpleasant sensation the guilt evoked, his body thrummed as he breathed in the man's heady scent. He needed to get away from this temptation… this… this….

Goddammit! I will not give in to such depravity. I won't!

Straightening, Tom took a step back and squared his shoulders. "I apologize, the storm has me a little unsettled," he said neutrally. "Please stay where you are, sir, while I get a lamp lit."

"You got that Dr. Jekyll and Mr. Hyde thing going on, don't you?"

"Never saw it. I don't go to the picture shows," Tom admitted.

"Probably don't read much either," the man muttered under his breath, but Tom heard it and chose not to respond.

Tom spun on his heel and stomped to the cabinet, a task easily done in the dark without tripping over anything. The room was small, housing three desks, a couple of filing cabinets, and a single holding cell. The place was kept warm in the winter by an old potbellied woodstove, and a single ceiling fan fought the heat in the summer. It was nothing fancy like they had up in Nashville, but Tom wouldn't trade a single thing with them city folks. They could keep their big fancy precinct, new cars, and modern weapons, as long as they kept their crime rate too. Ramer was a damn fine place without any of that mess—perhaps a little backward, a little remote, but the people were good and honest for the most part.

With a shaky hand, Tom grabbed the box of matches and fumbled to pull one out. *God, that was close.* It had actually been on the tip of his tongue to blame the stranger for the wayward thoughts he inspired in Tom. What the hell was wrong with him?

He turned up the wick on the lamp and lit it, filling the small room with warm light. He blew out the match and took a deep breath, exhaling slowly for good measure. He turned around to face his tormentor and groaned.

Much to Tom's dismay, the extra deep breath did little to calm his nerves, and he had to force his feet to move steadily back to the stranger, who watched Tom intently the entire time. Those dark, intense eyes were like a stroke of fire to Tom's tingling flesh.

Without a word, Tom grabbed the man's bicep and tugged. The stranger didn't say a word, nor did he resist, allowing Tom to pull him along until Tom opened the holding cell door and ushered him in.

Dark eyes shot upward, widening in alarm as the gusting wind caused the old building to groan and creak. "You're not actually going to lock me in a cell with a tornado about to hit, are you?" He glared at Tom.

"Just till I figure out what the hell I'm supposed to do with you." Tom gave the man a slight shove, getting him moving, then quickly shut the door and locked it.

"I know what I'd like for you to do with me," the man grumbled. At least it's what Tom heard, although he couldn't be sure it was what the man actually said or just his messed-up mind projecting crazy thoughts.

Tom turned away, hiding both shock and desire, shrugged out of his raincoat, and hung it and his cap on the coat-tree near the door.

"Could you at least unfasten these cuffs?"

"Sure," Tom agreed, strolling back toward the cell and pulling his keys from his pocket, twirling them. "As soon as you tell me your name and why you're here in Ramer, I'll consider it."

"It's Ben, and I told you, the highway is shut down," Ben said in exasperation and turned his back slightly, exposing the cuffs. "Now do you mind?"

"Ben what?" Tom stepped closer to the cell and met the man's eyes, searching for any hint of deception.

"Parker. Benjamin Parker," he responded evenly, holding Tom's gaze. "I'm a thirty-two-year-old salesman from Toledo, Ohio. Never been married, no kids, no commitments." Ben licked his lips as he raked his eyes up and down Tom's body. "What about you, Officer? You got anybody waiting at home for you?"

Tom clamped down on the shudder that threatened and refused to acknowledge the suggestive note in Ben's voice. "Turn around and put your wrist to the bars."

As Tom unfastened the cuffs, he noted the heavy calluses on the palms of Ben's hands as well as the numerous small wounds and old white scars covering his fingers and knuckles. *Salesman, my ass.* Tom stepped back quickly, trusting Ben even less now that his hands were free, and shoved his keys into his pocket.

"Thanks," Ben said, rubbing at his wrists. "Would you mind doing me one more favor?"

"Ask."

Ben cocked an eyebrow at Tom's clipped tone, his smile growing. "Could I get a towel or something?" He opened his coat, pushing it over his shoulders and slowly letting it drop to the floor. "I'm a little wet." He smirked.

Tom would *not* look at the way Ben's damp dress shirt clung to his muscular chest or the way his erect nubs were visible through the white material. Tom ripped his gaze away from the tempting sight before him, but it hadn't been quick enough. A deep rumbling chuckle proved Ben hadn't missed Tom's momentary lapse. *Shit!*

Cursing himself for a fool, Tom rummaged around in a small closet until he found a towel. "Here," he grumbled and threw it toward the cell.

Ben snatched it easily. "Thanks."

Tom's only response was a curt nod without looking toward the cell as he dropped down in the chair at his desk and grabbed the phone. "Hello?" He tapped the receiver several times even though he knew it was useless. The phone lines had gone down before he'd sent Frank home, and the storm had only increased in strength. He'd have to think about taking cover soon, but the thought of being confined in the small cellar with Ben scared him more than any act of Mother Nature. With a huff, he slammed the phone receiver down and scrubbed his hands over his face. He leaned his elbows on the desk and held his head in his hands.

Why? Why was this happening now?

Chapter 2

AS A young boy, Tom had been prone to impure thoughts. His teenage years had been agony, but he'd learned to deal with his… predilections. He'd pushed down the nefarious desires, locked them behind a thick wall of ironclad will. Not since his youth had he acted upon such things. So why was he considering it now? Why with this… this…. Why him?

"I don't mean to interrupt your nap there, Officer, but I'm thinking the big bad wolf is about to blow your house down," Ben advised.

Tom lifted his head and stared up at the ceiling. He'd been lost in his head, the rush of blood as his pulse raced drowning out the tempest raging outside. The lightning was a nearly constant flash, and the rain obscured the view beyond the windows.

"Get it together, Tom," he groaned.

"You okay?"

"Would you shut the fuck up and let me think for—" The words stuck in Tom's throat when he caught sight of Ben with nothing but a towel wrapped low on his hips, so low in fact, the dark bush above Ben's cock was visible. He'd tucked his pack of Lucky Strikes beneath the material against the juncture of hip and thigh. Ben's head was tilted back sensually as he took a long pull from his cigarette before opening his mouth wide and letting the smoke roll out slowly. Tom looked appreciatively up and down Ben's body—his chest smooth, his muscles well-defined. A dark trail of hair ran from Ben's navel downward, a path Tom longed to follow with lips and tongue. His stomach fluttered in reaction, and he swallowed hard, his pants a hell of a lot tighter than they had been only moments before. He sat there, his mouth agape, transfixed by the sexy fucker. Tom ached for him.

A loud crash outside the window forced Tom's attention away from Ben's tempting body, and he lunged to his feet, embarrassment, shame and anger propelling him toward the cell.

He pointed an accusing finger at Ben. "Put your goddamn clothes on now!"

"They're wet," Ben complained, his voice sounding innocent, but the mischievous glint in his eyes telling the opposite story.

The tentative hold Tom held on his temper slipped, and he pulled out his cuffs and shook them at Ben. "I am done with your games! Put your fucking clothes on now, or so help me God, I will cuff you to the tree out back!"

Ben's gaze shifted to the window that looked out back and then settled once again on Tom. Ben's smug grin was firmly in place when he said, "I'm pretty sure the tree is no longer standing." Ben rubbed a hand over his flat belly, sliding it upward, drawing Tom's eye. "Besides I told you—" Ben cocked his head to the side, his expression thoughtful as he stared at the front door. After a few seconds, he asked, "Do you hear that?"

Tom narrowed his eyes and concentrated on the sounds around him. "Sounds like a train."

"I didn't cross over any tracks coming into town," Ben pointed out as he stubbed out his cigarette between his fingers.

"What? No. Closest train track is about twenty miles over," Tom told him as an uneasy feeling settled into his gut. His head was still swimming from the conflicting emotions raging through his system, and it took him a moment to catch up with the turn in the conversation.

"Unlock this door!" Ben demanded, his voice rising, a panicked look in his eyes. When Tom only stood there, Ben clutched the bars and yanked, rattling them. "C'mon, man, let me out. If that's not an engine roaring down on us, then it's a fucking tornado!"

That got Tom throwing off the last of the fog of lust and anger, and he pulled his keys from his pocket. Adrenaline surged through his system as he fumbled to unlock the cell, his hands shaking nearly as hard as the walls.

"C'mon! C'mon! C'mon," Ben chanted, his knuckles white where he gripped the bars.

The instant the key turned in the lock, Ben shoved the cell door open, narrowly missing Tom. In full survival mode, Tom rushed to Frank's desk and shoved it out of the way, exposing the trapdoor in the floor. He gripped the metal ring and pulled it open.

"Here, take this." He shoved the flashlight into Ben's hand. "Get down there. I'm going to grab the lamp."

Tom didn't wait for a response and could only hope Ben wasn't stupid enough to ignore his instructions. Tom raced to the filing cabinet and snatched up the lantern just as the front window blew out. The room erupted in a swirl of flying papers, debris, and rain, the sound deafening. Keeping his head down and eyes shielded with one arm, Tom made it to the opening of the cellar, relief washing through him when he saw Ben standing below and shining the flashlight on the ladder.

"Take this," Tom screamed and held out the lantern as he started down. Ben rushed over and took it from him, freeing up Tom's hands so he could get the hatch closed. The floorboards shook violently, and Tom cried out his rage when the bolt initially refused to slide into the latch. It took every bit of strength he could muster—and more than a few ripe curses—but the bolt finally slid home, and Tom slumped down the ladder, breathing heavily.

"Whew! That was close," Ben whistled.

"It's not over yet," Tom grunted and pinched the bridge of his nose as his head began to throb.

The scents of damp earth and mold assaulted Tom's nostrils, and the chill of the underground room seeped into his flesh and bones, causing him to shiver. The building had been constructed before the turn of the century. Its original purpose prior to the town buying it and converting it to a police station in the thirties had been a general store. The small ten-by-ten room he now shared with a practically naked stranger who caused his blood to boil had once been used as cold storage. The irony would almost be funny if the threat of possible death by tornado wasn't looming over their heads.

"You're right," Ben said huskily. "It's only just the beginning."

Goose bumps blossomed across Tom's skin, and he shivered again at the suggestive tone of Ben's voice. Jesus H. Christ, was the man not afraid of anything? A deadly storm was wreaking havoc above their heads, bodily injury or even death was a real threat, and still Ben provoked him, taunted him with wickedness. Tom was afraid to turn around and face the man. He wasn't sure how he would react to Ben's nearness—throttling him and kissing him were equal desires.

Tom curled his hands into fists and, without turning around, asked, "Why are you here?" His voice sounded defeated, even to his own ears.

"I think it's pretty obvious, don't you?"

"No! No, it's not," Tom growled and spun around to face his tormentor. "Why the fuck are you in Ramer?" He let his anger take the forefront, his vision going red, blessedly blurring the hard, chiseled muscles of Ben's chest and stomach.

Ben didn't flinch away in the face of Tom's anger; instead he took a step closer. This bastard was either one crazy son of a bitch or had a death wish. Tom was vibrating with anger, face flushed, and he was armed. How could Ben be so calm? How could he have the balls to continue to taunt Tom? Tom's first instinct was to draw his nightstick, beat the man into submission, and force him to back down or at least show some signs of discomfort or fear. It was only fair, goddammit. He was done being intimidated.

He took a step closer. "I asked you a question. Why are you in Ramer?"

Ben set the lantern on the shelf and stepped up closer until there was only a foot of space between them. His dark eyes reflected the lamplight, as if fire burned within him. He studied Tom, stared at him as if he were looking through flesh and bone and contemplating the secrets of Tom's soul.

Maybe he was, because Ben's nostrils flared as he inhaled deeply and groaned, "Just looking for a little release."

"Goddamn you," Tom growled before he grabbed Ben roughly by the waist, pulling Ben against his body and smashing their mouths together.

Tom groaned the instant his lips touched Ben's firm ones, and he gripped Ben's side tighter, digging his fingers into the soft flesh. With his other hand, Tom grabbed Ben's head, fisting the dark, silky strands and forcing the man's head back as he shoved his tongue past those lush lips. He took Ben's mouth in a furious kiss and explored with the urgency of long-denied desire. The clash of lips, teeth, and tongue had a hard, painful edge, and Tom wanted more. He wanted to take it deeper, harder, just... fucking wanted more.

Blunt fingers dug into Tom's back, and he felt the power in Ben's hands and arms and body.... Christ, Tom needed to devour this man. The harder he tried to dominate the kiss, the more forceful Ben became, giving as good as he got. That alone pushed Tom's need to a feverish pitch. His anger and fear morphed into passion and desire.

Ben groaned loudly and finally surrendered, relaxing into the kiss and allowing Tom to control it, a task Tom accepted with relish. He released the hold he had on Ben's hair to cup his stubbled cheek and increased the pressure of his lips against Ben's. Tom feasted on Ben's mouth relentlessly, pulling needy sounds from him, which spurred Tom on.

Ben didn't give up the reins for long.

"Fuck!" Tom muttered when he finally pulled back from the kiss.

"Not yet," Ben chuckled and rubbed his cheek against Tom's. His coarse facial hair was rough against Tom's cheek, but it felt so damn good, Tom moaned at the contact. Before Tom had a chance to catch his breath, Ben grabbed Tom's head in both his hands and forced it downward.

"What the hell?" Tom bristled angrily and began to struggle out of Ben's grasp. His hands slid down Ben's body, dislodging the towel, and he grasped Ben's hips and dug his fingers in when his face was roughly pressed against Ben's chest.

"Suck it," Ben demanded as he held Tom's mouth against one dark nipple.

"Bastard," Tom growled, the sound muffled against Ben's flesh, but he complied, taking the hard nub into his mouth and sucking vigorously, teasing with his tongue.

"Ah, yeah," Ben moaned. "Harder but watch those teeth."

"These?" Tom mumbled and scraped his teeth along Ben's nipple.

"Fuck!" Ben shuddered violently. He dug his fingers into Tom's scalp but didn't pull him away, rather he shoved Tom harder against his chest.

This is a bad, bad, bad idea. Tom was a smart man, knew he shouldn't be doing this, but he couldn't stop. He ignored the alarms going off in his head and looked up to meet Ben's eyes as he began to suck and tease in earnest.

Ben gasped, his kiss-swollen lips parted as he stared back at Tom with lust-filled eyes. Heat rushed through Tom's body, and he slid his hands up Ben's sides, one hand moving to Ben's back to hold him in place and the other pinching and pulling at Ben's other nipple.

"Harder," Ben rasped, but the death grip he had in Tom's hair went from pulling to petting, encouraging.

Tom continued his assault on Ben's chest. He licked his way across Ben's breastbone to the other nipple, giving it the same harsh treatment. Tom opened his mouth wide and bit down on Ben's pec, teeth sinking in, not hard enough to break skin but enough to make Ben grunt in pain and tighten his hand once again in Tom's hair.

"Son of a bitch," Ben growled. "You like having your mouth full." He yanked Tom's head back and without warning, shoved him to his knees. "I got a mouthful for you."

Tom's knees hit the dirt floor with a painful thud. He started to protest, but just as he opened his mouth, Ben shoved his fat cock in. The feeling of his lips being stretched wide, the thick spongy head heavy on his tongue, and the bitter flavor overwhelmed Tom, obliterating any complaints. He hungrily swallowed Ben's cock an inch at a time, tongue working, tasting, until he'd taken it in to the root. Tom's eyes threatened to roll back in his head. It was pure, sweet heaven. He never thought he'd experience it again, and he hummed his pleasure.

"Such a good little cocksucker," Ben praised, hips snapping.

Why the naughty praise caused Tom's cock to throb and his belly to flutter pleasantly, he didn't know. He only knew he wanted to make this man lose control, unhinge him as Ben had done to him. Tom bobbed his head faster, his tongue and lips working Ben's cock as he slid a hand down to tug on Ben's heavy balls. Tom might have been the one on his knees, but he was the one making Ben's buckle.

"C'mon, give it to me," Tom ordered and swallowed Ben down again. Tom encouraged him to thrust with a hand on Ben's hip.

"Gonna fill your mouth so full you'll fucking choke," Ben snarled and thrust in earnest, pushing deep into Tom's throat.

Ben's harsh, naughty words sent a jolt straight to Tom's groin, and he could only moan his approval and beg for more with lips and tongue. Tom relaxed his jaw, his eyes fluttering shut as he allowed Ben to take what he needed. The anticipation of Ben keeping his word, pumping his load down Tom's throat, caused his skin to tingle and his pulse to quicken. Fuck, Ben wasn't the only one who was close. He gave his straining erection a hard squeeze through his trousers. He'd be damned if he'd come before he had gotten his fill of this man.

"Take it! Every fucking drop! Take it!" Ben howled as his back arched, and he went completely still, not so much as breathing as the first spurt shot down Tom's throat. True to his word, Ben's first blast choked Tom, but he recovered quickly, pulling back slightly to wrap his lips halfway up Ben's shaft. He sucked down every drop, tonguing the slit, searching out the last of Ben's flavor from his twitching cock, and still Tom didn't want to release him.

"Enough. Jesus, enough." Ben groaned plaintively as the stimulation to his overly sensitive cock seemingly became too much.

Tom let Ben slip from his mouth and pushed to his feet. "Nowhere near enough," he said against Ben's mouth before diving in for a wild and sloppy kiss.

Chapter 3

TOM HAD broken the promise he'd made to himself all those years ago. He'd no doubt feel the weight of his perversity later, but not now, not with Ben's arms around him and Ben's tongue sliding along his own as they shared Ben's flavor.

Ben was breathing hard and trembling against Tom as he recovered from his orgasm, but his mouth was hot and wet and willing, and in combination with the little moans and whimpers, it spurred Tom on.

Without breaking the kiss, Tom unhooked his utility belt and let it fall to the floor with a heavy thud. His pants and briefs soon pooled around his ankles. Ben pawed at Tom's shirt, fumbling with the buttons, then slid his hands past the cotton material and around Tom's body to pull him close. They were pressed chest to chest, cock to cock, and thigh to thigh. As badly as Tom wanted to bend Ben over and fuck him, he wasn't in any hurry to release the man. The hard body crushed against his own was boner popping and orgasm inspiring in and of itself, and an indulgence Tom wanted to savor. He broke the kiss, sliding his mouth over Ben's strong jaw and along his neck, nuzzling as he wrapped himself around the man, touching every inch of skin he could reach, stroking and kneading all those powerful muscles.

So hard he'd fought these unnatural desires, and as he held Ben, touching and tasting, he was dizzy with how right, how good it felt. The need and want surged within him, wiping out any and all rational thought until he became a wave of sensation.

How long they stood there, wrapped in each other, Tom couldn't rightly say, but a loud thud above them reminded Tom where he was far too soon. There was a storm raging above them, but it couldn't hold a candle to the tempest raging inside Tom. It was foolish, yet he wouldn't be denied. He'd allowed Ben to take what he wanted from his mouth, now it was Tom's turn to take what he wanted from Ben.

"I want to fuck you," Tom muttered against Ben's neck as he rocked against the man. "Any objections, say so now."

Ben continued to hold on to Tom's back, fingers kneading, digging in a little, humping against him. Although Ben had just found his release, he was already semihard, the friction causing him to swell again. Without a word, Ben tilted his head, giving Tom full access to his neck. It would be so easy to spin Ben around, bend him over a stack of crates, and shove himself home, but he wanted to hear Ben say it. He wanted to hear the cocky son of a bitch beg for it.

"Say it!" Tom bit down on the muscle at the juncture of Ben's neck and shoulder.

"Fucker!" Ben grunted, but just as he had when Tom had bit his pec, he pushed into the pain rather than pulled away.

"Yeah, I am," Tom snorted and bit him again. Tom was rewarded by a deep, husky groan that he felt all the way to his toes.

Forcing his mouth away from Ben's delectable flesh, Tom scanned the area, a smile spreading across his face when he spotted just what he needed. He licked and nipped at Ben's mouth as he steered them toward the shelf. Once he was within reach, he nudged Ben's cheek with his nose, encouraging him to look up. Tom's breath hitched as a pair of hungry eyes met his.

"Prove it," Ben said with a challenging grin.

Tom forcefully spun Ben around and roughly shoved him down until the cocky bastard was bent over the crates. Ben's chuckle was low and throaty, another challenge.

Holding Ben by the back of the neck, Tom kicked Ben's legs farther apart and situated himself between the man's thighs. Tom's straining erection pressed against the crease of Ben's round, tight ass, and he couldn't help but thrust against it a few times while he reached for some oil.

Pouring out a good amount on his cock and Ben's ass, Tom set the bottle aside as he continued to thrust, his gaze riveted to the sight of his glistening, engorged cock against the creamy mounds. He rubbed the oil along his length, slicking Ben's crease at the same time, not knowing how much time they had together but refusing to be rushed.

Ben squirmed beneath him, pushing his ass against Tom's hand, begging for more with his body and with the gravelly moans and whimpers that poured from him.

"Say it," Tom growled. "Tell me what you want."

He traced along Ben's crease and pressed the tip of one finger against his opening, tapping and teasing. When Ben's needy sounds increased in volume, Tom slowly pushed in just a little, twisting and rubbing against Ben's slick walls.

"Damn, that feels good," Ben gasped. "Deeper."

Tom withdrew his finger and slapped one taut butt cheek. "I'm in the driver's seat." Ben glared back at him, but before he could argue, Tom shoved two fingers deep, pulling back just slightly before pushing them deep again. "I got your number." Tom pulled his hand back till just the tips were breaching Ben. "You like it rough." He slammed into him again. "Raw and dirty."

Ben's response was unintelligible. He arched his back and breathed harshly as Tom plunged into his ass over and over. The muscular body was spread out before Tom like a feast, the wet, slippery ass clamping down on his fingers and the low, husky sounds making his nerve endings buzz, his cock throb.

Ben writhed, hips rolling as he stroked himself with the same hard and fast rhythm Tom used to work his ass. Tom grabbed Ben's forearm and yanked, snatching Ben's hand away from his cock.

"Hey!" Ben protested with a snarl.

Reaching around, Tom fisted Ben's hard cock and squeezed to what he knew would be just this side of painful. "Say it!"

Ben continued to move, heedless of the viselike grip on his shaft. Tom allowed Ben to fuck himself on Tom's fingers for a few more beats, then withdrew his fingers to dig them into Ben's hip and halt his movements.

"Bastard!"

"Not that I'm aware of." Tom laughed.

Ben planted both hands on the crates, lifting up, and shoved his ass back, hard. "Goddammit, will you just fuck me already!"

"All you had to do was ask," Tom replied wryly and bent and bit Ben's right asscheek. His effort was rewarded with a ragged groan.

Mindless of where he was, who the stranger was beneath him, or the threat of danger, Tom fisted his shaft and pressed the flared cockhead against the protective ring of muscles at Ben's opening. With a grunt, he buried himself deep in Ben's ass in one brutal thrust.

"Jesus!" Ben screamed, and he flailed, hands flying to the wall in front of him to stop from being slammed through it.

A man could only be prepared so much with slick fingers, especially when he was about to get fucked with something as large as Tom's cock, but Tom just couldn't find it in him to be gentle. He wanted Ben to feel it, to experience the pain and burn. He wanted to turn this arrogant man inside out, leave his body broken and hurting. Wanted him to share in the misery Tom would no doubt be feeling when it ended. At least Ben's battered backside would heal; physical pain rarely lasted as long as that inflicted on a man's soul. Part of him, the good man, the upholder of the law, was weeping, but another part, the part that had lived in the dark shadows, seething, reared its ugly head and sent the good side of Tom fleeing for cover. Without the restraint of his conscience or the courtesy of giving Ben time to adjust to the invasion, Tom began to pound into Ben with single-minded determination. Each thrust was deep and powerful, pulling all the way out before plunging in again, giving the man the full length of his cock with each stroke.

Ben's curses and grunts of pain soon enough turned to passionate moans of pleasure, and he met Tom's thrusts, grinding against Tom's groin each time he pressed against Ben's ass. Tom bent, pressed his chest to the hard ridges of muscles along Ben's back, and rubbed his stubbled cheek and chin against the back of Ben's neck, inhaling deeply the heady scent of masculine musk.

The new angle pushed Tom's cock deeper, and they both hissed. He slid his hands under Ben's arms to grasp his shoulders. Ben's ass clamped down on Tom's cock like a vise grip, and Tom found himself teetering on the edge.

Tom froze. "Don't move," he panted harshly and gritted his teeth as he fought to hold back his impending orgasm.

"Close," Ben moaned pitifully and undulated his hips.

"I said, don't fucking move," Tom growled and tightened his grip on Ben's shoulders and sank his teeth into the meaty flesh of Ben's shoulder.

Tom squeezed his eyes shut as his overly stimulated cock twitched, his balls aching with the need for release. *So long.... Too long....* God, how could he have denied himself such ecstasy? *Don't let it end. Not yet.*

They stayed pressed together for long moments, both breathing harshly. The sounds of the storm, the heat of their bodies, and the scent of sex in the air were heady, making it more difficult to get a firm grasp on the reins to pull himself back from the edge. Pure stubbornness eventually won out—the tingling along Tom's length finally subsided, and he tentatively began to move.

"Damn, that was close," Tom muttered and carefully leaned back, spreading his fingers wide across Ben's back and propping himself up.

Ben grunted with Tom's heavy weight, rested his head over the crates, and let his arms hang down. Although he was taking deep breaths, his muscles were still tense, body thrumming. Tom couldn't take his eyes from the man, captivated by the way he moved, the way his muscles flexed beneath Tom's fingers. He slid his hands down Ben's back to the top of his ass, pushed his thumbs into the dimples he found there. Ben grunted again and rolled his neck. Fuck, he was one sexy beast, all hard muscles, attitude, and a fine, fine, tight ass, massaging and stroking Tom's cock with each movement.

With one last huffed breath, Ben lifted his head to glare back at Tom. "Yeah, I was really fucking close," Ben grumbled, but the smirk he tossed over his shoulder ruined the angry effect he was obviously trying for.

"What the hell are you complaining for? You done got your nut, it's my turn," Tom said slyly.

"Goddamn right, I'm complaining," Ben snapped. "I'm still waiting for you to actually fuck me like a man," he goaded.

"You talk a lot of shit for someone bent over with a cock shoved up his ass." Tom chuckled and swatted Ben on the ass just because he could.

Ben growled, the sound deep and throaty, rumbling as it reverberated along the length of Tom's cock. Ben's brow furrowed, and a spark of the anger Tom had seen earlier glistened in Ben's narrowed eyes. Once again the feeling he had his hands wrapped around a deadly animal overwhelmed Tom, and he shuddered even as his cock pulsed in excitement. Tom also knew he'd pushed Ben to his limits and he wouldn't stand to be baited much longer.

Keeping his gaze locked with Ben's, Tom pulled all the way out of that perfect tight wet heat and hesitated for a heartbeat before he slammed back in. He slid his hands down the sinew along Ben's back and grabbed a meaty globe in each hand, pulled Ben's asscheeks apart to watch as his dick slid in and out of Ben's ass.

"Harder," Ben gasped and worked his own cock with a steady, quick pace.

This time restraint was futile, and Tom let go and pumped into Ben at a brutal pace. After only a few moments of mind-numbing pleasure, Tom threw his head back, arched, and with a long, drawn-out moan, unloaded. Ben's ass clamped down on Tom's cock as Ben shouted out his own release, the clenching channel demanding every last hot spurt from

Tom until he slumped, burying his face in the damp skin of Ben's neck as he caught his breath.

Boneless and breathless, Tom let Ben hold his weight until his trembling legs nearly gave out. Tom leisurely ran his tongue along the base of Ben's neck, indulging in one last taste of Ben's addictive flavor before he groaned ruefully and forced himself up. He slipped from Ben's body with a hiss.

Now that the sexual tension had seeped from Tom's body and the fog of lust began to dissipate from his mind, good sense returned, and he kept a wary eye on Ben as he bent and snatched up the towel. He swiped the terrycloth over his slick hands and wet dick, then threw it at Ben, who snatched it out of the air.

Tom pulled up his pants, buttoned and zipped up, then grabbed his belt and secured it around his waist. He fastened the buttons on his shirt without taking his eyes from Ben. Ben wrapped the towel around his waist and stalked toward Tom, a wicked grin on his face. Tom's first thought was to reach for his weapon, which, given the circumstances, seemed ridiculous—a notion he realized was even more ridiculous when Ben pressed his lips against Tom's, then traced the tip of his tongue around Tom's mouth. Tom grabbed the back of Ben's head and pushed his tongue deep. *Just one more time, one last kiss, and then no more.*

Ever.

Ben ended the kiss in small increments, licking, then nipping, and finally brushing his lips against Tom's in a ghost of a touch before leaning his forehead against Tom's and buttoning the rest of Tom's shirt for him.

"Well, that's two intense rides I survived today," he murmured, smoothing out Tom's shirt before stepping back.

"Two?" Tom asked in confusion.

Ben grabbed his cigarettes and lighter from the floor and tucked them back into his towel before he replied, "Pretty quiet up there. Looks like the storm's passed."

Tom tilted his head to the side and looked upward, straining to hear, but the room above them was eerily silent. It would have been nice to kick back and relax, maybe have another go at Ben's ass after he recovered a little. He truly was a sick bastard, thinking of himself when he should be worried about what Mother Nature had just rained down on the good folks of Ramer.

Best to be getting back to reality. With a resigned sigh, Tom grabbed the flashlight and trained the beam on the overhead latch. "After you."

Ben nodded and headed up the ladder. Tom couldn't help but give the man's ass one last appreciative once-over as he moved upward, unhooked the latch, and threw open the door.

"Yeah, it is that fucking good." Ben smirked when he caught Tom staring at his butt. "You want to hand me that?" he asked with a wave toward the lantern.

Tom turned to grab the lantern, grunting in affirmation and rolling his eyes at Ben's attitude. His expression was neutral when he turned back and handed it to Ben. "So am I," Tom said just as smugly. "Hope you don't have to do much walking today."

Ben's laughter followed him up and out of the cellar, and Tom joined in.

Tom's laughter died in his throat as he pulled himself up out of his hiding place and caught the first sight of destruction. The building was still standing, but the storm had left its mark. The front window had been blown out; glass and debris covered the floor. Tom ran a hand through his damp tousled hair as he turned slowly, taking in the room. Chairs were toppled, the shelves busted, their contents scattered around the room, the desk was askew, but he had walls, a roof, a sated dick, and his life. Not only had he survived the storm, he'd come out on the other side feeling pretty damn good.

"Gonna be dawn before long. Guess I should be heading out and checking on the rest of the town," Tom muttered, picking up the lamp from the floor and setting it back on his desk without looking toward Ben.

After a long moment without Ben responding, Tom finally turned around to face him. Ben had pulled on his clothes and was bent fastening his shoes. When he straightened, he slicked back his hair with both hands, his gaze locked on Tom's.

After a long tense silence that rivaled the eerie quiet outside, Ben licked his lips and grinned. "You going to be detaining me longer, Officer?"

The way Ben said it, the look in his eyes, caused Tom's heart to race. There was so much meaning in the simple question: challenge, dare, and perhaps even a little hope. *Dangerous.* Tom's gut was rarely wrong, and in that moment, free from the wicked temptation of flesh, Tom realized the gravity of what he'd done. It wasn't so much the mind-blowing sex he'd just had with another man, but who the man was, or at least who his gut was telling him this man was. The bile threatened to rise from his churning belly, but he swallowed it down. He needed this man gone. Now!

"Any reason I should?" Tom asked coolly, feeling anything but.

Ben picked up his jacket from where it lay on the floor in the cell, shook off the debris, and wrinkled his nose as he slid the wet garment on. "Only if you're predicting another storm sweeping in later," he said suggestively.

Keeping his steps measured, his jitteriness in check, Tom walked to the door, grabbed his raincoat—which miraculously still hung from the hook—and shrugged it on. "I think it's going to be blue skies here in Ramer for a long while."

"You sure about that?" Ben asked, a single eyebrow arched.

"Yeah, I am." He nodded toward the green duffel. "Don't forget your bag." He didn't want anything more than memories of Ben left behind and even those were no doubt going to come at a heavy price.

Ben casually strolled over and shouldered his bag. He studied Tom for a moment as Tom stood stoically at the door, hand resting on the knob. Tom had no idea what kind of reaction Ben was waiting for or what he was hoping to hear. Didn't matter. Tom refused to react or show any emotions.

Tom could practically see the calm façade being laid into place brick by brick, and the smirk that curled Ben's lip fell naturally into place. Ben pulled a smoke from his crumpled pack and slid it between his teeth. He lit it and moved toward Tom, blowing the first puff of smoke out as he stopped next to the door.

"You know, I do love me a good storm. The power, the danger, the thrill," Ben murmured as he ran his gaze slowly down Tom's body, his focus settling on Tom's crotch before he continued. "Sometimes it's those unexpected storms that pop up out of nowhere that leave you the most satisfied after they pass." Ben looked up at Tom with hooded lids. "Wouldn't you agree, Officer?"

Tom pulled Ben's keys from his pocket and handed them to Ben. "And sometimes they leave the most destruction," Tom said coldly and opened the door.

"Touché." Ben winked, placed the cigarette back between his teeth, and was gone.

Tom shut the door and slumped back against it. With a trembling hand, he rubbed at his tired eyes. The weight of what had just transpired between him and Ben slammed down on Tom with such force it nearly drove him to his knees.

"What the fuck have I done?"

Chapter 4

"YOU SURE you didn't get knocked on the noggin during that storm last week?"

"Huh?" Tom asked in confusion.

"You've been out of it ever since the tornado smacked down on us. You sure you're okay?" Frank asked with real concern in his voice.

Tom turned away from the window he'd been staring out. Only he hadn't been seeing the landscape beyond, but rather dark brown eyes, a lean, scarred face, and a perpetual smirk. The nightmares and erotic dreams were hard enough to deal with; the daydreams were killing him.

Leaning back in his chair, Tom propped his boots up on his desk, trying to give the outward appearance of calm. "I'm fine, Frank. Exhausted, but fine," he assured him.

It wasn't a lie. He was exhausted. The tornado had done a whole hell of a lot of damage. Tore the roof off the old church, a couple houses flattened, signs missing, massive amounts of debris scattered around town. Luckily there hadn't been any loss of human life. Over the last week, Tom had been helping out where he could after work. His own house had received damage to the roof, making it uninhabitable—and so Tom was staying at the station and had instructed his wife and son to stay with her family. He rarely had time for sleep, which in some ways was a blessing. Sleep had become less than restful, what with the dreams and all. Missing his son, the guilt over the betrayal of his marriage vows, his sins, and the desire to have Ben again didn't help either.

"You need to learn to tell people no," Frank chastised. "Why don't you head to my house and get some sleep in a real bed. Get the hell away from this place for a while. People are too busy cleaning up to be getting into trouble."

God, if only he could get a full eight hours of restful sleep. Tom knew it would go a long way to help him get a handle on his scattered thoughts. However, his brain simply wasn't shutting down, even in slumber.

Tom ran a hand over his unshaven chin and over his red and burning eyes. "Nah, I'm good. I'm going to help Pastor John for a couple of hours after dinner, then I'll get some sleep."

"Jesus, Tom. You keep up this pace and you're going to fall flat on your face."

That's the plan. "Just make sure you prop my head up on something soft, will ya?" Tom chuckled.

The door opened and Tom tensed, setting his feet back down on the floor and sitting upright in his chair expectantly. He rolled his neck and leaned back in his chair with a sigh when he spotted George Fremont entering the station. The dark-haired man who'd turned Tom's world upside down and inside out wasn't coming back, nor did Tom want him to. And yet he'd been both disappointed and relieved in equal parts each time the door opened over the past week and it turned out not to be Ben.

"Afternoon, gentlemen."

"Hey, George," Frank greeted the postman. "I was beginning to think you had run off and retired on us."

"Bite your tongue, young man," George said with an expression of horror on his face. He stabbed one withered old finger in Frank's direction and shook it. "And don't you be goin' and saying that where the missus can hear you. She's been after me to retire for years."

"So how come you don't?" Tom inquired, taking up his previous position, feet propped up. "Don't you want to spend more time with the grandbabies?"

"Sure I do," George said with a nod. "It's more time with the little woman that scares the bejeebers out of me."

That got both Tom and Frank to laughing and George to grinning, his toothless grin stretched wide across his face.

"Pull up a chair and sit a spell," Tom offered, still chuckling.

"Can't," George said regretfully. "Today's the first day back, and I got a week's worth of mail to deliver." He pulled out a large stack from his bag and plopped it down on Tom's desk. "I'll have to catch up on the gossiping tomorrow. See you boys then," he said with a wave and hobbled out the door.

Tom waved back, grabbed the stack of mail, and started sorting through it. Most of it he set aside. Bonnie Regan, their secretary/switchboard operator, would be back on Monday and would take care of it. *Poor thing, she and her husband, Jay, own one of the houses that was leveled.* Tom turned over the large manila envelope still in his hand and read the return address. It was from the Selmer county office. He brushed his fingers across the opening; a prickling sensation caused the hair on the back of his neck to stand on end.

"Looks like another storm is moving in," Frank commented from where he stood at the front window. "Just what this poor town needs—more rain."

Tom shook off the strange feeling and opened the envelope. "Yeah, guess I should be careful with what I wish for. Although, when I was hoping I wouldn't have to climb up on the roof of the church today, this wasn't exactly what I meant."

Frank crossed his arms over his chest and glared at Tom. "This is entirely your fault, you bastard! I'm never going to get my old tractor out of the mud."

"Yes, yes," Tom appeased as he spilled out the contents of the envelope. "I'll try to control my wishes."

"Damn straight you will," Frank huffed. "Ooh, wanted posters! Who made the list this month?" He moved around to grab one from the stack.

Tom picked up the first one and flipped it over. The photo showed an elderly man with thinning hair and a gentle smile. He looked more like—he scanned the info. Jesus, he looked more like a grandpa than a murderer. Just proved you couldn't judge a book by its cover. Tom set it aside and grabbed another one.

"Wow, this guy is pretty scary looking," Frank commented, scowling at the poster in his hand. "I wouldn't want to come face-to-face with him unarmed or without backup. Here, check it out."

Tom accepted the poster, and his heart stopped dead in his chest, his breath catching in his throat. Dark eyes stared back at him, a familiar scar curling a full lip into a smug grin. Pulse hammering, Tom read the description.

WANTED

Armed Bank Robbery

William Parker

"aka" Parker Williams - Willie Parks - Benjamin Williams - Ben Parker

Wanted in connection with the armed robbery of the First National Bank in Nashville, Tennessee on April 5th, 1952

A loud clap of thunder shook the walls, and lightning flashed in the darkening sky. A jolt raced down Tom's spine, causing him to shiver violently. *No! No! No! This can't be possible.* Yet even as Tom thought it he knew it was true. His gut had warned him, his instinct screamed it, he'd known. Known in the pit of his soul Ben had been dangerous, and he'd forced it away. Ignored it all so he could…. Jesus, he was a sick son of a bitch.

"'If a man lies with a male as he lies with a woman, both of them have committed an abomination.'

'Protect and serve'

'Forsaking all others'

'Thou shalt not commit adultery'

'Uphold the law'"

Tom squeezed his eyes shut as the room began to spin. It didn't matter how many passages popped into his head to swirl with the vows he'd taken as an officer of the law and as a husband. He was aware of what he'd done, knew the crimes he'd committed against his God, wife, and community. But God help him, seeing Ben's face caused his body to heat. The memories—Ben's body against his, his scent, his voice—overpowered everything else.

"Tom! Tom, are you okay?"

Frank's voice came to Tom as if he were speaking underwater—muffled but the words discernable. Tom could hear him, heard the concern, but he couldn't respond. He was drowning in guilt, regret, disgust, desire, and need. It was all so powerful, surrounding him completely, and Tom couldn't tell in which direction to swim. There was no light identifying the surface, not that his limbs would work even if he knew where to swim.

He couldn't breathe, heart stopped dead in his chest. The blackness began to press in around him, whispering to him to give in. There was peace in oblivion.

Tom agreed and no longer tried to breathe, stopped struggling to swim. There was nothing but pain and heartbreak waiting for him. He deserved to drown in the misery of his guilt.

"Goddammit, Tom, answer me!" Frank screamed. He grabbed Tom's shoulders and shook him hard.

The touch was enough to pull Tom to the surface, and he opened his eyes to stare up at Frank's horrified face. Tom sucked in a harsh breath.

"Fuck!" Frank muttered, his expression turning from scared to relieved. "You havin' a heart attack or something? Should I call Doc Masterson?"

Tom shook his head. He tried to speak, but it came out as a grunt. He cleared his throat and tried again. "No. I'm okay," he lied. "I suddenly felt really dizzy." Tom ran a hand across his face, wiping at the sweat that dampened his brow. "I think I've missed one too many meals, and the no-sleep thing is finally catching up with me." It wasn't a complete lie. He hadn't been eating or sleeping, but what he'd allowed himself to do with Ben was the real reason.

Fucking Ben, or whatever the hell his name was.

"Your face turned as white as a sheet and you stopped breathing!" Frank swatted Tom's arm. "Don't you be scarin' me like that again," Frank warned angrily. He stomped to his desk and snatched up his lunch box and coffee mug. "Here," he said, shoving the cup at Tom. "Drink this."

Tom accepted it and took a big swig of the lukewarm coffee as Frank rummaged around in his lunch box. "Sorry," Tom said feebly.

"Yeah, well, just don't do it again. Here."

Tom took the sandwich, and although his stomach was still roiling, the bile that had been pushed up still burning his throat, he took a big bite. It felt like sludge against his tongue, and he chewed it slowly, silently praying he'd be able to keep it down.

Tom did his best to take in slow, steady breaths as he ate, working hard to give the outward appearance of calm. However, the fear still gripped him and made it difficult to keep his shit together. His body trembled, his racing pulse causing a roar in his ears. He wasn't afraid of the new storm rolling in. The one that had blown through in the form of William Parker had already caused Tom's complete destruction.

THE THUNDER and lightning had been all flash and show. By the time Tom had been able to convince Frank he was fine and to head home to his family, there was a fine misting rain and little else. It was just enough that Tom wouldn't be climbing on a rooftop. He'd promised Frank he'd try to get some sleep—"try" being the objective. Tom, however, knew the attempt would be futile.

The effort and time it took for Tom to convince Frank he was fine had been the longest three hours of his life and pure hell. No matter how hard Tom tried to avoid the wanted poster of Ben—William Parker— Frank had hung on the wall, Tom found himself seeking out the dark eyes and smirking smile. The image staring back at him both infuriated Tom and excited him.

All alone, Tom leaned back in his chair and stared out the window. The raindrops on the glass panes distorted the road and building beyond. Didn't matter; Tom's mind wasn't even in Ramer. Well, that wasn't entirely true—it was in a small man-made cold cellar beneath the city of Ramer. As much as Tom hated it, tried to fight it… God help him, but part of him had no regrets. The dark place, the secret part of his soul he never told anyone about, rejoiced at the memories that assaulted him.

Tom tipped his head back and closed his eyes. The image of Ben looking down at him while he was on his knees, lips wrapped around….

"Shit!" Tom jerked upright, nearly jumping out of his skin when the shrill sound of the phone echoed around the small room. Heart thumping wildly in his chest, Tom snatched up the receiver. "Webber here," he said harshly.

"Officer Webber, this is Sheriff Cronkite of Davidson County." What the man said next paralyzed Tom with fear. "We have a William Parker in custody who has just named you as his alibi."

Chapter 5

BEN PARKER sat in a six-by-nine cell of concrete and iron bars, cursing himself for the fool he was. He had organized the robbery. He and John Walker had spent hours plotting out every aspect of the hit, had staked out the bank for weeks. Ben had no doubt it would have been the perfect crime, but then John had to go and run his big fat mouth to his cousin Carl. Carl was a fucking idiot, no two ways about it. The addition of Carl into the mix had been the reason Ben had backed out of the plan and cut his ties with the both of them.

The dumbasses had apparently used Ben's plan and followed through with the robbery, gotten caught, and were now naming him as the mastermind, which technically he was. *Fuck!* Ben took a long drag from his cigarette and blew it out slowly, trying to get his anger back under control. It pissed him off. He had been the intellect, the big cheese, so to speak, but he'd be damned if he was taking the fall. Ben had warned John what would happen due to his stupidity in telling Carl. Sure enough, the heist had gone smoothly just as Ben had expected. Yet, also as he predicted, Carl-too-fucking-stupid-to-breathe had started flashing around big wads of cash, and sure as shit, he was busted. How the hell would a part-time dishwasher suddenly having tons of cash when he didn't have a pot to piss in nor a window to throw it out of not be noticed?

"Goddamn country bumpkin," Ben muttered under his breath and took another pull from his smoke.

Ben and John had grown up together, been drafted together, and survived together. It was John's betrayal that stung the most. Ben would have sworn John would never do such a thing, their friendship too deep. And yet, the fucker had ratted him out, shown the cops the notebook Ben had written his notes in and claimed he was the one who pulled off the robbery with Carl. Ben couldn't deny it was his, the authorities already lifted his prints from the cover, and so no one seemed to care what he had to say, even if it was the truth. He'd backed out, hadn't even been in town when it all went down. He'd been holed up with the sexiest man he'd ever laid eyes on, having both his cock and his mind blown.

Ben shook his head and chuckled. He hadn't told them all the details of his time in Ramer. The authorities would have strung his perverted ass from the tallest tree. However, he'd had no choice but to give them Officer Webber's name.

Ben snubbed out his cigarette and lay back on the lumpy cot. He folded his hands behind his head, staring up at the ceiling as he wondered how Tom would take the news. No doubt there would be shock. The last time Ben had laid eyes on the officer, the man had been struggling to keep a neutral tone and expression, but Ben had seen the guilt swimming in those blue eyes, had witnessed the tension and trembling in the man's lean muscles and heard the slight crack in his voice when he'd said, *"And sometimes they leave the most destruction."*

Ben had thought a lot about those words since Tom had uttered them a week ago. Hell, it wasn't only the man's words Ben had been thinking about. If he closed his eyes, he could still see Tom's face clearly—the stubbled square jaw, regal nose, the lines around intelligent blue eyes. Could hear the deep drawl, smell his addictive scent. And if he tried hard enough, he could feel Tom's callused hands against his hips, gripping, blunt fingers digging in to his flesh. Ben's fingertips tingled with the memory of the hard muscles beneath them as he'd shoved Tom to his knees. The way Tom's light blond hair felt against his palms. Fuck! The way his tongue lapped at Ben's cock, the perfect suction of that warm, wet mouth. Everything about the cop was pure animalistic sexual perfection.

Ben groaned as the memories assaulted him, heating his flesh, causing his pulse to race and his cock to harden and twitch. He might not have intended to ever see Officer Thomas Webber again, never thought he'd have to name the man as his alibi, but a big part of him was rejoicing at the turn of events that would bring Tom back into his life. His body damn sure wanted to spend more time up close and personal with Tom. Hard parts, tingling and throbbing parts wanted lots and lots of attention from him. And truth be told, Ben was also curious about the man's life, his mind. He wanted to know the secrets hidden within, the ones that caused such pain to shine in his haunted blue eyes. The guilt and shame and every other thought or dream was burned into his orbs and showed in the lines on his rugged face.

Ben shook his head and reached for another smoke, lighting it with shaking hands. He inhaled deeply and blew it out slowly, felt the burn in his throat, the nicotine calming his nerves slightly. He was unnerved, confused, and yet so fucking turned-on. For the first time in his life—well, the second time, but the crush of a preteen boy didn't count—this was the first time as an adult that Ben pictured himself spending more than one night with a man. He'd had this crazy dream of waking with Tom's arms wrapped around him, and much to Ben's surprise, it hadn't been unpleasant.

"Alright, Parker," Sheriff Cronkite called out as he slapped the bars, causing Ben to jump. "Looks like you aren't a total liar. Officer Webber has confirmed your story."

"I told you," Ben said with a sneer. "I'm a lot of things, but I'm not a fucking liar."

Cronkite laughed, an ugly sound without humor. "I beg to differ, and somehow you've gotten Officer Webber lying for you too."

"Oh right, because it's so much more believable that I could corrupt an officer of the law rather than be telling the truth," Ben said sarcastically.

"You're a goddamn thief and con man, and you obviously have something on Webber." He pointed a finger at Ben, a deep scowl on his face. "This ain't over. I will find out what it is, and when I do…."

Cronkite let his threat hang in the air, and Ben clamped down on his reaction to it. He gritted his teeth to keep the ugly curse from passing his lips. Instead, he smiled as the sheriff continued to glare at him. *Never give them anything. Never let them see you sweat.* Ben put the cigarette between his teeth, folded one arm back behind his head, and stretched his legs out. He was projecting the perfect picture of relaxed without a care in the world, even though on the inside he was nauseous with the thought of this mean bastard going after Tom. Ben's heart raced, causing his chest to hurt, but he ignored the pain and sick feeling. *Never admit to anything.*

Ben was concerned about going down for a robbery he hadn't committed, but his other secret, the dark one he hid from everyone, the deviant part, scared him fucking senseless. The thought of being yanked from his cell and lynched for enjoying the pleasures of another man, or worse, exposing that other man, were much more difficult to deal with. They were much harder not to react to, but with an ironclad will born of pure fucking orneriness, he hid it. He took another draw from his smoke and blew it out, all the while forcing himself to act carefree and paste a sly smile on his lips.

"Don't you have some paperwork or something to do for my release?" Ben asked easily with a dismissive wave of his hand.

"You don't fool me, you piece of shit," Cronkite sneered.

"Why so hostile, Sheriff? I've done nothing wrong, and soon you'll have your proof."

"That remains to be seen," Cronkite growled and stormed off.

Ben squeezed his eyes shut and pulled the cigarette from his mouth, wincing when it stuck to his dry lips. So Officer Thomas Webber was on his way. The idea was both exhilarating and frightening. He'd have to work harder than he ever had to before at controlling his reactions to a man he found so incredibly attractive. One slip up, one telltale sign, and he wouldn't be the only one swinging from a tree. The thought of Tom dangling bothered him even more than his own demise. He wasn't sure why that was, since he'd never considered anyone's feelings before his own since he was a teen. He'd have to give it more thought when he wasn't so horny and tired.

Ben leaned over the cot far enough to snub out his butt, then returned to his reclined position. He hadn't slept more than a few minutes in the last couple of days, and with Officer Thomas Webber on his way to Nashville, he couldn't afford to allow any of his carefully constructed guard down. The only way he'd have a chance was to rest his mind, clear the fog that sleep deprivation always produced.

The sound of birds chirping outside the small window lulled Ben, and he yawned sleepily. He shut his eyes and blew out a long sigh. The calming sound of the birds was quickly replaced when the first thing he saw behind his closed lids was the image of Thomas Webber on his knees in full uniform, gun on his hip, badge on his chest, and Ben's fat cock sliding in and out of his sweet mouth. The seductive images followed Ben into slumber, making for sweet, erotic dreams.

TOM REPLACED the phone receiver, leaned back in his chair, and ran a shaking hand over his face. "What have I done," he murmured under his breath. He covered his face in his hands as tears burned his eyes. *Dear God! What have I done!*

Guilt, shame, and disgust assaulted him so powerfully, his breath caught and his gut roiled. Bile rose up in his throat as the tears spilled from his eyes. Tom lunged for the wastebasket, snatching it up just in time. Stomach acid burned his throat, coated his tongue, and spewed out of him in painful retching waves. His stomach cramped and churned long after the meager lunch he'd eaten was expelled. After his gut was empty, he continued to gag and retch, dry heaving, as if his body was trying to rid itself of the damnation Tom had soaked it in. It didn't matter that the logical part of his mind begged and pleaded with his body to stop, reasoning the damage to his soul could not be dispelled by something as simplistic as vomiting—it didn't listen. He heaved and cried and silently begged for it to end, although he dared not pray.

He had no right.

Deserved no pity.

No forgiveness.

How long he was held in that miserable state—seconds, minutes, hours, years—Tom didn't know. He only knew when it ended, when his stomach gave up the fight and his muscles released their constrictive hold, and he was left exhausted. The only thing he had the energy to do was wrap his arms around himself and silently cry. No great sobs, no hitch of breath, just a steady stream of tears. Perhaps his one last attempt to rid himself of evil? It wouldn't work. Nothing could save his mortal soul. He'd sinned against his wife, his child, his community, and his God, and he would lose them all. His punishment for allowing the devil in, for his weakness, for wallowing in the foulness of carnal temptation.

Do not be deceived: God is not mocked, for whatever a man sows, that will he also reap.

The only question now was whether he would do the right thing and admit to his sins, stand up, confess his wrongdoings, and take his punishment like a man? Or would he try to save the shell that now housed his corrupt soul and allow Ben to walk away?

Chapter 6

SHERIFF CRONKITE tapped his thick index finger against his desk, his dark eyes cold as he stared at Tom. Tom did his best not to squirm under the sheriff's scrutiny, but it was difficult. Cronkite was an imposing man. Although he appeared to be in his late fifties to early sixties, as evidenced by the deep wrinkles on his tanned face, Cronkite was built like a brick house. He towered above Tom at well over six feet tall, and his broad chest, heavy with bulk, was nearly twice as wide as Tom's. The muscles in his neck bulged against the collar of his tan uniform shirt, the veins straining. But what made Cronkite imperious was the hard expression on his face and the ice-cold stare he had trained on Tom.

"So let me get this straight," Cronkite said, leaning back in his chair and folding his arms across his chest. "You found Mr. Parker stranded on the side of the road at three o'clock?"

"Yes, sir," Tom lied. He'd made the decision to try and save his reputation for the sake of his family. No doubt he had a one-way ticket to hell, but the least he could do was try and spare his wife and son the embarrassment of the full truth. The shame and stigma of having a father and husband who was a disgusting faggot wasn't something he'd burden his family with if he could help it. It was unfair they should have to pay for Tom's transgressions.

"And you say he was locked up in your holding cell all night?"

"No, sir. I said he was locked up in the cell until the storm hit. He was then with me in the cold storage area beneath the floor."

"And you released him the next morning at dawn?" Cronkite asked, his tone disbelieving.

"Yes, sir. Just as dawn was breaking," Tom responded evenly.

"Now why in the hell would you do that, son?"

Tom bristled at being called son, but he swallowed down his irritation. "I didn't have anything to hold him on."

"And you didn't think to run his name, maybe obtain his prints?"

Tom leaned on the desk, holding that cold gaze with a fiery one of his own. "Well now, Sheriff, I had a bit of a problem, considering I had no phone lines and the front window of my station had been blown to kingdom come from a fucking tornado that had just ripped through my town. My first priority was to assist the citizens of Ramer, not some stranded motorist with a lost wallet. So you'll have to forgive my slip in protocol."

Tom had fucked up, he knew that, but allowing Ben—William Parker—to walk away that morning wasn't one of them. It was the one thing he didn't regret. His town was in ruins, his citizens hurt and homeless, and he'd be damned if he'd apologize for wanting Ben gone—whatever Tom's initial reasoning—so he could help those who mattered.

"I take it you informed Chief Harvey of your"—Cronkite scowled, his expression brooding—"disregard for procedure?"

"I would have," Tom informed him with a smirk. Tom hated what he'd done, the temptation he'd been powerless against, but he disliked Cronkite immensely. Tom wasn't sure why. There was something about the man that rubbed Tom the wrong way, and he relished in pissing the fucker off. Tom leaned back in his chair, stretched his legs, and crossed his ankles. Relaxed. Not a care in the world. "But you see, Chief Harvey passed away two weeks ago, and I'm interim police chief until we can hold an election. So yes, I suppose the chief of Ramer is aware of and has no issues or apologies for the disregard, given the circumstances." Tom entwined his fingers, resting his hands on his belly, and smiled broadly.

Cronkite glared at Tom, but Tom continued to smile. He saw the defeat in the man's eyes. They were still dark, cold, and intimidating as hell, but Tom noticed the way his shoulders slumped slightly and saw the twitch in the man's clenched jaw. Sheriff Cronkite would suck at playing poker. He wore his emotions on his face; his body language also gave him away. Cronkite was pissed but resigned to his defeat, at least for now. Tom had no idealistic dreams that it would end here.

It was only the beginning; that much he was sure of.

Cronkite slammed his hand on the papers on the desk in front of him and shoved them angrily at Tom. "Sign it," he barked, then slung a pen at Tom.

Tom picked up the pen, his grin never faltering. "You know—"

"Just sign the fucking papers so I can rid myself of you and that piece of shit stinking up my goddamn holding cell."

Tom considered taunting the man a little more, then thought better of it and snapped his mouth shut. He understood the whole big-dog territorial bullshit. He also got that Cronkite had convinced himself he was right, thinking he'd caught himself a wanted man and would be a hero, and Tom had come and shit in his yard. Tom signed the statement, dated it, and pushed it and the pen back toward Cronkite.

"I'll see myself out," Tom said, going to his feet. He tipped his hat— "Sheriff" —and walked out the door.

He'd done it—given the best performance of his life, lied his ass off without so much as batting an eye. With any luck, he'd be back in Ramer before nightfall and the whole fucked-up situation with Cronkite and William Parker would be behind him.

HEAVY STEPS echoed along the corridor, moving closer. Ben pushed his fingers through his tousled hair, smoothing it as he rolled his shoulders. Each footfall caused his heart to pick up in pace, the anticipation and excitement making his belly flutter. His gut plummeted when he looked up and saw the scowling face of Sheriff Cronkite. *Just the man I didn't want to fucking see.*

Cronkite rattled the keys in his hand, periodically twirling them around his finger, his icy gaze on Ben. The silence in the room was palpable as the man continued to stare at him. Ben refused to be provoked; instead, he leaned against the wall and met Cronkite's hard expression with a smug one. Ben consciously tried to keep his expression cool and collected, his stance relaxed. Whatever had happened between Cronkite and Webber, it hadn't gone as Cronkite had planned. The big mean goon was literally vibrating, the thick veins in his neck bulging and his face so red Ben wondered how long before the lawman exploded or dropped from a coronary or stroke. The thought of Cronkite's head exploding caused Ben to chuckle.

"Something funny, boy?" Cronkite snarled.

"Nothing you'd appreciate, I'm sure," Ben drawled.

Cronkite shoved the key in the cell door and turned it, not without difficulty, as evident by the shaking of his big paws, the jerky movements, and the deepening scowl as he ripped open the door.

"Grab your shit," Cronkite ordered.

"Oh. Am I going somewhere?" Ben feigned innocence.

"Get your ass up and grab your shit, or I'll slam this motherfucking door closed and you can rot."

"Temper, temper," Ben warned. He stood, grabbed his jacket, and shrugged it on. He'd best not poke the bastard. Cronkite didn't look like a man who made idle threats.

Ben stepped past the sheriff and nearly fell on his face when the bastard gave Ben's shoulder a nice, hard shove. He stumbled but grabbed the iron bars of the cell, hiding his grin by keeping his face averted, and moved to the door at the end of the hall. He stepped to the side, allowing the sheriff to unlock the door to the office. They stood so close Ben could smell the sweat and pipe smoke and anger. Yes, he could smell the anger: it had a sharp aroma, stung his nose, and kicked up Ben's fight-or-flight response. Adrenaline surged within him, heightening his awareness. He wouldn't win either scenario, so he kept his grin hidden, his eyes averted, and waited patiently.

Hand resting on the doorknob, Cronkite turned his head to look at Ben. "I know you have to be blackmailing Officer Webber in order for him to lie for you," he whispered in a menacing tone, "but rest assured, it is my top priority, my new mission in life to find out exactly what it is, and when I do"—he leaned just a fraction of an inch closer to Ben, the message clear—"I will bury you both."

"Understood," Ben acknowledged with a nod.

Ben followed Cronkite to his desk and accepted the duffel bag the sheriff held out for him, only Cronkite still held the strap, the tension on it pulling them together. "I don't want to see you back here. If I do, I will take it as a direct threat on the good folks of Davidson County and put a fucking bullet in you."

Ben clamped his mouth shut. The poison in the sheriff's tone was deadly, serious, and broached no argument. No need for comment.

Ben nodded again and tugged at the strap of his duffel; this time Cronkite released his hold. Without a backward glance, Ben hightailed it out of the precinct. He didn't slow down until he was behind the wheel of his sedan. With a shuddering breath, he turned the key in the ignition.

"Yes'm, sir, boss-man. Won't see my sorry ass back in this stupid fucking county," he grumbled as he revved the engine. He threw the car in reverse and gunned it, gravel flying from beneath his tires. He then slammed on the brake and clutch, shoved the shifter into gear, and stomped on the gas. Ben checked the rearview mirror several times as he flew down the highway, half expecting to see flashing lights behind him or bullets blowing out his back window. Only when he turned at the first intersection, checked the rearview mirror once more, and saw nothing did he let out a heavy breath and ease his foot from the gas pedal.

The landscape outside his window was a blur of color as Ben flew down the road. He couldn't get away from Cronkite fast enough. Still, he was disappointed he hadn't had the opportunity to see Tom again. If he had, being pulled over and hauled into jail and accused of bank robbery would have been worth it. It would have been fate bringing him and Tom together again. But it hadn't happened.

Fate was a fickle bitch.

Jesus, how many times had he thought of heading back to Ramer over the past week—Hundreds? Tens of hundreds?—only to quash the urge each and every time. It had been difficult, but he'd proven he was stronger than the allure, the desire, the need. God, how he had needed. He'd lain on a stinking mattress in a seedy hotel room with peeling wallpaper, cockroaches, and the smell of things he'd rather not think about or give name to. In his mind's eye, though, as he took himself in hand, he was beneath a small police station, the scent of earth and musk in his nostrils, the heat of that body against his, the wet warm mouth around his cock. He'd come so hard. He'd been left sated and boneless far away from the rotting hotel room, transported to another place, an unfamiliar place. When he closed his eyes that night, his pulse still racing, his body sweat and cum-covered, he'd drifted off to sleep against Tom, those big strong arms wrapped around him, holding him tight. Not fucking. Not restraining him or shoving him into a cell, but hugging him, Tom's strong and powerful yet loving embrace keeping Ben safe and warm as he slept.

Down the highway Ben flew, staying close to the speed limit, that much he was aware of. He didn't fancy another trip to jail tonight, but his mind was barely on the road, focused just enough on the asphalt before him. He was able to maneuver the car with ease, but his thoughts were still wrapped in the dream. He saw flashes of smooth, strong muscles, the rise and fall of a broad chest beneath his head. He heard the deep, husky voice whispering to him, telling him things he'd never hear outside his fantasy, beyond his dreams, and thought he would commit murder to hear them just once in reality. If he tried hard enough, concentrated deep enough, he could smell the clean sweat of his phantom lover, taste the earth and wind and sunshine on his skin as Ben ran his tongue along Tom's thick neck. He was hard, his need was strong, and he wanted. Ben wanted Tom like he'd never wanted anyone—why? Perhaps it was loneliness that was the driving force, or maybe he'd simply met Tom at a point in his life when he was tired of life on the edge and was ready to settle down. Could it be possible the crazy dream of warmth and safety had affected him more than he'd realized? Hell, he had no idea what it was about Tom that called to him so strongly. The only thing Ben knew for sure was Tom had both his logic and his emotions a complete mess.

He wanted…

Sorrow filled Ben, made his eyes sting and his chest ache. It was silly to think of such things, to wish for the impossible. People like him—con men, hoodlums, faggots—rarely found happiness. But what if he could change? What if he stopped conning people, stopped stealing, hitting, taking? Would he deserve happiness then? A relationship with another man was a dangerous thing to want, yet he couldn't help it. He'd been born with a noose around his neck, couldn't change that part of who he was, knew it for the impossibility it was. He had tried—hard—to no avail. No, he couldn't change who he was at his core—faggot, nancy, sissy—whatever term society labeled him with, he would never stop desiring the feel of a smooth hard, muscular body, stubbled chin, cock, but the other things…. Perhaps.

Ben took his foot from the gas pedal, depressed the clutch, slowly pushed down on the brake, and steered the car to the side of the road. When he came to a stop, he looked up at the large sign: *Welcome to Ramer.* Ben ran his hand over his chin, his two-day-old beard tickling his palm, as his grin spread across his face. He hadn't consciously set out to return to this town, but apparently that didn't matter. It looked like he was going to try and tempt fate, make his own destiny—or get himself killed in the process.

Chapter 7

THE SUN beat down on Tom's shoulders and back. His undershirt, long ago soaked through with sweat, clung to him as he worked. He focused on nail, hammer, and shingle, ignoring the exhaustion in his limbs, the blisters on his hands, and the fire along his back. He did his best to keep the events of the morning out of his head. He'd convinced himself he'd done what any good husband or father would have done. He'd protected his family, even if he was what they needed protection from. Done what was right. Expected.

You've always done what was expected of you, Tommy boy, haven't you?

Nail. Hammer. Shingle.

Married well. Fathered a nice strapping boy. Protector of the law.

Tom shook his head, the sweat rolling down into his eyes, burning them. He redoubled his efforts to focus, clear his mind.

Nail. Hammer. Shingle.

Helping to rebuild this church isn't going to save your soul, Tommy boy.

Tom gritted his teeth, swung the hammer harder.

Liar.

Nail. Hammer. Shingle.

Adulterer.

Nail. Hammer. Shingle.

Faggot.

The voice inside Tom's head was screaming, accusing, and no matter how hard he tried, he couldn't block it out. He swung with all his might, angry and defeated, and cried out when sharp pain radiated out from his finger, ran up his arm, and finally silenced the voice.

"Son of a bitch," Tom cut out angrily, tossing away the hammer and gripping his smashed finger as he jumped to his feet.

"Here, let me see," Pastor John said as he came over to Tom.

"It's fine," he managed to grit out between clenched teeth.

"I said, let me see it," the pastor demanded.

Without looking up and meeting those concerned eyes—he couldn't—Tom held out his finger. Fuck, it hurt! He felt each beat of his heart as a painful throb in the digit. Tom swayed on his feet, jaw clenched to keep from crying out as the pastor examined his finger, poked at it, moved it.

"Definitely broken. Gonna need to be set." He released his hold on Tom's hand.

Tom instinctively gripped his finger again, tucked it away against his body, protecting it.

"You think you can make it down the ladder on your own or you want me to get you some help?" Pastor John touched Tom's forehead, then his cheek. "You're lookin' a little pale. Best get you some help."

Tom shook his head. "Nah, I'm okay. Just hurts like a motherfu—I mean, I'm okay. Knocked the wind out of me for a bit." He released the hold he had on his damaged finger, but kept it close to his body. He could feel the blood soaking into his shirt. Tom pulled his bandana from his back pocket and carefully wrapped it tightly around his hand.

"You sure?" Pastor John asked. He didn't sound convinced.

"Yes, sir. I can make it down on my own," Tom assured him and went to his feet. He started to collect his tools, but Pastor John stopped him.

"I'll get those. You go on and have that finger looked after."

Tom nodded and slowly made his way down the ladder. He no longer had to try and focus on tools and work, the searing pain in his hand was enough to keep any and all thoughts at bay. As he moved down each rung of the ladder, he jostled his finger, making him wince, and he swallowed the nasty curses that wanted out. Sweat poured down his brow and stung his eyes. His good hand was slick with sweat, and he was dizzy as well. Losing his grip was a real concern. Maybe letting go would be wise. A two-story fall could end the pain in his hand, the fucked-up thoughts in his head, and the sin in his heart. He could make it all stop. *It's easy, no pain, no guilt, nothing but sweet oblivion. Let go.* Yet he tightened his grip, moved down another rung, kept moving.

Obviously the need to survive outweighed the easier choice, and Tom planted his boot on hard dirt, instantly moving his free hand to protect his injured one. Fuck! Not only was he a liar and a sodomite, he was a goddamn coward.

"Welcome to rock bottom," he grumbled under his breath.

Tom found Doc Masterson in an old rocking chair just inside the large open doors of the church, sipping on tea. As soon as Doc looked Tom's way, Tom held up the wrapped hand and shrugged.

Doc set his cup aside and stood, shaking his head as he came down the steps. "Sometimes I wonder who is the smarter of the two, the hammer or the damn fool swingin' it."

"I'm going with the hammer this time," Tom drawled, then winced when Doc grabbed his wrist and removed the bandana. Blood still oozed from the disfigured digit. "Not so rough," Tom yelped and instinctively tried to pull away. Doc tightened his grip.

"You ain't seen rough yet, boy," Doc muttered as he ran a critical eye over the injury. "Gonna need to be cleaned up, disinfected, set, splinted." He turned Tom's hand over and poked at the cut. "A few stitches."

Tom snatched his hand away, pulled it close to his body, protecting it again. "You ain't touchin' it till I've had a shot of that rotgut you keep in your desk drawer."

"That's strictly for medicinal purposes," Doc scoffed.

"Yeah, well, I got some purpose for your medicinal. C'mon."

Tom headed down the block with Doc Masterson on his heels. By the time they made it the small office at the end of the street, Tom was still drenched in sweat, dizzy, but now he was also nauseous, and his finger hurt worse. He stepped aside, swaying slightly as Doc unlocked the door, then pushed past him as soon as it was open. He headed straight to the desk where he knew the whiskey was kept and snatched open the drawer. Bottle in hand, Tom pried the cork out with his teeth and took a long pull of the booze. The cheap alcohol burned all the way down to his churning gut. He took a couple deep breaths as he fought to keep the disgusting shit from coming back up, then took another big gulp.

Tom wiped the back of his hand over his mouth. "Alright. I'm ready," he muttered, then walked over to the sink and held his hand beneath the faucet. "Start washin'," he said and tipped the bottle up again.

Thank goodness Pastor John hadn't accompanied Tom back to Doc Masterson's office. If he had, the pastor surely would have heard screaming and cussin' that would make a sailor blush. The five stitches had hurt like hell, but Tom had clenched his jaw, only allowing a grunt to escape with each pass of the needle through flesh. However, when Doc set the break, splinted it, and taped the poor abused digit to his middle finger, Tom had been unable to keep his agony inside.

"All set," Doc commented, brow raised, and chuckled. "Pun intended."

Tom didn't find any humor in the statement. He wiped the sweat from his brow with a shaking hand, then grabbed the whiskey, gulped a good measure, and handed to bottle to Doc.

"Thanks. What do I owe ya?"

Doc examined the nearly empty bottle. "Another fifth of whiskey," he said with a scowl.

"I'll drop it off tomorrow before work," Tom slurred. He stood and swayed, unsteady from both the alcohol and pain.

"You show up here at 6:00 a.m. and knock on my door, I'll beat you with that goddamn bottle," Doc warned.

Tom laughed and held up his good hand as if to ward off an attack. "Fine. Fine. I'll drop it off after work."

"Smart man," Doc said with a sly grin. "Now get your ass back to the station and no working this afternoon. Oh, and keep that hand propped up and iced. It will hurt like a bitch if ya don't."

"I'm thinking I'll head home," Tom said, keeping his bad hand up on his chest. More pain wasn't something he would take kindly to. The damn thing was still screaming.

"I thought your roof was gone?"

"Was. Is. But Frank had a couple old canvas sails and tarps. Rigged it up so I could at least sleep in a bed rather than that lumpy-ass cot down at the jail."

"The missus and I got a spare room. You're more than welcome to it."

"Thanks," Tom said sincerely and patted Doc on the shoulder. "I don't wanna be a burden." Doc started to say something, probably to assure Tom it wouldn't be a hardship. Doc and Mrs. Masterson were good people, but Tom wanted to go home. He wanted peace and quiet to lick his wounds and have a good cry, or even a lollipop, if he took a notion. *Stupid hammer, Stupid hammer swinger.* "Besides, we've had a couple reports of theft."

Doc shook his head. "Takes a real hoodlum to steal from a man while he's down."

"That it does, Doc. That it does." Tom stopped at the door, hand on the knob. "Thanks again for the patch up and the offer of a bed. I'll see you tomorrow."

"You sure you're okay to be driving?" Doc asked with a concerned expression.

"Yeah. I'm fine. Pain done burned off the whiskey."

"You want to take the rest of this for later?" Doc offered, raising the bottle.

Tom waved it off. "Nah. I got the good stuff at home."

"That moonshine's illegal, ya know. Careful not to get caught with it." Doc chuckled and waved.

So is lying and being a faggot. A bottle of hooch was the least of his worries. Tom didn't say anything more, just waved, opened the door, and stepped out. He closed the door behind him and shut his eyes. Christ! Couldn't he ever get that shit out of his head? It was over and done with. He'd better find a way to put it behind him or he was going to drive himself insane. Then again, going insane, ending up in a padded cell drooling and barking like a dog might be a blessing. With his goddamn luck, he'd end up in a straitjacket in a padded cell with nothing to chew on but images, lust, and a big fucking heap of guilt.

Tom hadn't been completely honest with Doc—big shock there, seemed he'd been lying to everyone as of late—the alcohol was indeed affecting his head. Everything was a little swimmy as he made his way home. He stuck to the back roads, nothing but dirt and trees and the occasional wild animal to worry about. And the pain. The pain was a new constant, both in his head and his hand. When he finally pulled into his drive and cut the engine, he let out a relieved breath. Tom rested his head against the seat, giving himself a moment to calm. He took in a long deep breath through his nose and let it out slowly past his lips. The moment he closed his eyes, the calm became impossible to achieve because images of Ben popped into his alcohol-hazed brain.

"Goddammit! I hate you!" Tom shouted and jerked himself upright, opened his eyes, and cursed again when his injured hand was jostled. "I hate you. Hate me. Hate this fucking splint. This whole fucked-up situation."

Tom stilled and went silent when he caught a glimpse of movement. He scanned the porch, the area around it, but saw nothing. An uneasy feeling tickled its way down his spine as he continued to stare out the front windshield, checking each window, door, the ruined roof. There. Tom started to laugh when he realized it was the tarp on the roof that had moved in the wind.

"Add scaredy-cat to my list of pathetic attributes." He laughed harder and stepped out of his cruiser.

Still, as he made his way up the stairs to the front porch, the tickling sensation along his spine increased. He stood silently next to the door, straining to hear any sound that would clue him into what had him so jumpy. Nothing. He turned in a slow circle, taking in his surroundings, concentrating hard as he scanned the area once again, searching for anything out of the ordinary, but still nothing seemed out of place. He could find no source for the strange feeling. Tom continued to turn, searching, listening. The last time he'd ignored the warning signal in his gut he'd.... Nope, he wasn't going to think about that night.

Convinced it was the alcohol and the events of the morning that had him spooked, Tom pushed open the front door and stepped inside. The living area was devoid of any furnishings; everything had been moved into the garage until the roof could be repaired. Leaves and debris blew around along the scarred hardwood floors. Everything looked as it had the last time he'd been home. With the odd jittery feeling still riding him, Tom cautiously moved through the kitchen, his son's bedroom, and bathroom. All was as it had been. As he moved to the door to his bedroom, his nerves went nuts, and Tom instinctively reached for his gun. *Fuck!* He'd left it locked in the trunk of his cruiser. The goose bumps that bloomed across his flesh were a warning. He should take heed, retrieve his gun first, and yet he turned the knob, heart hammering in his chest. Adrenaline surged through him; the sensation scared him, yet was oddly arousing, his body heating in anticipation. Anticipation of what? This was getting ridiculous. Tom shoved the door, and it slammed into the plaster, the loud sound echoing off the walls in the otherwise silent room.

The heavy curtains drawn over the windows along with the tarps and sails acting as a roof were enough to darken the room, and Tom blinked several times as his eyes adjusted to the gloom.

"Evening, Officer." It was a familiar voice, that of a stranger from a stormy night along a deserted road. It was deep and smooth with a hint of a northern accent.

Tom's breath caught in his throat as he focused on prominent cheekbones in a thin face and dark eyes Tom knew were liquid brown.

The dark brown pompadour was slicked back—not a hair out of place—unlike when Tom had grabbed it in his fists, disheveling it as he slammed into the man. Tom's lips knew well the slight scruff on his jaw and chin. A thin scar ran from one temple down a cheek, curving at the tip of a full upper lip, curling it into a sly grin. Tom had ached to trace it with his tongue one night not long ago. Since then, he'd dreamed of him. Wanted him. Hated him.

Ben.

Chapter 8

FROM HIS chair in the corner of the room, Ben watched Tom come through the door, recognized the moment Tom spotted him, and held dead still, scarcely breathing. For fuck's sake, the man was an officer of the law, armed, could justifiably shoot Ben dead as an intruder. He hadn't really thought out his plan beyond seeing Tom again, ruled by his libido. Jesus, his cock was going to get him killed. He was unarmed, just spooked a man with a weapon, and there he sat, hard as steel as he ran his gaze down the familiar body. This was the man he wanted so damn bad that he couldn't see straight, couldn't think, sleep, or eat without the bastard in his head. And now he was going to die. He was sure of it.

"What the fuck are you doing here?" Tom barked.

Ben stared unblinking, his body tense, waiting for the explosion of pain that would precede his death. But it didn't happen. In fact, Tom had one hand against his chest, the other at his side, and instead of raising his weapon, taking up a shooter's stance, he took a step back.

So maybe Ben had a chance. "I wanted to see you."

"What?" Tom asked, his tone disbelieving. He took another step back as if Ben had slapped him, his back hitting the doorframe.

"I wanted to see you," Ben repeated.

Tom stared at Ben, his eyes wide, his lean chest rising and falling rapidly in apparent shock.

"Wanted to personally thank you for what you did for me," Ben added. He shifted in his chair, Tom's presence, his scent, and the sound of his voice, all ramping up Ben's arousal. He ached to touch, to lick and kiss and fuck, but he fought the urge. He was crazy, but not crazy enough to tempt the man into shooting him.

After a long tense moment, Tom finally muttered, "I didn't do it for you." He took a step to the side, clearing the doorway, and pointed at it. "Now get the fuck out of my house."

Ben hesitated, ran a hand across his mouth to hide the grin. He'd heard the catch in Tom's voice, the uncertainty, the fear. Ben also couldn't help but notice the thick bulge in the man's trousers. Ben licked his lips and held up his hands in a show of being unarmed and defenseless.

"I haven't stopped thinking about you," Ben murmured seductively. He slowly rose to his feet. "Not since the moment I first laid eyes on you." He took a carefully measured step. "Can't stop thinking about how you felt when you—"

"Don't you dare fucking say it," Tom growled. "Nothing happened except I made the mistake of not leaving you cuffed and locked in that goddamn cell."

Ben took another step closer. "Is that what you've been telling yourself? How you've been dealing with missing me?"

"Missing you?" Tom sneered and laughed, the sound ugly and without humor. "I haven't thought of you once until that fucking phone rang and Cronkite informed me he had you in custody."

Another step. "Then why did you come? Why did you make yourself my alibi if nothing happened?"

Tom's scent was stronger now—sweat, cheap whiskey, fear—and holy shit, it was a hell of an aphrodisiac. Ben briefly wondered how long it would take him to have Tom bent over the mattress with his pants down around his ankles and his firm ass in the air. The man was dressed in dungarees, no service belt, no weapon, and injured; he saw the splinted fingers. *I bet it wouldn't take much to overpower him.* Within seconds he could be ramming himself deep into that perfect ass or feeling Tom's fat cock deep within himself. Either one worked for Ben. He groaned as the images assaulted him, made his cock surge and his flesh burn.

"Nothing fucking happened," Tom screamed, his face red with rage, muscles in his neck straining. "Now get your sorry ass out of my house, or I'll put a bullet in you!"

Ben moved closer, putting only a foot between him and the pissed-off man vibrating with rage. Tom wasn't the only one vibrating; Ben was too, but for a completely different reason. "Why do people keep threatening me with a bullet?" Ben kept his stance nonthreatening, hands hanging at his sides, his grin teasing.

"You deserve one," Tom hissed.

The anger was evident on Tom's face; it contorted his features, his sneer aggressive. Never one to back down from a challenge or allow a little threat to deter him, Ben stood his ground. He really fucking wanted this man like he'd never wanted another. Ever. Plus, anger and lust often mimicked each other—darkened eyes, quickened breathing, trembling bodies. But what encouraged Ben the most was the hard cock pressing against the front of the officer's pants.

"I deserve a lot of things," Ben murmured and pressed his hand against Tom's hardness. "But a bullet isn't one of them."

Ben's muscles coiled, tensed for a fight or a fuck. Ben hoped it was the latter, but expected the former. For one long, drawn-out moment, then another, they stood silent, still, barely breathing. Waited. Wanted.

"I fucking hate you," Tom shouted.

The air rushed out of Ben when he was suddenly spun and slammed against the door. Pain exploded across his skull when his head hit solid wood. He was dazed, the blood roaring in his ears, and panicked as he fought to catch up with the abrupt shift. The sensation was fleeting, as a new awareness, a pleasurable one, took over when Tom pressed his body hard against Ben's. Then he felt a new pain as teeth sunk into the meaty flesh between his neck and shoulder. Ben cried out, and he dug his fingers into Tom's muscular back, pulling Tom closer, encouraging him to rut. Ben sought out the soft silky strands of Tom's hair with his other hand; he curled his fingers and pressed Tom's face even harder against his own skin.

"Now this I deserve," Ben groaned.

Tom jerked back, eyes wide. "No!"

Ben was acutely aware of the absence of heat and friction and hardness as Tom pulled away. Jesus, his cock was hard and pulsing, and his body protested the loss in the form of a violent shiver. Whatever lust-filled spell Tom was under was broken with Ben's spoken words. *Shit!* Why the hell had he opened his mouth?

"No," Tom repeated, looking horrified, and took another step back. He ran the back of his hand over his mouth as if he were attempting to wipe away Ben's flavor.

"Why?" Stupid question, but it was the only thing Ben could think to ask.

Tom just stood and stared at him with that panic-stricken look. Ben's chest tightened. He needed to say something that would cut through Tom's consternation. But what? He curled his hands into fists and fought the urge to reach out and grab the man. Ben wanted to rut and fuck and get off so bad he could taste it, but something deeper, something he couldn't quite understand, stopped him. He had no witty remark, no demand or sly, seductive grin to give. Ben was shocked to realize he wanted to hug Tom, smooth away the furrow between his brows, kiss away that frown, and assure him everything was okay. But he knew tenderness would not be welcomed.

"Why?" Tom echoed. He shook his head and wiped his mouth again. "Because I won't let you tempt me again." He scanned the area, eyes wild, then sat on the edge of the bed, forearms resting on his knees, head hung. "I can still fix this," he muttered in a low, barely audible voice, apparently talking to himself.

"I want you, you want me. Way I see it, the only thing that needs to be fixed is the distance currently between our bodies."

Tom's head snapped up, his mouth agape. "I'm…. I'm…." He pointed an accusing finger at Ben. "I am not like you," he sputtered with indignation.

Rage, hot and fiery, flared within Ben, made him see red. He was sick and tired of people looking at him with disgust in their eyes, but for Tom to look at him with revulsion, it was all the worse. He'd felt Tom's arousal, had the man's cock up his ass, had his cock down Tom's throat. How dare he look at Ben like that?

In a blink of an eye, Ben propelled himself across the room and tackled Tom. Ben had his hands wrapped around Tom's wrists, pinning them over his head, and he pressed the full weight of his body down on Tom. He ground his hard cock against an equally hard one.

"You're exactly like me," Ben snarled. "The only difference is you're too fucking chicken-shit to admit it."

"Fuck you!" Tom arched his back and kicked his feet in an attempt to throw Ben off.

Ben held firm. He locked his legs around Tom's in a complete submission hold and snapped his hips with brutal force. He ignored the pain that shot up his spine and down his legs. He wanted to punish the son of a bitch.

"You'll get your chance," Ben snapped, then smashed their mouths together. Tom gasped, still fighting, and Ben used the opportunity to shove his tongue deep. Lips split against teeth, the coppery tang of blood—his? Tom's? Both? Didn't matter, Ben was too pissed off, too turned on to care—in his mouth. He'd be goddamned if he'd turn the bastard loose—screw the pain—until Tom responded, gave in, admitted.

Ben pulled back from the kiss, licked the blood from his bottom lip, and bared his teeth before latching on to the same spot on Tom where Tom had bitten him. He sunk his teeth in, not enough to break the skin, but enough to hold Tom and cause pain. Then he soothed the area with lips and tongue. Tom bucked at the bite, but stilled with the press of lips to his flesh, so Ben did it again. He kissed and licked until he pulled a deep groan from Tom.

Ben released one of Tom's wrists without a word. Moving carefully, ever so slowly, like one would with a spooked animal, Ben slid his hand between their bodies. He undid his pants, rolling his hips now rather than thrusting and pushing the pants down. Then he popped the button on Tom's pants and exposed his cock, all the while kissing, licking, nuzzling.

Ben bit back a moan as soft, hot skin over steel rubbed together. He held their cocks together in one hand, adding pressure and friction.

"Fuck," Tom hissed and pushed hard against Ben's hand. Defeated.

Not like me, huh? Ben hid his grin in Tom's neck, the irritation draining away and being replaced with desire with this victory.

Ben kept his rhythm slow and deliberate, the pressure on their cocks just enough to be pleasurable, but nowhere near enough friction to be more than that. The slow slip and slide was maddening. He wanted to bury himself deep within Tom, wanted to rise up and watch the pleasure play across Tom's features, see the lust in those amazing eyes. But he didn't dare. He had to force himself to go slow; he couldn't afford to spook the man again, break the spell again, not until they found their pleasure. Ben had to prove to Tom how good they were together, how much they needed each other.

HEAT AND friction and male and…. Damn, Tom was so lost to the pleasure rippling through his body. His mind reeled, fought, and balked, but his body kept reacting to Ben's ministrations. The sensations overwhelmed him—the calluses sliding along his length, the feel of Ben's cockhead sliding against his own, the man's breath, tongue, and lips against Tom's neck, the heavy weight on top of him. He was helpless against the onslaught, a wild animal, acting on instinct, need, want.

He thrust into Ben's fist, moaning wantonly. He was so hard. So very fucking hard he couldn't think beyond the pleasures of the flesh, his need for release.

Weak.

Doomed.

Tom stretched his arm out, and his fingers brushed against cold steel. *Gun.* The gun he kept beneath his pillow. The weapon he kept close at night to protect his family. His wife. His son. Dear God, he was rutting against a man—a criminal—in his marital bed.

No!

As the gravity of what he was doing, the sin he was committing in the very bed where his son was conceived, set in, Tom wrapped his hand around the gun, his finger against the trigger as he pulled it from beneath the pillow. In a split second of clarity, he weighed his options. Press the weapon to his own depraved head and squeeze… end it. Instead he pulled the hammer back and pressed the barrel against Ben's head.

Coward.

Ben went dead still; Tom couldn't feel Ben's breath or the rise and fall of his chest for long, drawn-out moments. After what felt like an eternity, the battle of right and wrong still waging within Tom, Ben slowly released his hold on their cocks and lifted his head. Wary dark eyes looked at Tom with confusion and question. The expression on Ben's face almost stripped Tom of his resolve to do the right thing, but he squashed the feeling. He refused to give in to his desires.

"Get off me," Tom demanded, his voice surprisingly even.

Tom kept the gun trained on Ben as he slowly slid off the bed and raised his hands.

"What the hell?"

Tom choked down the disgust when his hard cock throbbed at the sight of Ben standing there with his pants open, erection straining upward. He needed this man gone, needed to take control of the situation and of himself, something he couldn't do with the temptation standing before him. He was weak. He knew in his gut if he allowed Ben to stay, they would be fucking, marital bed and family be damned.

"Get out," Tom ordered as he pulled himself to a sitting position and steadied the gun with his injured hand to keep it from shaking. "Get out of my house, off my property, and out of my town."

"Tom—"

"I said get the fuck out! Now!" Tom roared.

Ben fastened up his pants and adjusted his shirt, never taking his gaze from Tom.

Please! Please just go. Goddamn you, please! Tom silently pleaded.

"This isn't over," Ben warned, then turned and left the room.

Tom kept the gun trained on the empty hallway long after he heard Ben's footsteps move through the house, the front door open and close, and the distinct sound of boots tromping down the porch stairs. He held it at the ready long after everything was silent, until his arms began to shake so hard he could no longer physically do so.

Easing the hammer back into place, Tom stared at the gun as it slipped from his fingers and hit the floor with a thud. Ben was right. It wasn't over, because Tom was too fucking weak, too much of a coward to end it.

Chapter 9

DARK EYES and a smirk stared back at Tom from the wanted poster. He wasn't sure how he'd found the strength to force Ben to leave his home the day before. It would have been so damn easy to give in to his desires, but somehow he'd managed to overcome his urges. Perhaps he wasn't as weak or as helpless as he'd thought. Maybe, just maybe, he could beat this… this demon within him that had resurfaced. He'd been able to hold it at bay for years. Tom might not be able to rid himself of it, but dammit, that didn't mean he had to allow the devil to control him.

Tom ripped the wanted poster from the wall. He couldn't stay strong with those eyes constantly staring at him, demanding things from him, urging him.

"Hey, did they nab that guy?" Frank asked.

"Wrong guy," Tom informed him and crumbled the poster before tossing it into the trash can.

"What do you mean wrong guy?"

Tom sat at his desk and avoided Frank's gaze. "Come to find out he's the guy I picked up the night of the big storm." Tom hadn't told Frank everything about Ben, William—whatever. But he had told him about detaining a subject that night. "I was his alibi."

"Christ, Tom. How the hell didn't you recognize him when I posted that damn photo? He's one scary-looking fucker."

"He looked different," Tom lied. "Besides, I wasn't really paying much attention to specifics. I was a little busy trying not to get my ass wiped out by a tornado."

"So a case of mistaken identity?" Frank shook his head and leaned back in his chair. "Wow! What are the chances there would be two guys who look like that. Hell, the scar alone I would have thought was one of a kind."

It is. "I'm not sure of the chances, Frank. My guess would be that someone accused the wrong man." *Or I may have helped the right guy get away with robbery.*

Frank nodded. "That seems more likely. Still…."

When Frank didn't say anything further for a long moment, Tom looked over at him questioningly. "Still what?"

"The guy looks like a criminal," Frank concluded with a shrug.

"Looks can be deceiving," Tom muttered. Hell, if Frank only knew the secrets Tom was hiding, he'd realize just how significant the statement was. Needing to change the subject as well as needing to move, get some fresh air or something, Tom went to his feet and grabbed his service revolver out of his desk drawer. "As long as you're okay here, I'm going to run down to Tony's and grab that bottle I owe Doc Masterson." Tom slid his weapon into his holster and grabbed his hat from the desk.

"Sure, go ahead. How's your hand feeling?" Frank asked with a nod toward Tom's splinted hand.

"Hurts like a son of a bitch, but I'll live," Tom assured him. "Plus, it was worth it. No more roofing for me for a while." He chuckled.

"That's one way to get out of work," Frank said wryly. "Although I don't know if I would have gone to that extreme."

"Still better than being up on that damn roof. You need anything while I'm out?" Tom offered.

The phone rang and Frank groaned. "Not unless you can pick up Bonnie. I'm about tired of playing secretary," he grumbled.

"You ain't got the legs for it either," Tom teased.

Frank waved him off and answered the phone. "Ramer Police Department."

Tom stepped out and closed the door behind him. He was lucky Frank wasn't one to pry. Frank was a smart man and a good cop. He was always aware of what was going on around Ramer. But he wasn't one to gossip nor did he have any desire to be a know-it-all. He and Frank had also been friends most of their lives, both having grown up in Ramer. He and Frank hadn't hung out a lot as youngsters once Frank married Vivian when he was only sixteen and became a father eight months later. But after Frank had discovered farming wasn't for him and joined the police force seven years ago, the two of them had been closer than ever. Frank trusted Tom and would never dream of doubting or questioning him. Another thing to add to the pile of guilt Tom had been collecting all his life. He didn't deserve Frank's trust.

With a sigh, Tom headed down the street to Tony's. The cars that had been damaged and overturned during the storm were now gone, having been towed to the salvage yard. Most of the garbage, wood, glass, and other debris had been picked up and swept away. Still, his town was a wreck.

The marquee from the movie house was gone, swept up in the tornado and dropped in Old Man Matthews's cornfield. Perry Pharmacy had sustained structural damage and was boarded up. It would be months before the store would reopen. The saloon was nothing but a pile of rubble. As Tom made his way past one damaged building after another, he couldn't help but feel as if the storm that had caused such destruction to the stores and homes belonging to the good folks of Ramer had also left their local officer in ruin. It seemed fitting.

"Hey, Tony," Tom said as he stepped through the door of the liquor store. It was ironic that it was one of the few stores that hadn't been affected by the tornado.

"Hiya, Tom. How you doing today?" Tony asked from where he was stocking wine.

"Can't complain. Doesn't do any damn good anyway," Tom surmised.

"Ain't that the truth," Tony agreed, standing and wiping his hands on his pants. "What can I do you for?"

"Need a bottle of Doc Masterson's brew," Tom informed him. He held up his injured hand. "I may have depleted his stock."

Tony laughed heartily. The balding, middle-aged Italian with a potbelly was a bit arrogant and well known around Ramer as a womanizer, but surprisingly, given the nature of his business, wasn't a drinker.

"I heard about your accident," Tony said. He grabbed a bottle of whiskey off the shelf and set it on the counter. "How's it feeling?"

"Hurts like hell." Tom smirked. "How about you grab me a bottle of the good stuff there too," he added and nodded toward the Old Crow.

Tony shook his head and grabbed the booze. "This stuff will kill ya," Tony chastised lightly. "You ever drink Jack Daniel's? I hear it's smooth."

"Not on my salary," Tom joked and pulled his wallet from his back pocket. "What do I owe ya?"

"Not a thing," Tony announced and placed the bottles in paper sacks and handed them to Tom.

"I can't let you do that, Tony. How you gonna make a living giving away your profit?"

"Thank of it as a thank-you gift for all your hard work on the church. You're a good man, Officer Webber."

Tom's gut flopped painfully. He felt like such a fake. Each time someone paid him a compliment, he wanted to roar, to scream at the absurdity of their statements.

But he held it back, planted a convincing smile on his face, and said, "That's right mightily friendly of you, Tony, but I insist." He pulled out a few bills from his wallet and threw them on the counter. "Don't feel right, you paying off my debt to the Doc."

"Alright," Tony gave in. "Next one is on me," he insisted and took the money.

"Deal." Tom grabbed one of the bottles and tucked it under his arm, then palmed the other. "I'll see you later," he called out over his shoulder.

"Take care," Tony replied just before Tom closed the door.

He'd just turned to head down to Doc Masterson's office when his heart skipped a beat and the air rushed out of his chest. Leaning against the wall, cigarette between his lips, was Ben.

"What the fuck are you doing here?" Tom hissed between clenched teeth.

Ben took a puff from his cigarette and blew the smoke out, seemingly unaffected by the dangerous tone of Tom's question. "Afternoon, Officer," Ben drawled.

Tom started to reach for his weapon, then cursed. His good hand was full of booze, and his injured hand was ineffective. And what the hell would he do with the damn weapon if he had been able to draw it? Shoot the bastard? While it would solve some of his problems, he knew he wouldn't shoot the man, and waving the damn thing around wouldn't intimidate Ben.

"This better be the last time I see your face in my town," Tom spat and started to walk by.

"Well now—"

Tom spun around and glared at Ben. "This is not open for discussion. I want you gone."

"Aw c'mon, Tom." Ben smirked. "The way I see it, your town could use all the help it can get." Ben took another draw from his smoke, then stubbed it out. "Pastor John sure was appreciative of my offer to help."

"What the hell is your angle?"

"No angle other than gonna be working to get the roof back on the church this week."

"No the fuck you're not," Tom said vehemently. "You're going to get in your car and forget you ever heard of Ramer."

Ben ignored Tom's anger, his smirk firmly in place as he stepped up close, his mouth only inches from Tom's ear. "No way I'll ever forget you or this town," he murmured and walked away.

Tom stared at Ben's back as the bastard sauntered down the street. Tom was so goddamn mad he was vibrating with it. The idea of dropping the booze and shooting the fucker in the back was appealing. Instead, Tom clutched the bottles and stomped off angrily down to Doc Masterson's office.

"Goddamn stupid motherfucker," he grumbled.

Who the hell did Ben think he was? A better question was, what the hell was Ben up to? What did he hope to achieve by staying in a town where he clearly wasn't wanted? This wasn't going to end well. Too many things could go wrong for Tom. Too many secrets could be exposed. Somehow he had to figure out how to get Ben to leave. Only then could Tom try to put the man out of his head. Forget him and move on.

HIS SMILE was firmly in place as Ben strolled down Main Street. He didn't care what Tom had said, Ben could tell from the look in his eyes that he didn't mean it. Or perhaps on some level he did. Tom was scared, that much was obvious. Yet there was a desire in the man that he couldn't hide. Ben had learned years ago that no matter how hard you tried to fight your true nature, it was futile. And why should he have to fight it? Why the hell did Tom have to fight it?

Ben nodded to an elderly woman who stared at him warily, moving closer to the wall as Ben passed. He'd always had that effect on people. People saw his scar and his dark eyes and assumed he was a bad man—and maybe he was. He sure as hell had done enough robbing, fighting, and drinking in his lifetime to warrant people being wary of him. People assumed Ben had received the disfigurement to his face because of a criminal lifestyle, but they were wrong. He'd received it during a time he no longer wished to think about and refused to talk about. However, once he returned home—had survived the nightmare—he figured if he was going to be looked upon as if he were a shuck, accused constantly of being a hoodlum, he might as well use his looks to his advantage. He'd reap the benefits, so to speak.

Now, not only was it the way he made his living, he enjoyed being a bad boy, tormenting and tempting. And oh how he wanted to be a bad boy with Officer Webber.

Ben might be pushing his limits as he shoved open the door of the Ramer station, but if he planned to understand Tom, to get what he wanted from the man, then he needed to know all he could about him.

"Can I—" The officer at the desk jumped to his feet. "Hey, I know you."

"My reputation precedes me, does it?" Ben smirked. "Benjamin Parker," he said and held out his hand as he stepped up to the desk. "And you are?"

The cop behind the desk studied him for a second, his expression apprehensive. This was a look Ben was used to. "Officer Frank Compton," he responded and accepted Ben's hand and shook it. "What can I do for you, Mr. Parker?"

"Ben. Please call me Ben."

"Okay," Frank said with an arched brow. "What can I do for you, Ben?"

Ben pointed to the chair on the other side of Frank's desk. "Do you mind?"

"Not at all, please have a seat," he said warily and sat back down.

Ben sat on the edge of the chair and rested his forearms on the desk, leaning forward. "I'm going to be working with Pastor John, helping to rebuild the church, and I'm looking to find some lodging for a while and hoping you can point me in the direction of someone who might be taking in boarders."

Frank shook his head. "Housing is a little sparse around here, as you can imagine. Some of our residents are having to live in the old schoolhouse."

"I don't need much," Ben assured him. "Just a place to lay my head at night for the next week or so."

Frank thrummed his fingers against his desk, a thoughtful expression on his face. "Well, I can ask around. My partner says you were falsely accused of bank robbery," he pointed out with a challenging look. "Any reason I should be worried about recommending you as a tenant?"

Ben did his best to give Frank a charming smile. "Don't let my looks fool you. I'm completely harmless, I assure you," he chuckled. "I know what it's like to have such a devastating storm hit your town. I lived through one about fifteen years ago, and had it not been for so many good folks coming in and volunteering their time, I don't know if we would have ever recovered. Plus, Officer Webber saved my life." Ben ran a hand over his stubbled jaw. Damn, he needed a shave and a shower. "Just want to repay the kindness."

"That's mighty noble of you, Mr. P—"

"Ben," he interrupted.

"Ben," Frank said with a grin, and Ben knew he had set the officer at ease with his charm. "Let me do some asking around, and I'm sure I can find you a place to sleep and shower while you're in town."

"I rightly appreciate your hospitality." Ben held out his hand again as he went to his feet. "I best be heading over to the church."

Frank shook his hand. "I'll stop by later and let you know what I find."

"Thank you. You have yourself a good afternoon."

"You too, Ben."

Ben ran his hand through his hair and whistled as he headed to the church. Tom was going to go nuts when he discovered Ben had talked Tom's partner into finding him a place to stay. He laughed out loud at how that chat would go down.

Chapter 10

THE TENNESSEE sun was relentless in the cloudless sky, beating down on the exposed skin of Ben's back. Sweat rolled down his spine as he sat on the edge of the roof, his feet dangling, taking a break. Using his undershirt, Ben wiped across his brow and down his chest. His hand halted against his stomach as he spotted Tom walking down the opposite side of the street talking with an unfamiliar man. To Ben's shock and confusion, jealousy reared its ugly green head at seeing Tom walking so close to the young man. Jealousy wasn't something Ben had a lot of experience with. Tom brought out a lot of feelings in Ben he wasn't used to. Some pleasant, others... not so much.

What the hell am I getting myself into? Ben knew he should be moving on. He was low on funds, and there was that little issue of dealing with John and Carl's betrayal. But as he watched Tom walk down the street, a smile on his handsome face as he spoke to the stranger, Ben simply couldn't find it in himself to leave. Not yet. Not until he could either figure out what it was about Tom that had him so intrigued or he had his fill of the man.

Ben knew the second Tom was aware of Ben's presence. Tom's smile fell as he looked up and met Ben's gaze, his steps faltering. Ben lifted a hand and saluted Tom. Tom scowled and turned his head away. Ben couldn't help but chuckle. Tom could act as pissed as he wanted to, but Ben could see beyond the anger Tom used to hide his true feelings. Ben had felt the way Tom's body responded to his, had seen the want and desire in Tom's eyes. Somehow he had to figure out how to get past that angry façade Tom was hiding behind. Dammit, they deserved to be together, to explore whatever the hell it was that connected them.

"Stupid fucking society and their damnation," Ben grumbled. He wiped the sweat from his brow again. It wasn't fair. He and Tom didn't deserve to be scorned. They shouldn't have to fear what others might do to them simply because they desired someone of the same sex. He simply had to convince Tom of it and why they should turn their back on a world that would sentence them to such a fate.

"Hey, Ben! Can I get a hand?" someone called out from behind him.

"Be right there." Ben watched Tom walk away for a second longer, then sighed. He had no idea how in the hell he was going to get through to Tom, only that he wasn't going to give up until he did.

TOM DID his best to avoid Ben, but it seemed he ran into the bastard everywhere he went. Seeing him today without his shirt, the sun glistening off his sweat-dampened skin, had been nearly too much to bear. Tom had done his best not to let Ben's sexy ass affect him, but he hadn't been able to control his body's reaction. He could only hope Gene didn't notice the bulge in Tom's pants. *Damn it to hell anyway.*

"How much longer do you think it will be before the church reopens for services?" Gene asked.

Not soon enough, Tom mused. He hoped Ben would move on once the roof was complete. "Pastor John says the doors should be open come Sunday."

"Darn," Gene muttered. "I was hoping for another Sunday off. Simon and I found a great place to fish."

"Don't you let your ma hear you say that," Tom warned with a sly grin.

"And don't you go telling Pa either. He thought Simon and I were working on fences."

Gene was Frank's oldest boy. He was the spitting image of his dad— tall, lean, dark hair. He might look like a grown man, but he was still nothing more than a playful kid of seventeen.

Tom gave the boy a disapproving look as they tromped down the sidewalk.

"It was just a bit of a fib," Gene sputtered, his eyes going wide. "I mean, we did fix some fences, but darn it, sir, we deserved us a break. I would have thought having the week off school would have been fun, but all I've been doing is working my fool butt off. I tell you what, if I could get me a little money, I'd be gone and wouldn't do nothing but fish all day."

"You let me know how that works out for you," Tom chuckled.

"I'm serious! I'm just not cut out for hard labor." He held out his hands palms up. "Look at all these blisters," Gene whined.

"Alright," Tom laughed. "I won't tell your daddy, but you damn well better be in church come Sunday morning."

"I will," Gene assured him. "I gotta run. I'm helping Mr. Regan with his pump today." Gene raced ahead, but tossed back over his shoulder, "And thanks."

Tom smiled. Gene was a good kid. Lord knows Tom had spent more than a few afternoons down at the fishing hole avoiding work when he was a young'un. Everything had been so much simpler then. He'd had no worries beyond getting his chores done and keeping his grades up. At the time, both had seemed like the hardest things in the world to endure. Now he knew better.

Tom stood outside the station and took a deep breath. That fishing hole—hiding—sounded much more appealing today. He was relieved to find the door locked when he tried the knob. He pulled out his keys and opened the door, thankful Frank wasn't in. Tom hung his hat on the hook and slumped into his office chair. He scratched his head, his fingers tangling in his too-long hair. He was letting himself go. His hair needed to be cut, his face shaved, and his uniforms pressed. He also needed to start eating, sleeping, and getting his mind off a certain someone and back on his family and town.

The phone rang and Tom answered it on the first ring. "Officer Webber."

"I understand Mr. Parker is back in your town."

Tom tensed at the familiar sound of Sheriff Cronkite's voice. How the hell did the man know Ben—William was in town? "Good afternoon, Sheriff," Tom said coolly. "Why the interest in Mr. Parker's whereabouts? Is he a suspect in another bank robbery?"

"I know he pulled off the robbery in Nashville. I plan on nailing his ass and, as an added bonus, having you in the cell next to his," Cronkite hissed. "I'm watching you." Cronkite's threat was followed by the sound of the phone being slammed down on the hook.

"Jesus H. Christ," Tom grumbled and returned the phone to its cradle.

Just what he didn't need right now. Wasn't his life complicated enough without a pissed-off sheriff wanting his fucking head on a stake?

Tom rested his elbows on his desk, closed his eyes, and rubbed at the throb in his temples. He'd give anything to go back to that night of the storm. There were so many things he would have done differently, the most important of which was leaving Ben, or whatever the hell his real name was, stranded on the side of the road.

Tom's life was crumbling around him, one brick at a time, and he had no idea how to stop it.

The door of the station opened, and Tom looked up to find Frank coming in with a covered plate held high and a huge grin on his face. "I got a cure for what ails ya. Bonnie's homemade brownies," Frank said excitedly.

Tom's gut churned at the thought of food, and the throb in his head intensified. "I'm not hungry."

"You don't have to be hungry to enjoy these delights." Frank set the plate on Tom's desk and pulled off the towel. "It's brownies!" He grabbed one and shoved it into his mouth, leaving the plate behind as he headed to his desk. Tom didn't take one.

"I found your little friend a place to stay," Frank informed him with a mouth full of sweets.

"My little friend?" Tom asked in confusion. "What friend?"

"You know, that guy from the storm. The one falsely accused of the robbery."

"You did what?" Tom spat.

Frank looked taken aback as he stared at Tom with wide eyes. "Is there something wrong with the guy? Something I should know?"

Yes! He's a goddamn criminal and hell-bent on ruining my life! Though his heart thumped wildly, Tom forced himself to appear calm. "We don't know anything about him," Tom said neutrally and rubbed at his tired eyes.

"He's helping with the church roof," Frank said, still looking at Tom suspiciously. "Wanted to repay your kindness for saving his life."

How ironic Tom had saved the life of the man who was destroying his. "That's kind of him," Tom muttered, fiddling with the files on his desk to avoid Frank's questioning gaze. "Who is he staying with?"

"One of Mr. Matthews' hands left town, so Ben will be staying in the bunkhouse helping with the fences when he's not at the church."

"That's rightly kind of Mr. Matthews giving him a place to stay," Tom said, trying to sound disinterested, while inside a tempest was raging.

He wouldn't be able to relax until Ben was far away from his town, and it didn't look like that would be happening anytime soon. *Shit!* He didn't know how long he'd be able to maintain his sanity.

"Oh, you know that old coot isn't doing it out of the goodness of his heart," Frank chuckled. "He'll get his money's worth out of that poor guy."

Tom relaxed a bit as he latched on to the idea of Ben having to work his ass off. Between the church, fences, and whatever else the old farmer could find for Ben to do, it wouldn't leave the man much time to be bothering Tom. Yeah, okay, this might not be as bad as he thought. However, Matthews might be a bit of an asshole, but Tom just wouldn't feel right if something happened to him, if he lost money or property because of Ben. Ben was not who he claimed to be, that much Tom was sure of. As for how dangerous Ben was to others, Tom was unsure of that as well. He couldn't sit back and do nothing.

"I'm going to take a drive around town," Tom informed Frank. "Check out the progress out at the schoolhouse."

"I went by there this morning," Frank replied. "I think you'll be surprised."

"Yeah?" Tom asked, grabbing his hat and setting it low over his eyes. "Looking good, is it?"

"Kids will be back in class come Monday, and according to the wife, not a day too soon. The little ones are driving her batty."

"After all the years she's put up with you, I'd think Vivian would be used to batty," Tom teased.

"Hardy har, har," Frank called out, his voice muffled by the door as Tom pulled it closed.

Tom waited at the corner until he spotted Ben step out of the church and start walking down the road alone. Tom put the car in gear and pulled up next to him. He reached over and opened the passenger-side door. "Get in," he ordered.

Ben didn't seem surprised to see Tom, but rather gave him that infuriating smirk and slid easily into the car. "Afternoon, Officer," he drawled.

The scent of man and sweat filled the car, and Tom had to grit his teeth and roll his window down. "I want to know what the hell you think you're doing," Tom demanded as he pulled away from the curb.

"I'm just getting off work," Ben said easily and shifted in the seat till he was facing Tom, his back resting against the door. "I appreciate the ride. I find myself too tired to drive." He cocked his head, grin growing.

"Goddamn," Tom growled and slammed his hand against the steering wheel. "You know what the hell I'm talking about. Why the hell are you sticking around Ramer? And don't give me the same bullshit excuse you gave Frank."

"I want you. I'm sure I could muster up a little energy if you stop in a secluded spot."

Tom snapped his head to the side, and he glared at Ben. "Are you fucking insane?"

"I've been called worse."

"Like con man, robber, hoodlum," Tom pointed out.

"To name a few," Ben said with a shrug. "Doesn't change the fact that I still want you and I aim to have you."

"No!"

"I don't take no for an answer when I want something," Ben said confidently. "And I want you more than I think I've ever wanted just about anything."

"You can't have me. Jesus," Tom groaned and wiped his throbbing hand over his face. "You're going to ruin my life."

"You don't have a life, Tom. You're simply existing and trying your darnedest to ignore who you are, but you can't keep it up forever."

Tom looked down to see the speedometer pushed to the limit, so he eased his foot off the gas to a speed closer to normal as he headed out of town. "What I am is an officer of the law, a husband, father, and respected member of this community."

"And a homosexual, don't forget that."

"Goddammit, how many times do I have to fucking tell you? I'm not like you. I made a mistake. I let the devil overtake me, but it won't ever happen again. I… I…." Tom pulled off onto a side road and stopped the car. "I want you out of Ramer by nightfall."

"You don't actually believe that shit, do you?" Ben asked, sounding incredulous.

"Oh I assure you, I want nothing more than you being gone."

"No. I mean all that crap about being taken over by the devil?"

"Yes, I do," Tom said confidently. He'd been fighting practically his whole life, and he'd have kept the wickedness from overcoming him if he hadn't met Ben.

"Why? Because someone told you that?" Ben shook his head.

Tom looked away, refusing to answer.

"Let me guess, you were sitting in a pew, a happy little boy, and some son of a bitch damned your soul to hell?"

"It's unnatural," Tom responded flatly. It was the same argument he'd been telling himself for years.

"Please tell me you're not one of those cops who go around preaching homosexuality is contagious like small pox. That we're lurking everywhere, and we're murderers. That the public needs to protect their little boys from us."

Tom looked into dark, challenging eyes without flinching. "You *are* dangerous."

"I've never chased a young boy. I've never murdered anyone. Never gave my fucking disease to anyone," Ben snarled. His hands were curled into fists, and daggers were shooting out of his eyes as he stared at Tom. "Have you?"

"I'm not—"

"I swear to God, Tom, if you say you're not like me, I'll pop you in your lying face," Ben interrupted. "Aren't you sick and tired of having to hide who you really are? It doesn't have to be this way."

Tom wanted to scream, rage, and deny, but the hint of sadness in Ben's voice stopped him. It didn't matter if Ben knew what it felt like, if he had experienced the doubt and shame. None of it mattered. Tom put the car in reverse and backed onto the main road.

"Yes, it does," Tom said sadly and put the car in gear.

Chapter 11

NO MATTER how hard he'd tried, Ben had been unable to get Tom to say a word as he'd driven Ben back to his car, nor had he spoken to him in nearly a week. He'd seen Tom in passing, but the stubborn man had refused to even meet Ben's eyes.

That was about to change.

With the roof now complete on the church, Ben had volunteered to join the crew repairing Tom's house. Come hell or high water, Ben would get Tom to acknowledge his presence and talk to him.

Ben sat in his car and waved to the last crew member as he pulled out of Tom's driveway. Ben let his car engine idle as he watched the truck in the rearview mirror. As soon as it disappeared, Ben turned off the ignition and stepped out of the car. His clothes were damp with sweat, and his hands and dungarees were filthy. He'd sell his right nut for a hot shower, but he didn't dare enter Tom's house. The last time he'd tried something so foolish, he'd ended up with the barrel of a gun pressed against his temple.

Grabbing a towel and some clean clothes from the trunk, Ben made his way around to the back of the house. He'd have to settle for rinsing off the majority of the grime with cold water from the pump. Ben left his boots and dirty clothes on the porch steps and hung his clean ones, as well as his towel, on the railing.

Ben pumped the handle a few times until the water flowed, took a deep breath, and stuck his head beneath the stream. "Holy goddamn hell," he sputtered and shivered as goose bumps bloomed across his flesh. The ice-cold water droplets running down his chest and back caused him to shiver again. *Damn!* The things he'd go through for Tom. Ben chuckled and pumped the handle again. This time when the water began to flow, he used his hands to scoop up water and rinse off his body. It was still cold but a little more tolerable. Barely.

Rushing but doing a thorough job, Ben washed the dirt and grime of the day away. He pushed his wet hair from his face and reached for his towel when he caught a glimpse of movement to his right. Leaning against the railing at the other end of the porch, arms crossed over his chest, stood a scowling Tom.

"I did some investigating, and there is no thirty-two-year-old salesman from Toledo, Ohio, named Ben Parker." His tone was cool, but Ben didn't miss the way Tom's gaze roamed over Ben's naked body.

Ben wrapped the towel around his waist and wiped the water from his face. "That's because my name isn't Ben Parker. It's William Benjamin Parker."

"I'm not a fool," Tom snapped. "I tried all of your aliases. Who the hell are you?"

"I'm Ben Parker—"

"You want me to be honest with you, then you damn well better start being honest with me," Tom growled.

"That's fair," Ben replied with a nod.

He rummaged around in his dirty clothes till he found his pack of smokes and lighter, and lit up. It wasn't the nicotine he needed so badly but a moment to decide what and how much he should tell Tom about his past. He was asking Tom to be completely honest with him, the least he could do was to return the favor. He sat on the edge of the steps, took another pull from his cigarette, and blew it out before speaking.

"My name really is William Benjamin Parker, but I prefer Ben. I am also thirty-two." He rolled his cigarette through his fingers, finding it easier to stare at it rather than meet Tom's eyes. "I'm not from Toledo. Passed through there a couple times, nice place. I was born and raised in Detroit. One of my first jobs when I was a teen was a salesman. Sold meat and cheese door-to-door, if you can believe that." Ben chuckled and shrugged. "I made a fairly decent living until Uncle Sam shoved a weapon in my hand and shipped my ass overseas. When I returned home in '45, I was pretty fucked up and more than a little pissed off at—" Ben took another puff as he fought to keep the horrors of what he'd seen in Normandy and other parts of Europe from surfacing. "—pretty much everyone." He sighed.

"Is that where you got the scar?" Tom asked and sat on the step next to Ben.

"There was an explosion. Flying piece of metal nearly cut my face off." Ben ran his hand over the scar that had contributed to the direction his life had taken once he'd returned home—or perhaps he would have chosen the path he did even without it. "At least that's what they told me when I woke up in a hospital with over fifty stitches. What about you? You serve?"

"No," Tom responded with a shake of his head.

"You're one of the few lucky ones."

"I would have gone. At first they didn't draft only sons, but I wanted to go. Hell, the whole town was fired up wanting to do their part. Patriotism was pretty high." Tom was staring out over his land with an expression that caused Ben's chest to tighten.

"What happened?" Ben asked cautiously.

"Influenza epidemic hit us in '43. I recovered, but many in town didn't, including my parents," Tom muttered sadly. "I took over this place, and instead of wanting to go fight the Germans, my new mission was to help my town recover."

"I'm sorry about your parents," Ben said sincerely.

"Thanks."

Tom continued to stare toward the back of his property, but Ben wondered if he was seeing anything. Tom's expression was thoughtful, the lines around his eyes more prominent. They sat there silently, each lost in his own thoughts, Ben battling to push down the memories that threatened. No doubt Tom was trying to do the same. Ben snubbed out his cigarette and grabbed his clean clothes. When he'd first spotted Tom staring at him, his eyes roaming appreciatively down Ben's body, he'd planned to use Tom's lust to his advantage. Now he suddenly felt foolish wearing nothing more than a towel. He silently stepped into his trousers, pulling them up and fastening them, then shrugged into his undershirt. He pushed his damp hair out of his eyes and sat back down next to Tom, who was still staring at the landscape.

"I've been thinking a lot about what you said the other day," Tom said, finally breaking the silence.

"I said a lot the last time we talked. Which part?"

"All of it," Tom admitted. "About me not being like you, God, lies, that it doesn't have to be this way." Tom pulled his hat off and ran his fingers through his hair. "I admit, I haven't been able to think about much else the past few days."

"And have you come to any conclusions?"

"Nope," Tom mumbled and set his hat back on his head. "I need a drink." He abruptly stood.

Ben watched him as he went up the stairs, opened the door, and disappeared inside. Ben exhaled a heavy breath. Saddened by having obviously been dismissed, he started gathering up his clothes. It didn't seem like the right time to push Tom. He'd leave the man to his memories, but he wouldn't give up. Maybe tomorrow.

"You gonna join me?" Tom called out from inside.

Ben halted and he stared, blinking at the open door, until a smile began to curl his lip. He dropped the clothes onto his boots and bounded up the stairs.

Tom had set out two glasses on the kitchen table and was pouring two good measures of Old Crow as Ben stepped into the kitchen. Tom tipped his glass back and downed his drink in one gulp. He poured himself another one and pushed the other drink toward Ben as Ben took a seat at the table.

"Thanks." Ben took a small drink and coughed as the alcohol burned all the way down to his gut. He'd never had a taste for whiskey, preferring rum, but he wasn't about to turn down an opportunity to share a drink with Tom.

Ben was eager to learn more of what Tom had been thinking about since their last meeting, but he didn't press. Ben didn't want to say or do anything that would rock their tentative truce. Instead, Ben stayed quiet and sipped the foul booze. As the silence stretched to an uncomfortable level, the urge to prompt Tom grew maddening. He couldn't read the expression on Tom's face, Tom's longish hair hiding his features as he stared down at his drink and swirled the amber liquid in his glass.

The long days of work combined with the tension, the booze, and his lack of sleep over the past week had started to take their toll on Ben, and he yawned and rubbed his tired eyes. "Maybe I should head back to the bunkhouse."

"I was twelve," Tom mumbled without looking up.

"Excuse me?" Ben asked in confusion.

"I was sitting in between my parents on Sunday morning when Pastor John had a sermon on the sins of homosexuals. I swear, it felt like he was looking right in me. That he knew the dark thoughts I'd been having. So when he started preaching about it being a sin against God, unnatural, an abomination, I knew right then and there I was going to hell."

Red-hot rage bubbled up in Ben, and he tightened his grip on his glass. Goddamn men preaching hate in their sermons, damning young boys to hell before they even understood what they had done wrong. The idea of any man or woman planting the seed of hate inside a child, dooming him to a future of self-loathing, doubt, and fear, infuriated Ben.

"He's wrong," Ben said adamantly. "God is supposed to be all about love, and any proclaimed man of God who preaches hate is nothing more than a hypocrite."

"Yeah, well, I didn't question it," Tom muttered solemnly and finished his drink. "And then you showed up and…. Dammit, Ben, why'd you have to break down in my town?"

Ben met Tom's sorrowful gaze. He'd asked himself the same thing numerous times. Ben understood Tom's confusion and pain, had seen the same questioning look in his own reflection.

He gave Tom the only conclusion he could come up with. "Fate?"

"If that's the case, if it's my fate, then maybe Pastor John is right. What other reason could there be for my fate to be complete destruction?"

Tom reached for the bottle of whiskey, but Ben stopped him by grabbing his forearm. "I used to think the same thing," Ben admitted. "But not anymore. I can't change who I am, and if society can't accept me, then fuck society."

Tom shook his head. "If everyone felt that way, there would be complete anarchy."

"I don't mean murderers or child molesters." Ben's voice went lower as he leaned in close to Tom until their lips were practically touching. When Tom didn't pull away, Ben pressed a gentle kiss to Tom's mouth and spoke against his lips. "I'm talking about this," he murmured before deepening the kiss.

Tom responded to the kiss with a deep moan and threaded his fingers through Ben's hair, holding him. Tom needn't worry; Ben had no plans to go anywhere or to end the kiss anytime soon. Ben explored Tom's mouth unhurriedly, savoring the feel of Tom's tongue sliding along his. Even the alcohol flavor was pleasant.

They were both breathing hard when Ben finally ended the kiss, but he didn't stop tasting and savoring Tom's flesh. Ben kissed his way along Tom's stubbled jaw, the coarse hairs tickling his lips, then, licking his way up Tom's neck, he nipped and kissed at the sensitive skin beneath his ear and around the shell. Tom shuddered and moaned, the husky sound going straight to Ben's hardening cock.

The hand in Ben's hair tightened its grip as he moved his way back down Tom's neck to place a kiss on the exposed flesh of Tom's chest in the V of his shirt. Carefully, slowly, silently, Ben moved from his chair to kneel on the floor next to Tom. He slid his hand along Tom's thigh, over his hip, and up his flat stomach.

"How can this be wrong?" Ben asked with his lips against Tom's skin as he unbuttoned Tom's shirt, exposing more of his warm, lightly furred chest.

"I don't kn…." Tom's words turned into a long, drawn-out moan as Ben sucked Tom's left nipple into his mouth, sucking hard and teasing with tongue and teeth. He gave the other hard nub the same treatment as he continued to remove Tom's shirt, then began working on his belt and pants.

Tom's cock was hard, the flared head ruddy and seeping precum. It was a delight Ben couldn't, wouldn't deny himself. He groaned loudly as he swiped his tongue over Tom's cockhead, his bitter flavor filling Ben's mouth. Hungrily, he wrapped his lips around Tom's shaft, sucking it deep into his mouth.

"Damn that feels good," Tom groaned and pushed down on the back of Ben's head.

Ben took his time, exploring every inch of Tom's cock. He carefully scraped his teeth along the length, ran his tongue along each bulging vein as he slowly bobbed his head, his lips stuttering over the spongy head with each pass. The moans, whimpers, and curses pouring from Tom as well as the sting of pain in Ben's scalp from Tom fisting his hand in Ben's hair caused Ben's cock to throb, but he ignored his own need and concentrated on Tom's pleasure.

Tom began to thrust as he pushed down on the back of Ben's head, shoving his cock deep into Ben's throat. Ben didn't fight it; he opened wide and allowed Tom to fuck his mouth, to take what he needed.

Ben's eyes watered and his jaw ached, but he took deep breaths through his nose. As Tom continued to thrust, Ben worked Tom's pants down his legs and ran his fingertips along the soft hairs on the inside of Tom's thighs and over his balls.

"Oh! Ah fuck! Ben," Tom gritted out, the movements of his hips losing their finesse. "Stop! You gotta stop," he panted harshly. "You're gonna make me come."

As the last word passed Tom's lips, Ben slid his finger back behind Tom's balls and pushed the tip of one finger into Tom's ass. Tom roared.

The first blast choked Ben, but he recovered quickly, taking Tom fully into his throat and swallowing every last drop until the tension seeped from Tom and he slumped back in the chair.

Ben let Tom's cock slip from his mouth and licked his lips as he stroked Tom's trembling thigh. Tom's eyes were closed, his lips parted, his breathing harsh. Ben laid his head on Tom's thigh, a satisfied smile stretching his face. He'd never seen anything so gorgeous as a sated Tom, and knowing he'd been the one to put that look on Tom's face—all the better.

Chapter 12

WITH HIS eyes closed and his heart hammering, Tom stroked Ben's hair, enjoying the moment of satisfaction and contentment before the guilt settled in. However, as his breathing returned to normal and his pulse slowed, Tom didn't experience any of the expected signs of guilt or remorse. His stomach wasn't roiling, there was no bile rising up in his throat, and his head wasn't throbbing. There was only peace.

He'd spent the last few days contemplating his life, his beliefs, and how he felt about Ben. Tom had spent so many years—a lifetime—refusing to look too closely at the temptations he fought so hard to quell. He'd learned while still young to control the dark side of his being, pushed it down beneath the denial so completely that even he'd begun to believe it.

Deny. Deny. Deny.

"You okay?"

Tom opened his eyes and met Ben's gaze. Ben stared up at him with real concern in his dark eyes. Ben didn't look evil. Tom ran his fingertips along Ben's cheek. He didn't feel evil. Ben wasn't evil, and neither was he.

"Yeah, I'm okay," he murmured and gave Ben a genuine smile.

Ben returned the smile. "Good. I'm glad you didn't feel the need to pull your gun again and demand I get out."

"I considered it for a split second." Tom chuckled.

Ben sat back on his calves and smirked. "Well, thank you for not shooting me."

Tom pulled up his pants, tucked his softening cock back in, then buttoned and zipped up. He leaned forward and pulled his belt out from behind him and set it on the table. When he looked back down at Ben, he couldn't help but notice the large bulge in Ben's pants. Tom stood and held out his hand to Ben, helping him to his feet.

"How about we get you a proper shower?" Tom suggested. "One with soap and hot water."

Ben arched one brow, looking a little stunned, but recovered quickly and asked, "You going to wash my back?"

"And your front," Tom informed him and pulled him along to the bathroom.

"Hot damn," Ben hooted, causing Tom to chuckle.

Tom couldn't remember feeling this good, this relaxed, or this content in a long, long time. Maybe ever. It certainly had never felt this good or this right with Marna. As Tom set the taps on the shower, he waited for the guilt that would surely come with the thoughts of his wife, but once again the feelings stayed dormant.

Tom caught Ben's wary expression in the mirror as he kicked off his shoes and removed his pants. "What?"

"I'm just not used to this side of you," Ben admitted.

"Neither am I," he said slyly.

Tom noticed the tension in Ben's muscles, the way his fingers gripped the counter. The usually cocky, confident man who didn't flinch when a gun was shoved in his face looked completely unsure. Tom stepped up close and grabbed the hem of Ben's undershirt and pulled it over his head. He understood why Ben was so hesitant, considering Tom's behavior in the past. But something had shifted in Tom over the last few days. Or rather, pieces of Tom had fallen into place, and for the first time in his life, he understood what and who he was.

Pressing a gentle kiss to Ben's lips, Tom unfastened Ben's pants and pushed them down his lean hips as he continued to place soft kisses to Ben's lips, cheeks, and chin. Ben stayed tense but allowed Tom to undress him and pull him into the shower. They both groaned when they stepped under the warm spray, then laughed. The laughter seemed to relax Ben a little.

Grabbing the soap, Tom lathered up his hands and ran them across the sinew of Ben's back, shoulders, and arms. Tom took his time touching, washing, and exploring Ben's body. Taking his time, showering with another man was a pleasure he'd never experienced before, had never allowed himself to indulge in. Tom took full advantage of the long-denied opportunity. He loved the way Ben's lean muscles flexed and rolled beneath his fingers, the way the hair on Ben's chest felt against his palms, and the power and strength in Ben's body. All the while, Ben watched him, his dark eyes full of lust and wonder. Tom's cock made a gallant effort to fill as he took Ben's hard length in hand, stroking it in his soapy fist.

"That feels good," Ben moaned.

"Yeah you do," Tom agreed. He leaned in and licked at the water droplets running down Ben's chest, then rubbed his cheek against one of Ben's hard nipples as he increased the speed of his strokes.

Ben began to tremble, and he clutched Tom's shoulders as he thrust into Tom's hand. "Not going to take much," he groaned, his fingers digging into Tom's flesh. "I nearly came just sucking you off. So sexy when you come. Ah! So fucking sexy," Ben panted.

Soap rinsed away in the spray, Tom's hand stuttered over the wet skin of Ben's cock where it throbbed against his palm. Tom wouldn't be denied tasting Ben, so he went to his knees, looking up at Ben with heavy-lidded eyes.

"So are you," he whispered and took Ben into his mouth.

Ben's hand landed on Tom's head, not restraining or encouraging, only petting as he thrust in and out of Tom's mouth. Moans, pleas, and praises rumbled out of Ben, spurring Tom on, and he bobbed his head faster. Tom greedily feasted on Ben's cock as he rolled Ben's balls in his hands. All too quickly Ben tensed, the loss of rhythm and the increased volume of Ben's moans the only warning Tom got before Ben shouted Tom's name and came.

Tom continued to suck and lick until he'd drained every drop from Ben. Placing one last kiss on the head of Ben's cock, Tom stood. He wrapped his arms around Ben and held him, giving him his strength until Ben stopped trembling.

Ben buried his face in the side of Tom's neck. "I like this side of you," he murmured.

The temperature of the water began to cool, and Tom turned off the taps. He wasn't sure how to respond to Ben. Hell, Tom wasn't even sure how he felt about this new side. Yes it felt good, natural, and right, yet he was still having a hard time wrapping his mind around it. He'd spent his entire life denying his desires, and he wasn't sure what would happen next. Without responding, Tom stepped out of the shower and grabbed a couple of towels. He tossed one to Ben and ran the other over his head and down his chest.

"Was it something I said?" Ben asked hesitantly.

"No. I'm just struggling to get a handle on all of this," Tom confided. "I'll be fine. You hungry?" he asked, wanting to change the subject.

"I could eat," Ben said with a nod.

TOM SERVED Ben the beef stew one of his neighbors had delivered. They ate in silence, but it wasn't uncomfortable. Tom had never been one for idle chatter and was learning quickly that Ben wasn't big on small talk either. Dinner eaten, dishes done, they sat on the couch shoulder to shoulder, their bare feet on the coffee table, before their talk returned to weighty topics. Tom hated to disturb the low-key feeling, but he had to know.

"I'm hoping you can ease my conscience a bit," Tom confessed.

"I know what you're going to ask," Ben jumped in. "And the answer is no."

Tom cocked his head and gave Ben an exasperated look. "I didn't even ask the question yet."

"I didn't do that bank job," Ben told him without blinking an eye.

"Cronkite sure in the hell thinks you did it, and he sounds pretty damn adamant."

"He's too full of himself and an asshole," Ben grumbled.

Tom didn't miss the way Ben glanced away, nor the way he ran his hands down his jean-covered thighs. "What's he got on you?" Tom pointed a finger at Ben. "And you better be telling me everything, because Cronkite not only wants to take you down, but he's now got a vendetta against me."

Ben grabbed Tom's finger and kissed the tip of it, which shocked the shit out of Tom. Ben often did things that shocked him, and he was still not used to it. Tom's shock grew when Ben entwined their fingers and held his hand as he spoke.

"I'm sorry for getting you involved. Honestly, it wasn't my intention. But I had no choice. Look, I'm not saying I'm pure. I've done my share of bad shit, but I didn't do this. I planned it, wrote out the entire plan in a journal, but backed out when my buddy told his cousin about the robbery. The guy is a complete fucking idiot, and I knew we'd get caught so I walked." Ben waved his free hand in a dismissive manner. "I was right! Fools got caught when the cousin went around flashin' big wads of cash, but my prints were lifted from the journal.

"When you found me the night of the storm, I was coming back from Nashville. So I had been in town, and my prints were on evidence. If I were Cronkite, I'd want to nail me too." Ben squeezed Tom's hand and held his gaze, the look in Ben's eyes sincere. "I didn't make you an accessory. I know you may not believe me, but I promise you, I didn't do this."

Tom had no doubt that Ben was one hell of a con man, so he was sure Ben had fooled more than one man in his day. However, something inside Tom told him Ben was being truthful this time.

Tom stared down at their entwined fingers. He liked the way they fit together; the calluses on Ben's hands were rough against Tom's palm, but it wasn't unpleasant. *A good fit.*

Tom nodded, then looked back up at Ben. "I hope to hell I don't regret this, but I believe you."

Tom's stomach fluttered when Ben smiled broadly and pecked Tom's cheek. "You won't regret it," he said confidently.

There was so much more to Ben than Tom had first thought. Oh, he wasn't so naive to think that Ben was innocent of everything. The man was still dangerous, but there was something good in him too. Knowing more about Ben's past—his service in the war, the injury, the secrets he'd carried, the burden of being something society and religion deemed unnatural—Tom had a better understanding of why Ben had made some of the choices he had. He understood why Ben had taken the path he had into a life of crime. His anger against man and the system found an outlet in being a criminal.

"Can I ask you something?"

"Sure. You can ask me anything," Ben offered.

"Do you know many—" Tom swallowed hard, the first aloud admission the hardest. "—men like us?"

"I've met a few in my day. There are even some underground groups in the bigger cities, but for the most part, many are too afraid. Who the hell can blame them?" Ben spat angrily. "It's bad enough they have to worry about losing their jobs or being sent to a mental institution, but they have to live every day with the very real possibility of being jailed, attacked, beaten, and even killed." Ben met Tom's gaze with a challenging look. "You ever jail a man for being a nancy boy?"

"Oh, simmer down. Ramer's so damn small I only knew of one. Richie Lenox," Tom said with fondness. Richie had been Tom's first kiss, his first sexual experience. His only kiss from a male until Ben. He and Richie had experimented, rubbed off on each other, mutual blow jobs, touching, but nothing like he'd experienced with Ben. It had been mainly fumbling fingers, shyness, embarrassment, innocence. Experiences Tom had been able to convince himself were simply silliness of childhood that had meant nothing, were nothing. "He lived just outside of town, but he and his family moved away when we were teens."

"Cripes! You really have lived a sheltered life," Ben barked with disbelief.

"Not too much is secret in a town this size," Tom commented. "I learned to control my urges, hid them, and did my best not to think on them too much."

"Do you love her?"

Tom looked at Ben questioningly. "Who?"

"Her," Ben responded and nodded toward the fireplace.

Tom followed his gaze. Old photographs of Tom's parents and grandparents were on the mantel, and in the center was one of him and Marna on their wedding day. "She's a good woman."

"That's not what I asked," Ben clarified.

Tom pulled his hand from Ben's and scrubbed it across his face. He'd forever regret lying to her, not being the kind of husband she deserved. But as he looked at the photo of his young son, his pride, his namesake, he knew he had made the right choice.

"I care for her" was all Tom could offer.

Ben patted Tom's thigh before he pulled himself to his feet. Tom didn't say a word as Ben pulled on his shirt, nor did he try and stop Ben when he heard the back door open and close. They had shared something special, a moment in time Tom would forever cherish, but in the big scheme of things, it changed nothing.

Tom tipped his head back and stared up at the ceiling. He wasn't sure if having met Ben had enriched his life, given him a brief moment to be completely free and at peace, or if it would forever haunt him. Tom now had a taste of what it could be if things were different. If…. Tom squeezed his eyes shut, nearly choking on the sad reality of it bearing down upon him. They weren't different and never would be.

Chapter 13

SUMMER HAD come early to Ramer, the temp well into the eighties. Tom pulled his cap from his head and wiped the sweat from his brow as he looked up at his completed roof. Day by day, his beloved town was one step closer to being restored. The storm that had ripped through Ramer a month ago had crippled the town, destroyed buildings, shaken foundations, but it couldn't break the spirit of the people. They had come together as a community, supported each other, and the evidence of their generosity and hard work was in the new roof and shingles. His house was once again a home.

"It looks great," Ben commented, coming to stand next to Tom.

"That it does."

"I can't stay any longer," Ben said, his tone full of sadness.

Tom studied Ben's profile as Ben continued to stare up at the roof. He wanted to ask him to stay, but Tom knew it was wishful thinking. His family would be home soon, and it wouldn't be fair to anyone if Ben were to stay.

"Where will you go?"

"I got me a little spread up near Louisville." Ben turned to meet Tom's gaze and smirked. "Gonna try going legit, settle down, make an honest living raising cattle."

The smile on Ben's face didn't reach his eyes, the sorrow evident in the brown orbs. Tom wanted to wrap an arm around Ben, pull him close, and hug away his sadness, but he didn't dare. They had come together by fate, their lives entwined by a powerful storm, and in their brief time together had found a slice of happiness in the middle of destruction. Tom was forever changed; whether that change was for the good or not, he hadn't yet decided.

"I'm sure you'll do the right thing," Tom murmured. "You're a good man, Ben." Tom held out his hand. It was all he could offer in way of a good-bye.

Ben took the offered hand, but he didn't shake it; instead he gripped it hard. "Come with me," Ben offered. "My land is far out from town, away from prying eyes and judgmental folks. Be just you and me working the land, side by side. Dammit, Tom, all we've had to endure, we deserve some happiness. Some peace."

Tom's heart clenched painfully as he stared back at Ben's hopeful expression. It would be so easy to accept Ben's offer. The idea of spending time with Ben on a hidden piece of land had its appeal. A place where he didn't have to worry if his eyes lingered too long on a strong masculine body, a place he could stop pretending to be something he wasn't. But, no matter how alluring it sounded, as he had done his entire life, Tom put the needs of others before his own. In a perfect world, he wouldn't question it or hesitate to go with Ben. But it wasn't. For men like them, it was ugly and dark, full of secrets and hiding. Tom might not ever be able to find peace or real happiness, but he could have a small slice of them here in Ramer by helping others find theirs.

A quick glance around to confirm they were alone, Tom pressed a soft kiss to Ben's lips. "Safe travels," he whispered. Without a look back, Tom forced one foot in front of the other. He fought the urge to give in, to take Ben up on his offer and run. With each step up the back stairs, his effort became all the harder, but somehow he made it.

"This isn't over," Ben yelled as Tom opened the back door.

Tom hesitated midstep and closed his eyes. He took a deep breath and, with a wistful grin on his face, stepped inside, shut the door, and leaned against it as his pulse hammered. This time, he believed Ben's parting warning.

One day they would meet again, if only in Tom's dreams.

Chapter 14

TOM PULLED the crumpled pack of Lucky Strikes from his shirt pocket and dug one out. He placed it between his teeth, struck a match against the wooden railing, and lit up. He'd never cared much for cigarettes; he preferred cigars. But when Ben left behind a pack, Tom hadn't been able to throw them out. Nor had he been able to throw out the small slip of paper that he'd found with the pack. The map of a small spread of land near Louisville, Kentucky, was safely tucked away in his wallet. He'd have been smart to have thrown both out, but obviously he wasn't playing it smart these days. A train whistle sounded in the distance, announcing the arrival of Tom's family. He took a deep draw, the smoke burning his throat and lungs, and tried to find a little calm, the effort futile. While he'd missed his family, especially his son, Tom wasn't all that excited about their return. The guilt clawed at his gut; even worse was the thought of having to go back to a role he no longer had a desire to play.

An elderly couple strolling arm in arm approached. "Good afternoon," the gentleman greeted pleasantly.

Tom plastered on a fake smile. "Afternoon," he responded with a nod as they passed.

It wasn't only his smile that was fake. He'd spent the majority of his life as an actor. He was good at it, and no one suspected what lay beneath his carefully constructed façade. Hell, he hadn't truly known—refused to look, refused to accept, refused to acknowledge. Ben had stripped Tom bare, forced him to not only look at who he was, but accept it. Ben had showed him, if only for a brief moment, what it felt like to be whole. Sadly, knowing made it worse.

The train came into sight, and Tom took one last deep draw from his cigarette before dropping it to the wooden platform and stubbing it out with his boot. Billowing puffs of thick smoke, the screech of metal against metal, and the train came to a halt.

The conductor stepped from his perch and pulled out his pocket watch. "Welcome to Fleming," he bellowed.

Showtime.

Tommy barreled down the stairs, eyes scanning. Tom could tell exactly when his son spotted him by the huge smile that spread across his small face.

"Pa!"

Tom crouched down and opened his arms. His son nearly knocked him over, jumping into his arms and wrapping his little arms around his dad's neck. "Well, I do believe you've grown a foot," Tom teased and hugged his boy.

"I think it's 'cause Granny made me eat spinach," he said and wrinkled his nose. "I think I'd rather be little than eat spinach again. It was gross."

"Don't tell your granny, but I never ate my spinach." Tom chuckled and ruffled the boy's curls.

"And you're plenty big enough. Can we go home now?" Tommy asked and tugged at Tom's hand.

"Soon. We gotta wait for your mama and the luggage."

"Let's leave her here. Ma's been mean to me."

Tom gave his son a disbelieving look.

"She made me take a nap. On the train, Pa! What if outlaw robbers woulda come? I was doing what you told me. I was protecting Ma, and she made me take a nap. She's mean, I tell ya."

Tom couldn't help but laugh again. "Well, it's a good thing they didn't come then, huh?"

"She's lucky for sure," Tommy said adamantly. "Can we go now? Are we going to take the police car? Can I turn on the siren? Oh look, there she is." Tommy bounded off to undoubtedly try to make her hurry.

Tom smiled fondly. His boy had always been a bit of a handful, and it was good to see his time away hadn't dampened his enthusiasm, or as Marna called it, his "spirited nature." Marna looked worn, dark circles under her eyes, and her clothes were wrinkled after hours on the train. Still, she was patient with her son as he tugged at her and gave him a soft smile as he continued to rattle on.

"Welcome home," Tom said by way of greeting.

"Thank you," she said politely.

Tom turned away from the hopeful and expectant look in his wife's eyes and picked up the suitcases. "How was your trip?"

"She made me take a nap," Tommy repeated.

"Smart woman, your ma," Tom told him.

Tommy's bottom lip pushed out into a pout, and he crossed his arms over his chest, but his ire didn't last long. "Oh look, balloons! Can I have one, Ma? Can I? Please, Pa. Tell her I can have one, please."

Marna looked to Tom for guidance as she often did when it came to buying frivolous items. When Tom nodded, she allowed her son to pull her along. "If you promise to be a good boy."

"Oh I will, I will," Tommy promised.

Tom took the opportunity to load the suitcases into the back of the truck. Once on the road, Tom had little opportunity to speak to his wife, his son chatting excitedly the entire way back to Ramer about the train, his time with his grandparents, and the new things he'd seen. It was fine by Tom; he had no idea what to say to his wife. He found it difficult to meet her gaze without being reminded of what he'd done. Instead he half listened to his son and kept his eyes on the road before him.

Tom had spoken with Marna after the storm had hit. He'd given her a full report of the damage that had befallen Ramer and knew she had spoken with some of the women from the church, but still she gasped when they pulled into town and she got to see the destruction for herself. The town looked better than it had, but for someone seeing it for the first time, Tom could understand Marna's response. Even Tommy went silent.

"Oh dear Lord," Marna said mournfully and covered her mouth with her hand.

"It looks much worse than it is," Tom assured her. "Everyone is okay, and we're slowly rebuilding. In fact, we're done with the church. We'll swing by there."

Marna had always been a very active member of the congregation. She spent much of her free time with the other ladies, planning bake sales, teaching Sunday school, and even singing in the choir. Tom knew, next to Tommy, it was the one thing that brought true happiness into her life. Tom's guilt had him pulling into the church parking lot and cutting the engine. He couldn't welcome his wife home properly, but he could at least give her this.

"Doesn't it look great?" he announced as he stepped out of the truck Tommy on his heels.

"It's beautiful," Marna commented as she took in the new roof and paint with what looked like awe. "I received a letter from Bonnie. They're organizing a group of volunteers to replant flowers around the church this weekend."

"Did you volunteer?" Tom inquired.

"I'd like to, but I'm sure I'll have too much to do getting resettled at home."

"I think you should," he told her. "You have plenty of time to get unpacked and settled. Besides, I was thinking I would take Tommy fishing this weekend. Give you a break and spend a little father-son time with him. It will be good for the boy."

Marna wrung her hands, still looking up at the grand church. The newly washed stained-glass windows cast a colorful glow on her skin. "I was hoping we could spend some time—"

"Pa! Look! Look!" Tommy squealed excitedly, pointing at a large backhoe. "Can we go see it, Pa? Please!"

"Go ahead," Marna said patiently without turning her gaze from the church.

Tom hesitated. The sadness in Marna's expression clawed at him. *Dammit.* Why in the hell couldn't things be different? Why couldn't he wrap his arm around his wife and comfort her?

"C'mon, Pa. C'mon," Tommy shouted and grabbed Tom's hand. "Ma said we could. C'mon."

Tom allowed his son to pull him along. There had to be some way he and his wife could live together and if not be happy, then at least be... not unhappy. Tom might not deserve it, but Marna did, only he had no idea how to achieve his goal of giving her at least a fraction of what she deserved. He could no longer pretend providing a home and food on the table was enough for Marna, just like he could no longer pretend he was a good man.

"HE'S OUT cold," Tom informed Marna as he rejoined her in the living room, taking a seat across from her in his worn-out recliner.

It had been an exciting day for his son—the train ride, playing at the church, running around his house and yard, screaming in delight with every new discovery. Tom had been able to set aside everything in his troubled mind in the wake of his son's youthful wonder and excitement. But now he found himself once again feeling as if he were a stranger in his own home.

From where she sat on the couch, Marna set her needlepoint aside, curled her feet up under her, and picked up her mug. She nodded to the steaming one on the table next to Tom. "I made us some tea," she commented before taking a sip.

"Thank you," he responded politely but didn't reach for it. Instead he pulled out the crumpled pack of smokes from his pocket and slid one between his lips.

"When did you start smoking those?"

Tom stared at the pack of Lucky Strikes. His first thought was *when Ben left them behind*, but instead of answering right away, he struck a match and lit up, ignoring the tightening in his chest. "Just something different," he finally said.

"You seem distant," Marna commented. "Anything wrong?"

Everything. "It's been a trying time. Between work, helping out where I can, and spending my evenings fixing this place, I'm exhausted." It wasn't a lie: he *was* exhausted. Weary in his bones, in his mind, and in his soul.

"You did a great job," she complimented. "The house looks nice."

"Thank you."

"As does the church," Marna pointed out. "I'm really looking forward to Sunday morning service."

Tom took a deep draw from his cigarette, tilted his head back, and blew it out slowly, watching the smoke swirl around above him. "Thank you," he repeated. "I'm sure the ladies' auxiliary as well as Pastor John will be glad to have you back."

The uncomfortable silence that followed was as thick as the smoke filling the room and as heavy as the weight of Tom's heart. It was nearly unbearable, suffocating. He snubbed out his cigarette and picked up his tea, taking a tentative sip of the hot brew. "Marna?"

"Yes?"

"Are you happy?" he asked without meeting her gaze.

She didn't answer right away, no doubt carefully choosing her words before she spoke. Marna had always been a gentle soul. Even when things were bothering her, she never complained and always did her best to avoid hurting anyone's feelings. Tom already knew the answer. How could she be? Prior to meeting Ben, Tom had believed that, although the marriage wasn't perfect, Marna could have done worse than having a man who provided for her yet didn't love her. Now he wasn't so sure.

"I'm a very lucky woman," she finally answered.

"How so?"

"I have a healthy, beautiful son, a nice home, and I'm married to a good man. I have so much more than most, and for that I am thankful."

Tom nearly choked on Marna's compliment. A good man, a proper fella, had a wife and kids. His neighbors and family expected it. And yet Tom found himself wishing it all away. Does a good man fuck another man in his marital bed? Does he dream of running from his family, leaving his wife to bear the stigma of divorce or worse, making her an outcast as the woman whose husband was a faggot? Did a good man want to run to a small spread of land—leave his son behind to grow up without a father— and spend his life in hiding with another man? Give up everything for a virtual stranger?

The all too familiar anger and disgust rose up in Tom. "But are you happy?" he snapped.

Marna visibly shied away, and Tom instantly regretted his tone. He set his mug aside and joined his wife on the couch, laying his arm over her shoulder. "I'm sorry, I shouldn't have snapped," he said with true regret.

Marna nodded, but stayed tense next to him, no doubt wary from the comfort Tom was showing, something he rarely did, as much as the harshness in his voice. Another thing he rarely did was raise his voice to his wife. He had no excuses other than he was losing it. The stress was shredding his control.

"A lot has happened since the storm. One minute everyone was living their lives, seemingly without much of a care, then in the blink of an eye, everything changed. Homes were leveled, businesses lost, livelihoods stolen. It makes a man realize how quickly everything can be taken away."

"And yet even in such tragedy, we must thank our loving God for protecting us. No lives were lost."

"That's just it, Marna. Life isn't guaranteed. This time it was the buildings, next time it could just as easily be a tragedy of human life."

"We must put our faith in God that he'll protect us from such a fate," Marna responded quietly yet with conviction.

"But don't you want to be happy? Not just content, but truly happy?"

"I do not promise you happiness in this world, but in the next," Marna responded, quoting her religious teachings.

"Dammit, Marna, stop it! Why does your God allow you to suffer?" Tom closed his eyes and ran a hand over his face in frustration.

"*My* God?" Marna asked, sounding shocked. "Don't you mean *our* God?"

"Yes, yes," he placated. "But what value is there in suffering? Don't you want to be happy now?"

"Yes, of course, but—"

"No buts. You deserve to be happy," Tom informed her. "You and Tommy both deserve happiness, don't you see?" he said pleadingly.

Marna stared at him, her eyes glassy, holding back tears. "I don't understand where all this is coming from. I don't know what you want me to say."

Tom's head began to throb. "Nothing for you to say," he said softly. He gave his trembling wife a gentle squeeze and placed a chaste kiss to her cheek. "I just want you to be happy is all."

Tom grabbed his mug as he passed and took it to the kitchen. He poured his tea out and filled his mug with a good measure of whiskey. Downing it in one gulp, he poured another and took it and the bottle out to the porch.

With his feet propped up on the railing, Tom sipped at his whiskey from the old worn rocker. A million tiny stars danced in the cloudless night sky. It was beautiful and peaceful, yet Tom felt no joy, no peace. The only thing he knew was his family didn't deserve to suffer, God be damned. Only he had no idea how to change the course of their lives.

Chapter 15

TOM TRIED his best to put the past few weeks behind him, to carry on with his quiet life as he had before the storm. But try as he might, he wasn't able to get Ben out of his thoughts. So he stayed busy. He volunteered to continue helping rebuild Ramer, spent more time with his son, and worked on being more sensitive to Marna's needs and her feelings.

He stared at the empty pack of Lucky Strikes in his hand—it was the only thing he had that belonged to Ben. *Dear God, man, it's trash, let it go.* Disgusted with himself, he curled his hand into a fist, crumpled the pack, and tossed it into the garbage can. It was time to move on and let go. It was the right thing to do.

The door to the station opened, and George entered with a big toothless grin. "Afternoon," he said happily.

"Afternoon, George. How are you this fine, sunny day?" Tom greeted, returning the smile.

"Fine, fine. You better enjoy the sun while you can. Rain's a-coming."

"There's not a cloud in the sky," Tom pointed out.

"Damn arthritis is acting up," George said with a grimace and rubbed at his shoulder. "Only thing that makes it act like this is the rain."

"Can't be your age," Tom teased.

"Nope," George said adamantly and plopped a stack of mail down on Tom's desk. "I'm in my prime. Just ask the missus."

Tom wrinkled his nose. "I'll have to take your word for it."

"Hey, Bonnie," George called out and waved at the secretary as she chatted away on the phone.

Bonnie acknowledged George with a wave but continued with her conversation.

"She's been on the phone all morning organizing the ladies for the beautification project at the church," Tom told him as he started sorting through the mail. "I figure as long as she's chattin', she won't be asking me to help out."

"The missus has been trying to recruit me for that nonsense. I told her, woman, that's old man and lady-folk work," George huffed. "Anyway, gotta get this mail delivered before bad weather sets in. See ya tomorrow, Tom." He headed out the door, still grumbling. "Plantin' flowers."

Tom waved and shook his head. *Crazy ol' coot.*

Tom turned back to the stack of mail where a letter addressed to "Officer Webber, Ramer, Tennessee," with no return address caught his attention. He turned it over, but the back was blank. He took out his pocketknife and slid it beneath the flap, careful not to destroy the contents. Inside was a single piece of notebook paper. Handwritten in large block letters was a single word that caused Tom's heart to stop dead in his chest and his lungs to seize.

FAGGOT

Tom quickly checked to make sure Bonnie hadn't moved from her desk, then shoved the letter in his pocket. Sweat beaded on his brow at how lucky he'd been to intercept the mail. Bonnie tended to open all the mail that came into the station, and the thought of her opening the letter made his gut roil. He studied the envelope, the cancellation stamp showing the letter had been sent from Ramer. That it had to have been sent from someone he knew made it all the worse. It couldn't be a coincidence, but how could they know?

"Mail's on the desk," he called and rushed out the door without waiting for a response. As soon as the door was closed, he scanned the area, his heart thumping wildly. His instincts were telling him to run. Run as far from Ramer as he could get. *Run! Run! Run!*

But where?

The envelope! "Fuck," he groaned under his breath and went back in to retrieve it. Bonnie gave him a questioning look, but he ignored her, snatched the envelope off his desk, and shoved it in his pocket along with the letter. Adrenaline had kicked in his fight-or-flight response, causing him to shake. He held his breath, forcing himself to take one normal— *Nothing about this is normal! Run, you stupid fool. Run! Run! Run!* Tom clenched his teeth and took one step at a time.

Once again outside, he leaned against the closed door and blew out a heavy sigh. He needed a minute to catch his breath and get his panic under control. Somehow, someway he had to get a grip and figure out what to do, but he knew there was nothing he could do. The message was clear. Tom's carefully guarded secret was out. The only question now was what the sender of said message wanted and what he or she planned on doing with the information.

"Afternoon, Officer Webber."

Tom looked over to see Mrs. Warren strolling down the street with her young son, who was happily licking a lollipop. They were going about their lives like his wasn't crumbling around him.

"Afternoon," he managed to get out with a curt nod and pushed away from the door and head in the opposite direction.

Dammit, he needed to get his shit together. His mind was still screaming for him to run, but he forced the urge down. There was nowhere to run to. *Think. Think. Think.* Who could have sent the letter, and what did they want? The first thing that came to mind was blackmail, but Tom quickly dismissed it. If it was someone from Ramer as he suspected, then it couldn't be blackmail. Everyone in town knew Tom didn't have any money or anything of real value. The salary he made was enough to support his family, but he'd never made enough to have any savings. What little extra he did have usually ended up in the plate being passed around on Sunday mornings or used to feed those less fortunate than himself in the form of a few extra cans on the food bank shelf. He racked his brain trying to come up with anyone who would have it in for him, who would do something like this, and came up empty.

Tom looked up and realized he'd unknowingly stopped outside Tony's liquor store. Oh yeah, he needed a drink in the worst way. It wasn't going to help him with his problem, but maybe it would help his shaking hands and ease his racing mind enough to come up with a plan and figure out what the hell he was going to do. If that didn't work, then maybe if he drank enough, he wouldn't fucking care.

"Hey, Tom," Tony called out from behind the counter. "How you doing today?"

Tom waved and started to ask for a bottle of his usual, then spotted the whiskey Tony had suggested the last time he'd been in the store. Screw it. "I'll take a bottle of Jack Daniel's."

Tony tilted his head and studied Tom, his expression full of concern. "You okay?" he asked, grabbing the bottle of booze and setting it on the counter.

"Fine," Tom responded and pulled his wallet out. "What do I owe you?"

"You don't look so good. Looking a little pale," Tony commented. "You need to take better care of yourself."

"I said I'm fine. Now how much do I owe you?" Tom snapped in irritation. The look on Tony's face caused Tom's anger to drain from him as guilt replaced it. "Christ, I'm sorry, Tony. It's…." He ran a hand over his face and blew out a heavy breath. "Working too much and not getting enough sleep is obviously catching up with me," he said as an excuse.

"You work too hard. You got to learn to say no, my friend." Tony put the booze in a brown paper bag and slid it across the counter. "That'll be four dollars."

Tom dropped a ten and took his whiskey. "I really am sorry I snapped at you, Tony, and I promise I'll work on cutting back a little," Tom assured him. "Keep the change."

"No, no, that's too much," Tony complained and shook his head.

"Think of it as a bribe for not telling anyone you saw me playing hooky," Tom said with a wink.

"My lips are sealed. Now shoo! Go enjoy some downtime and get some sleep."

"Will do," Tom lied and waved good-bye.

No way would he be sleeping anytime soon. Get piss drunk and pass out? Hopefully. But sleep? Doubtful.

Since he was not one to take any time off—even with half the town telling him he needed to take a break—Bonnie looked almost relieved when he informed her he was taking the rest of the afternoon off. Tom changed out of his uniform, then took his booze and hopped in his old truck. As soon as he was on the dirt road that led to the swimming hole, he opened the bottle and took a long pull. He coughed as it burned his throat, heating his gut.

"What the fuck am I going to do?" He took another big swig.

The sun was out, but the cooler temperatures and early hour on a school day ensured no one would be out swimming. Tom found a quiet spot near the water's edge and plopped his ass down and leaned back against a large rock. He took another big swig of whiskey, and this time he welcomed the burn.

He'd already come to realize he was a fucking coward, so it was appropriate that he had run and was now not only hiding from others, but from himself in a bottle of whiskey. But fuck, what else could he do? Nothing but keep drinking and hope. He didn't dare pray. It sure as hell hadn't gotten him anywhere in the past.

TOM WAS able to accomplish at least one task. Although he'd been drinking more over the past month than he normally did, half the bottle of whiskey was enough to knock him on his ass as well as knock him out cold. Blessedly, during his alcohol-induced slumber, he hadn't been tormented by nightmares, but a solution to his problem hadn't bestowed itself upon him either.

It was dark by the time he made it back home. He felt a little off-balance as he stepped out of his truck. His mouth felt stuffed full of cotton, nasty stale-alcohol-soaked cotton to boot. He ran a hand through his hair, pushed the door shut, and leaned against it. A light burned within the house, but he wasn't quite ready to go inside. He pulled the new pack of Lucky Strikes from his pocket, tapped one out, and placed it between his lips. He lit up, took a long draw, and blew it out slowly. As he smoked, he stared at the star-filled sky, his mind once again beginning to race. During the drive home he'd come to the decision that whatever was coming his way, he'd face it with his head held high. He'd learned one thing from his time with Ben—he might have to hide his true nature, but he was no longer ashamed of who or what he was. If it were just him, no ties, no home, no family, he'd already be gone. But he had them all, and he'd do right by them.

He took one last pull from the cigarette, dropped it, and crushed it under his boot as he headed up the porch steps. Hand on the knob, he rolled his neck, straightened his shoulders, and pushed the door open.

A lamp on the table next to the couch was on, but the room was completely silent other than the sound of the wind rustling the trees outside the windows and the creak of floorboards as Tom made his way across the room. He slumped down on the couch and let out a heavy sigh.

"Pa?"

Tom looked up to see his young son peeking around the corner of the doorway, and smiled gently. "C'mere, boy."

Tommy rushed from the hall and jumped on the couch at Tom's side. He placed a single finger against his lips. "Shh. Mama is sleeping."

"I figured as much. It's late. How come you're not sleeping?"

"I was waiting for you. I wanted to show you my treasure," Tommy whispered. With a large smile on his face, he opened his little hand and held it up. A copper penny sat in his palm.

"Wow. Where were you treasure hunting? Did you come across any bandits?"

"Not a single one." Tommy giggled. He glanced over his shoulder, no doubt looking to see if his ma had woken up, then leaned in close. "I found it under the porch."

Tom gave his son a stern look. "Are you supposed to be under there? Last time you ended up with the knees of your trousers torn and a bump on your head."

"I had to, Pa!" Tommy whined, then lowered his voice when Tom raised a brow. "I had to. I lost the button on my britches and it fell through the cracks."

"You did, huh?"

"Uh-huh."

"Did you find it?"

"Yup and this too," he said, proudly holding the penny up again.

Tom ruffled his son's curls and pulled him onto his lap, wrapping him in a hug. Tom smiled when Tommy snuggled into him and laid his head on Tom's chest. "Okay, I won't tell your ma this time. But there's lots of stuff under there you can get hurt on, so no more going under the porch, okay?"

"Okay, Pa," Tommy yawned.

Tom leaned his head back on the couch as he rubbed Tommy's back. The little guy was out cold in seconds, making small snuffling noises that warmed Tom's heart and brought his protective instincts to the surface. Tom hugged him tighter. The excitement on his son's face when he'd spotted Tom, the trust he had in his dad, and the way he felt in Tom's arms as he rocked him—this was why he'd do the right thing.

Chapter 16

AMAZING WHAT a little snuggle, a full night of sleep, and a warm sunny morning could do for a man's mood. Tom actually found himself whistling as he drove slowly through town, waving to those who were out building, raking, or otherwise working to clean up the devastation that had befallen Ramer. They had a long way to go and some things were gone forever, but the people were still here, and they were making progress every day.

Tom came to a halt outside the church when he saw Pastor John sweeping the front walk. "Morning, Pastor. Beautiful day, isn't it?"

"Sure is," he agreed and leaned on his broom. "How are you and your family this morning?"

"Good. Good," Tom responded with a nod. "Left the boy trying to plead with his poor ma about why he shouldn't have to feed the dogs. His arguments were sounding pretty good when I pulled out."

Pastor John chuckled. "He's too smart for his own good."

"You got everything you need for the big gardening event this weekend?" Tom inquired.

"Yup. Bonnie has been great at organizing everything. I have no doubt it will be a big success. You should stop by if you get the chance. They're having a bake sale as well."

"You're a sly one," Tom accused and shook a finger at the pastor playfully. "Tempting men to work with delicious home-baked treats."

"Well, you know what they say. The way to a man's heart is through his stomach."

"And you're hoping the same thing goes for his back-breaking labor too, no doubt." The pastor smiled and shrugged. Tom returned the smile and waved. "You have a great day. I'm sure between Bonnie and Marna, I'll be there."

"See you Saturday," Pastor John called out and returned the wave.

Tom continued to cruise around the small town, waving to townspeople and inspecting the progress. He didn't have to worry about crime, not that Ramer ever had that much to speak of, but lately even the teens were kept busy and were too exhausted to cause much of a ruckus. He pulled up in front of the station shortly before ten and headed in. While he was feeling better, he still had the letter from the day before nestled at the back of his mind, and he wanted to be there before the mail arrived.

"Morning, Bonnie," he called out as he shut the door behind him.

Bonnie nodded in greeting from where she sat at her desk and chatted away on the phone as usual. Tom hung his hat on the hook next to the door and went to his desk. He riffled through his messages: a reminder about the garden event, a call from Ruth Simms checking on the progress of her missing cat, and an invoice that needed his signature for office supplies.

"That was Connie Norton from Nashville," Bonnie informed him as she hung up the phone. "She's sending the flyers and banners out this week."

Tom cocked his head and blinked.

"You know, for your campaign?"

Shit. With all the mess and distractions, he'd completely forgotten about the election. "Do you really think that's necessary? It's not like anyone is running against me," Tom chuckled.

"You never know," Bonnie sniffed. "Some whippersnapper may get too big for his britches and try to take the job that's rightly yours."

Tom felt his cheeks heat. "I don't know if I'd go that far, Bonnie."

"Nonsense," she said and waved at him dismissively. "You've given more to this town than anyone, worked harder than anyone to rebuild. Hell, Tom. You've been the chief of Ramer the last five years while Harvey spent his time at the diner gossiping." She made the sign of the cross. "God rest his soul."

He'd never been good with compliments, so he just shook his head without comment. He also wasn't one who did things for the pat on the back or even the acknowledgment, but because it was the right thing to do.

Still, it felt good to hear it. Especially after the last twenty-four hours Hell, after the last month, truth be told.

He scanned his in-basket and desk and found them empty. "Did the mail come?" he asked, trying to keep the trepidation out of his voice.

"Not yet," Bonnie said as she looked into her compact while patting her nose with the sponge, then tried to check her hair using the wee thing.

Tom sighed internally.

"Oh, that reminds me," she exclaimed and snapped her compact closed. "You hear about any problems with the mail between here and Davidson County?"

A tickling sensation began at the base of Tom's neck. "None that I'm aware of. Why?"

"Sheriff Cronkite called yesterday saying he was expecting mail from Ramer and asked if we were having problems. I told him the same thing."

The phone rang and she answered it without looking over at Tom. It was a good thing, since he could feel the blood draining from his face and the air rushed out of his lungs. It couldn't be a coincidence. What were the chances that he'd call on the same day Tom had received the anonymous letter? *None. There was no fucking chance. None!*

Dammit, why hadn't he thought of that? He'd pissed the man off rightly. He'd seen it in the way the bastard's face had turned bright red, the way the veins bulged in his neck. If that hadn't been enough, the man's eyes had bugged out of his head when Tom had dared to challenge him. Tom scrubbed a hand over his face and through his hair. Jesus H. Christ, why had he taunted the man? Tom knew the kind of man Cronkite was; he'd dealt with enough of them throughout his life. Cronkite was big, mean, in a position of power, and hated to lose.

It made sense, and even while he struggled to figure out what the man had on him, how he could know or if he was only grasping at straws, Tom found he was relieved that the letter hadn't come from one of his townsfolk. It didn't make him any less frightened to know he had a pissed-off sheriff out for his ass, but it did make it less painful.

"Tom!" Bonnie hissed.

Tom jerked his head and met her quizzical gaze. "Sorry. Daydreaming," he lied.

"It's Ruth Simms again," she said quietly, holding the palm of her hand over the phone receiver. "She wants to talk to you. Should I tell her you're out?"

It took him a couple seconds to catch up to the conversation, his heart still beating rapidly, hands a little shaky from the news of Cronkite. "Um, no…." The door opened and George came in, his toothy grin leading the way. *Perfect.* "You know what? Tell her I'm on my way out," he told Bonnie and pushed out of his seat. "I don't have anything going on today anyway."

"Morning, Tom," George said in greeting.

"Morning. Here, let me take that for you," Tom offered and took the stack of mail. He scanned through it quickly, relieved he didn't see another anonymous letter, and set the stack on Bonnie's desk.

"I think Bonnie has a question for you, George," Tom said as he patted the postman on the shoulder. "Gotta run."

As Tom grabbed his hat and closed the door behind him, he heard George's muffled voice saying something about woman's work. That should go over well with Bonnie.

Tom hurried to his car, and as soon as he was behind the wheel and heading out of town, he finally unclenched his jaw, but the tension in his neck remained, as did the throb in his head. He tapped his thumbs on the wheel, ignoring his first inclination to head to his truck and grab his bottle of whiskey. He was done with that solution.

He ran through every possible moment when Cronkite could have possibly seen Tom and Ben together and came up blank. They'd been extremely careful and there was absolutely zero chance they'd been seen behind the closed doors and drawn curtains of Tom's home. When they were in public during the time Ben had been helping to rebuild, they'd barely even acknowledged each other. Ben was just another one of the numerous outsiders who'd come to town to help.

"You're grasping," Tom muttered. Still, the tickling sensation didn't ease up. He'd have to wait and see what the bastard threw at him next. He had no other choice.

As he continued down the road, his thoughts turned toward Ben. He was glad Ben had gotten out of town before this bullshit started. He was having a hard time picturing Ben riding horses and driving cattle—maybe rustling them. The image that popped in his head of Ben as a cattle rustler made him chuckle out loud. It wasn't that Tom didn't believe Ben had every intention of going straight or that he would no doubt make an honest go at it. But Ben looked more like a bad guy. Like a James Cagney, Edward G. Robinson, or—oh damn, he could so see Ben as Paul Muni, especially in *Scarface*.

Tom pulled into Mrs. Simms's drive with a smile on his face, but a heaviness had settled in his chest. He'd never see that smirking grin again, those haunting brown eyes, or that mass of dark hair. He'd never feel those strong arms—Tom forcibly pushed those thoughts away and stepped out of the car. *It is what it is*, he reminded himself. Thoughts of Ben, good or bad, had no business being part of his working or even daylight hours.

Setting his hat on his head, Tom made his way up the walk to the small bungalow. He raised his arm to knock and jumped when the door opened.

"Did you find her?" Mrs. Simms asked, sounding hopeful.

"Sorry, ma'am, I haven't found her, but we'll keep looking. Do you happen to have a picture of her?"

"Oh, why yes!" Mrs. Simms exclaimed excitedly, her weathered face lighting up. "Come in," she offered and shuffled out of the way.

Ruth Simms had been a fixture in Ramer since before Tom was born. She claimed she'd been the queen of the speakeasy and could give any flapper a run for their dancing shoes even if she'd been in her fifties at the time. Tom had no doubt she could. Even in her eighties, she was still full of piss and vinegar. It was sad to see her mind giving away to dementia.

"Did I tell you about the time I won a dance contest?" Mrs. Simms asked from where she sat on the couch, a large photo album on her lap.

"No, but I'd love to hear about it," he placated.

Ruth patted the couch, the lost cat forgotten for the moment. Tom had no doubt she'd call again. She'd been looking for that damn cat for three years. It was happening more often since Mr. Simms had passed summer before last, but he didn't mind so much. She was just lonely.

Tom took the seat next to Mrs. Simms as she chatted away about the photos Tom knew by heart. He'd seen them a hundred times.

Chapter 17

THE SOUND of gunfire had Tom jerking straight up in bed and reaching for his gun.

"What is it?" Marna asked, sounding as panicked at Tom felt.

"Stay here," he demanded and cautiously got out of bed. He went to the window and carefully eased back the curtain enough to peek out.

"Tom?"

"Shh," he hissed. The moon was out, lighting up the yard, but he saw no movement other than the trees swaying in the wind. As quietly as he could, he made his way around to the window on the other wall and again saw nothing.

"Stay here," he ordered in a low tone. "I'm going to go get Tommy."

Marna pulled the covers up close to her chin. He couldn't make out her face in the darkness, but he could hear her rapid breathing over his rapid heartbeat. Keeping his gun poised, he made his way across the hall to Tommy's room and pushed the door open. The curtains were open, casting an eerie light into the room, but it was enough to see his son's small form. Keeping to the shadows, Tom eased over to the window and scanned the front yard. He didn't see anyone, but something was covering the windshield of his truck.

"Damn kids," he grumbled.

Careful not to wake him, Tom picked Tommy up with one arm and quietly but quickly carried him to his room. Marna opened her arms and accepted the boy, pulling him to her chest.

"I think it's just some kids with a bushel of rotten tomatoes needin' a good swift kick in the ass," he whispered.

"What if it's not?" Marna complained.

"Maybe we should call the police," Tom said lightly as he pulled on a pair of trousers and shirt.

"Just be careful," she huffed, obviously not finding the humor in the joke.

"Always am." He lifted his gun to show her as he headed out the door. He closed it behind him and was still cautious as he made his way to the front room. Everything was as it should be, which made it all the more eerie considering the gunfire that had awoken him.

Tom pulled on his boots, then slipped out the front door, careful not to let the screen door bang shut. It was a moot point. He was standing on his porch in the glow of a nearly full moon; anyone standing in the trees would have a perfect shot. No shot came. Whoever had been shooting was either gone or watching. As he tromped down the stairs, he hoped it was the former.

When Tom approached his truck, all the caution, unease, and worry drained from his body in a rush, chased out by the anger surged through him. "That no good, rotten motherfucker," he cursed acidly.

His old truck was covered in rotten eggs and tomatoes, but what had ignited his rage was the word "fag" spelled out in the goo on the windshield. Tom raised his weapon as he turned slowly in a circle.

"Where the hell are you?" he snarled.

Silence.

He snatched up part of a tomato and ran it through the mess, obliterating the ugly word before angrily throwing it toward the trees. "Goddamn coward."

Tom swiped his hand across his pants as he stomped back up the porch steps. He wasn't about to sit idly by and wait for a third event. This had already gone beyond ridiculous. Come morning, he'd be taking a little trip to Davidson County and paying the good sheriff a visit.

Tom headed back into the house, making sure the door was locked behind him, and laid his gun on the counter in the kitchen. He washed his hands and pulled down the bottle of whiskey. He studied it for a moment, debating the soundness. Figuring there would be no way he'd get back to sleep without it, he shoved away the doubt. He tipped up the bottle and took a healthy swig, welcoming the burn in his gut. He wiped the back of his hand across his mouth and started to put the bottle away.

"Fuck it," he grumbled and took another long pull. He took the whiskey and his gun to the couch, propping his feet up on the coffee table.

He had no idea what he was going to say to Cronkite, but one thing was for sure—he'd be damned if he'd let the arrogant bastard intimidate him. He sat in the quiet of the room sipping his whiskey and thinking on the best way to deal with his tormentor, enjoying the fantasies of some of the more extreme things he'd like to do—tar and feathering being one scenario that brought a smile to his face. Of course, he wouldn't do any of them, but he could dream. Nothing wrong with dreaming, as long as it didn't involve things he shouldn't be doing. Not that a public forum around a whipping post was something he should do, but thoughts of getting back at Cronkite were much safer than where his thoughts had been wandering to as of late.

"Tom? Is everything okay?" Marna asked from the hallway.

"Everything is fine. Go back to bed."

Marna tightened her robe around her, clasping it below her neck, and padded into the room. "Are you sure?" she asked as she glanced at the bottle in Tom's hand and the gun resting on his lap.

"Yeah, I'm sure." He sat up, putting his feet on the floor, and set both the bottle and the weapon on the table. "Some hoodlums covered the old truck with tomatoes and eggs. Just a foolish prank."

Instead of returning to bed, Marna sat at the opposite end of the couch and tucked her legs up under her. "I've been worried about you," she admitted. "You've been... I don't know, different since Tommy and I returned."

"I'm exhausted, Marna. There is so much to do and not enough hours in the day to do it all."

"I know you are. You've been working so hard, but...." She looked down at her lap, picking at a stray thread on her robe.

"But what?" he asked, trying to keep the irritation out of his voice. This had nothing to do with her, and he wished she'd just take his excuse and go back to bed.

"You get this look."

"I get a look? What the hell are you talking about?"

Marna met Tom's gaze. Her expression puzzled Tom. It was full of sadness, and yet there was a stubbornness he rarely witnessed on his normally meek wife's face.

"I can't quite explain it, but you get this faraway look on your face and such longing in your eyes."

"I'm sure it's longing for sleep you're seeing," he demurred.

Marna shook her head. "No, Tom, it's not."

"I—"

"Let me finish," she said, holding up a hand.

The fact that Marna interrupted him was enough to shock Tom into silence for a few heartbeats as he stared at her. She so rarely ever stood up for herself where Tom was concerned, and she never questioned him.

"Sorry, go ahead."

"I've been doing a lot of thinking about what you said. You know when you asked me if I wanted to be happy. Not just content but truly happy." She looked down, drew in a deep breath, then let it out. When she looked back up at Tom, there was conviction in her eyes. "I haven't been truly happy for a very long time. Content, yes, but not happy, and neither have you. I'd go as far as to suggest you haven't been happy since we married."

"That's not true," Tom said guiltily. "There have been times."

"No, Tom, you haven't. I'm not talking about the love and joy your son brings you or the pride you take in providing for us and in your service to this community. I'm talking about being truly happy in your heart." She tilted her head, a sad smile playing at her lips. "Happy with yourself."

Was it possible that he'd assumed her complacency would be the end of it? That she wouldn't try to look beyond what he allowed her to see and take what he showed her at face value? Tom suddenly felt exposed, vulnerable, as if she had been picking away at his exterior and was finally breaking through. Or worse, that she somehow already had. He didn't know how to respond to what she was implying, so he gave the only answer he could come up with—none. He chose instead to pick up the bottle again and take another good swig and avoided looking her in the eye.

"I've always known you were different than other men," she said without scorn.

"What do you mean?" He still couldn't look at her, instead staring at the bottle in his hand.

"Women talk, Tom."

Tom squeezed his eyes shut. Just what he needed. Along with the big heap of shit already on his brain, now he had to hear how he wasn't living up to his duties as a husband. "Marna, do we really need to have this talk right now?"

"Tom," she said softly. She scooched down the couch and laid a gentle hand on his shoulder. "I wasn't complaining, just making an observation and letting you know I understood."

I highly fucking doubt that. Tom squeezed the bridge of his nose as his head began to pound. Again, he found himself not knowing how to respond.

"For a long time I thought it was me—"

"Marna," he said pleadingly.

"Stop interrupting me and let me finish," she snapped.

Tom whipped his head up, and he stared at his wife. He half expected her to have grown a second head since the chances of that were about the same as her raising her voice to him.

"I got over that," she continued without commenting on Tom's shock. "I then thought maybe you were visiting one of those women like some of the other husbands have or maybe having an affair. But that's not you, Tom. I've never even seen your eyes linger over Sally McCarthy, and every man's eyes linger over Sally McCarthy. Especially her chest." She chuckled.

Tom cocked his head and studied her. She didn't appear to be upset. In fact, there was a light in her eyes he hadn't seen in many years. "What are you trying to say?"

"I'm saying you were right. Life is too short not to be happy. I spent a lot of time with Donna while I was away."

"Who?"

"You don't know her. She lives down the block from my brother. Anyway, she and I talked a lot about that very issue. Her husband ran off with another woman and left her to raise her daughter on her own. Do you know her church asked her to leave? Can you believe that? Her husband was the sinner, and yet she was asked not to return to the congregation. It's not right, Tom, and I asked Pastor John about his feelings on the matter, and he agrees with me. Divorced women shouldn't be shunned from God's house, but welcomed in, supported."

"I still don't see what this has to do with us or about being happy," Tom admitted.

"Donna was still happy, Tom. Her husband left her, her church turned her back on her, and she was still happy because she knew she was a good person and had God in her heart."

Marna hadn't answered his question. Still confused, he continued to stare at her.

"I'm just saying that wherever our lives lead us, I know we'll be okay, and hopefully at the end of the journey, we will both find happiness." She shrugged and pecked him on the cheek. "We're both good people, and no matter what happens, we'll be okay." She went to her feet, pulling her robe tight. "I'm going back to bed and getting some sleep before Tommy wakes up. You coming?"

He blinked up at her, still trying to figure out what the hell had just happened. Unsuccessful, he pushed himself up off the couch. "Sleep sounds like a good idea. I'll just take care of my stuff," he told her and picked up his gun and bottle.

Marna smiled and without another word went back to bed.

Tom stared after her for a long moment. She'd given him a lot to think about, not only with her words, but also the expression on her face when she said them and the implications behind them. He finally got his feet moving, took the bottle to the kitchen, and started to return it to the cupboard when he thought better of it. He poured the remainder of the whiskey down the sink and tossed the bottle in the trash. The stuff was obviously more powerful than he'd thought.

His normally meek wife had stood up to him, even raised her voice to him, something Tom had never heard. Not only had she done those things, but he was pretty sure she'd been hinting about the fact that she knew his deepest secret.

He checked the safety on his gun as he headed to the bedroom. No more booze for him; it was beginning to make him hear and see things. Not a good idea, considering in a few hours he needed to clean his truck, get to work, and deal with real problems.

Chapter 18

TOM CUT the ignition of his car and jumped when something banged against the trunk.

"Dammit, Frank, you scared the shit out of me," Tom grumbled.

Frank leaned his arm on the top of the cruiser and looked down at Tom with laughing eyes. "I'm not the least bit sorry. Do you know how hard it is to sneak up on you?" he asked with a satisfied expression. "You're losing your edge."

"You're lucky I didn't shoot you in the ass," Tom growled without any real heat. "Running a little late, are you?"

"Yeah, didn't get much sleep last night. Sick kid kept us up. Talking about tired, you look like you haven't had much more than I have," Frank pointed out.

"Had some problems with hoodlums," Tom informed him. "You have any problems with kids out at your place?"

"What kind of problems?"

"Just stupid kid shit. My truck was covered in rotten eggs and tomatoes this morning." Tom left out the rest of the events, such as the gunshot and message. He was still hoping it was simply nothing more than teenaged pranks, including the letter.

"Haven't had any problems out at my place, and no one has called with any complaints, but I just got here," Frank told him with a shake of his head. "Did you ask Bonnie if she's had any calls?"

"Was just heading in to ask," Tom said and pulled his keys from the ignition, grabbed his hat, and opened the door. Frank stepped back, allowing him to exit, a strange expression on his face. "What?" Tom asked as he set his hat on his head and adjusted it to block the bright early morning sun.

"I did get a strange call last night. Sheriff Cronkite called me."

"What the hell did he want?" Tom snapped. Just the mention of that bastard's name was enough to set Tom's blood boiling again.

Frank looked taken aback for a second and his eyes narrowed. "What's going on between you two?"

"I don't like him," Tom demurred. "The guy just rubs me the wrong way."

"I didn't think you knew him."

"I don't," Tom admitted and rolled his shoulders, the anger causing the muscles to tighten. "I only met him the once, but he was a complete asshole. What did he want?"

"I don't know. He said he'd be stopping by later this afternoon and asked if I'd meet him for a cup of coffee."

"What?"

Frank shrugged. "I told you it was a weird call. He wouldn't say why he wanted to meet me, only that he had something important to discuss with me."

The tension increased exponentially with his anger. "What did you tell him?"

"What could I say? I said yes, of course."

Tom blew out a pent-up breath, struggling not to start growling, raging, and screaming. As he'd washed his truck earlier, he'd almost convinced himself that it had been nothing more than punk kids, but now with Cronkite wanting to talk with Frank, not at the station, but over coffee, Tom could no longer hold on to the denial. He could no longer ignore the obvious. Cronkite was after him. The only thing he wasn't sure of was how the man had found out his secret.

Turning away, Tom headed toward the station. "Just be careful. I don't trust that man," he tossed over his shoulder.

"Why not?" Frank called out and ran to catch up with Tom. "Is there something going on I should know about?"

"I think he had himself convinced he'd caught himself a bank robber, and he's pissed off at me for knocking him off his high horse."

"So why the hell isn't he out trying to find the dirt on the guy if he's convinced he's guilty? Why go after you?"

Tom held the door open for Frank. "Because he thinks I lied to him. I don't know, Frank. I had the guy's number two minutes after meeting him. He likes to toss his authority around, and he hates anyone who questions him or goes against him. I think he will say anything to make me look bad. I wouldn't even put it past him to make shit up. Just don't trust the guy, okay?"

"Yeah, okay," Frank said with a nod. "If he thinks he's going to use me to get his revenge on you, he's got another think coming. Sheriff Cronkite doesn't know how we do things here in Ramer. We protect our own and don't take too kindly to strangers causing problems." Frank patted Tom on the shoulder. "I got your back."

"Thanks," Tom responded with a genuine smile. He greeted Bonnie with a wave and sat down at his desk. While Frank's kind words had made him smile, the unpleasant churning in his gut didn't subside nor did the feeling of foreboding. The emotional highs and lows he'd been experiencing lately were taking their toll on him, and he was truly beginning to fear for his sanity.

Tom spent the morning obsessively watching the clock as he tried to catch up on long-overdue paperwork. He still had a ton of reports to file from the storm but couldn't concentrate on any of it. It only got worse once Frank left for his meeting with Cronkite. Tom paced around the small station like a caged animal. Every ring of the phone, every flash of movement outside the window caused him to jump and his heart to race. He was itchy, as though he were trapped in his own skin, and it felt like his head was going to explode and quite possibly his heart as well. He needed a distraction—something, Jesus fucking Christ, anything to keep from thinking of all the scenarios that could play out between Frank and Cronkite.

"I'm going to take a walk," he grumbled and snatched his hat from the hook.

"Thank heavens," Bonnie sighed dramatically. "You're plumb drivin' me crazy with all that pacing."

Tom didn't respond. He stepped out the door, pulled his pack of smokes from his pocket, and lit up. He'd already smoked nearly a pack since arriving at the station, and his lungs protested on the first deep pull. Tom coughed and spit. Instead of doing the smart thing and putting it out, he brought the smoke to his mouth with a shaking hand and took another long draw.

He paced and smoked and paced some more until Frank's cruiser finally pulled back into the lot. Tom was filled with both relief and trepidation, the conflicting sensations causing him to shake harder, and sweat broke out on his brow.

"Bonnie run you off for smoking?" Frank chuckled as he stepped out of his car. "You really should give that nasty habit up again."

Tom tried his damnedest to appear calm but knew it wouldn't do much good even with the light sound of Frank's voice. Instead he pulled his hat farther down on his brow and took another draw of his smoke as he leaned against the wall.

"She thinks it stinks," Tom responded as coolly as he could.

"It does." Frank leaned against the wall next to Tom, propping one foot up on the brick and looking up and down the street. When he saw no one, he grabbed the cigarette from between Tom's fingers and took a deep draw. "Don't tell the wife," he muttered as he blew out the smoke.

"My lips are sealed," Tom assured him. "Your meeting go that bad?"

Frank took another pull before handing the cigarette back. "You're right about Cronkite. He does have it out for you." Frank's eyes narrowed "I don't like him, and I sure as hell don't trust him."

Tom felt vindicated in his dislike and mistrust of the sheriff, but it didn't do anything to settle the dread surging through his system. "Doesn't surprise me. So what did he want?"

"He spent the first fifteen minutes pumping sunshine up my ass Told me how great I am, praised me on my impeccable service record, and offered to back me if I was willing to run against you for police chief Even guaranteed me a win."

The implication behind Cronkite's offer was obvious to Tom, but he acted like it wasn't a big deal. "You gonna run? Hell, Frank, I'll be more than willing to step aside and let you take the title. I never asked for the job in the first place. I was appointed the interim I'm sure based on seniority, but if you—"

"Hell no, I don't want it. Too much paperwork," Frank balked. "I didn't tell him that. Just let him run his mouth and nodded a lot. Trying to feel him out, ya know?"

Tom took one last puff from his smoke, then crushed it under his boot. "And how'd he feel?" he asked with a smirk.

"As slippery as a tub of lard." Frank chuckled, and Tom couldn't help but do the same.

"Well, if you ever want the job, just let me know. I have a lot of paperwork on my desk I'd be more than happy to give you," he offered and pushed away from the wall.

"No, thank you. I don't know if he was convinced by my acting skills, but he did ask me to give you this," Frank said as he held out an envelope.

Tom didn't reach for it right away, almost afraid to take it, as if it were something much more dangerous than a simple envelope. Hell, it was much more dangerous or at least was something he wasn't going to like, and more than likely it would send him a little closer to the edge of insanity.

"What is it?"

Frank held it up to the sun, turning and twisting it in his hand. Tom held his breath, afraid the secrets within would be revealed, yet not daring to snatch it from him. "An envelope would be my guess," Frank finally said with a raised brow and handed it to him.

This time Tom did snatch it away. "Ha, ha, funny guy." He shoved the letter in his back pocket without opening it.

"Aren't you curious about what's inside?" Frank asked as they fell in step with each other.

"Well, I see it this way," Tom drawled. "I got work to do, important work, and since I can't get you to do it for me, I best get on it. Cronkite's little game of intimidation isn't high on my list of priorities today."

"See, that's why you are much better for the job than I am," Frank commented.

"Why is that?" Tom inquired and held the door open for his partner.

"Because my curiosity would be driving me nuts right now, and I'd have ripped it open, work be damned."

"I just figure I'm not going to let him upset my day." Truth was, Cronkite had had Tom messed up for days, but he wasn't going to share that bit of info with Frank. "Not going to give him more importance than he's worth."

"Again, that's why you're perfect for the job."

Tom rolled his eyes. "You just hate paperwork."

"That too," Frank answered, completely unapologetic.

What Frank couldn't have known was the entire time Tom forced himself to write reports and sign his name, the envelope was burning a hole in his pocket, the weight of it heavy. He didn't dare reveal the contents of it in front of Bonnie and Frank, though. Tom was sure it was something that would be along the same line as the last two messages. He hadn't completely lied, he really didn't want to give Cronkite power, but more importantly, he didn't want the contents to be something either Frank or Bonnie witnessed. He didn't want to have to lie to either one of them any more than he already had.

"Tom."

"What is it, Bonnie?" he asked without looking up.

"It's Marna."

The mention of his wife had Tom pushing up out of his seat. "What is it?"

Bonnie held out the phone to him. Tom rushed over and grabbed it. "Marna, what is it?" he asked in concern. She never called the station. Ever.

"Will you be home soon?" she asked quietly, but her voice was tight. Tom instantly knew there was more to the question.

"Marna, what is it?" he asked again.

"I went out the back door to hang the wash, and there is a box sitting on the porch with your name on it."

"Did you open it?" he asked with fear skittering down his spine.

"No," she whispered. "There is a very foul odor coming from it, Tom."

"Don't touch it, I'm on my way." He hung up the phone.

"Everything okay?" Bonnie called out after him.

"Yes, it's fine. Marna saw a raccoon running around the backyard, and being it's out in the daylight, she's worried it may have rabies. She's afraid Tommy is going to get hurt or bit." To Frank he said, "Can you hold down the fort tonight?"

"Yeah, I got it. Go rescue the family."

"Thanks, Frank. I'll be at the house if either of you need me." He waved and headed out the door.

Behind the wheel of the car, he pulled the letter from his pocket and laid it on the seat next to him. He then fired up the car and headed down the road before he picked it up again. He slid the tip of one finger beneath a corner of the flap, ripped it down the side, and pulled out the contents, a small piece torn from a photo. At first Tom had no idea what he was seeing. Dirt and boots. Two sets of boots facing each other, attached to calves, so close that the two figures could be hugging.

Bile rose up in his throat, and Tom swallowed several times, forcing it back down. Those were his boots. His boots toe-to-toe with Ben's. "Oh fuck," he groaned as the second in time captured by a camera came rushing back. It was the last day he'd seen Ben. The day he'd kissed him good-bye. He crushed the section of photo in his fist and stomped on the gas. The photo was no doubt the first brick from the structure of his carefully constructed life. Once one brick was pulled from a foundation, it was only a matter of time before the whole structure weakened and eventually collapsed.

Chapter 19

WITH THE little surprise package—a dead cat with a noose around its neck—and a shovel in hand, Tom headed out beyond the tree line. He walked until he was far enough from the house that Tommy wouldn't stumble over the grave, then set the box down and began digging. He found an outlet for the anger simmering in him with each hard slam of the shovel and strain of muscles as he tossed the dirt away. Notes and rotten food was one thing, but to kill a defenseless animal was crossing a line Tom simply couldn't tolerate.

He was still sure Cronkite was involved but now knew there was at least one other person working with him. Marna had been out on the back porch before lunch and the box hadn't been there. When she'd gone back out later after putting Tommy down for his nap, she'd discovered it. Cronkite had been with Frank at the time, so either he wasn't involved or he had a partner. Tom's gut told him the sheriff was involved, so that meant there was another, most likely local, fiend at work. The back and forth, the uncertainty, and the constant worry was grating on his nerves. Something had to give. He simply couldn't continue on this same path. He slammed the shovel down and dropped the box into the large hole.

"It's got to end," he growled and began filling the hole in.

Sweat poured down his face as he left the site, leaving tracks in the dirt. He wiped the filth from his eyes as they burned. As he came through the trees, he dropped the shovel and broke out in a dead run toward the squad car.

"What the hell do you want?" Tom snapped.

"Well, good afternoon, Officer Webber. I was hoping I'd find you at home," Cronkite drawled, leaning against his car, looking completely relaxed and at ease.

"You knew damn good and well I would be after I got your little message," Tom snarled. He curled his hands into tight fists, fighting the strong urge to punch the smiling bastard in the mouth. "Now, I'm going to ask you one more time what the hell you want before I consider you a trespasser and physically remove you from my property."

"I see I've gotten your attention," Cronkite said with a mocking tone.

Tom began to tremble with the sheer effort it took not to swing. "Just fucking say it, Cronkite. I don't have the time or the patience to play games with the likes of you."

"Oh, but we've only just begun to play," he responded snidely.

"Tom, is everything okay?" Marna called from the front porch.

"Everything is fine, Marna. Get back in the house," Tom ordered.

"Pretty wife," Cronkite commented.

The way the sheriff said it made Tom's skin crawl, and he lost his hold on his control. He snaked a hand out and grabbed the front of Cronkite's shirt and drew his other arm back.

"I wouldn't advise you go through with that thought, unless you want your pretty little wife knowing what you've been up to."

Tom glared at the arrogant fucker who wasn't so much as batting an eye in the face of Tom's rage. Indecision caused Tom to pause. God, how he wanted to follow through and connect his knuckles to bone.

"Take your fucking hand off me, or we're going to have a serious problem here," Cronkite demanded in a low, dangerous tone.

They stared at each other for a few more heartbeats before Tom grudgingly pried his fingers from the man's shirt. "And just what is it you think I've been up to?" Tom hedged.

"Not think, know. Now, I suggest you listen closely." Cronkite smoothed down his shirt, then pulled a stogie from his pocket and ran it under his nose, sniffing it loudly, no doubt for effect. He bit the end off, spitting it at Tom's feet, and lit a match, puffing repeatedly until he had a bright ember glowing at the end. He took another draw and blew it out slowly toward Tom, holding his gaze the entire time.

Tom gritted his teeth and breathed harshly through his nose, ignoring the stench that burned it. Cronkite was obviously either waiting for a reaction or was just trying to be an ass. He wouldn't get the former, and he was most certainly the latter. Tom increased the pressure on his jaw, refusing to give the bastard the satisfaction.

After a long moment, Cronkite rolled the cigar in his fingers, staring at it. "Here is what you're going to do. You're going to recant the statement you made about Mr. Parker's whereabouts on April fifth, tell me where I can find him, then you're going to resign and disappear." Cronkite ticked off his points as if he were placing a dinner order.

Tom stared at him, unblinking, too shocked to respond as he struggled to process Cronkite's demands. Give up Ben? That one registered first and had Tom unclenching his jaw.

"The hell I will," he growled.

"Oh, I think you must have misunderstood me. It wasn't a request," Cronkite said coolly and held out his hand, a torn photo between his index and middle fingers.

Tom knew instantly what it was. He snatched it and stared at it. His heart skipped a beat, and he squeezed his eyes shut, trying to shut out the image of himself and Ben in a tight embrace, sharing a deep kiss. He crumpled the photo in his fist and blew out a heavy breath.

"No."

"What do you mean no?" Cronkite asked incredulously.

Tom opened his eyes and met Cronkite's unerringly. "I said no. I won't allow you to blackmail me."

"Don't be a fool. How long do you think you'll survive in this town once the good folks of Ramer find out their police chief is a faggot?" he asked, his voice dripping with disgust. "Hell man, one of your own took the damn picture. When his pocket money runs out, I suspect he'll be looking for more."

Cronkite's declaration caused Tom's heart to plummet to his gut sickened him. Yet it also brought clarity. It was inevitable that his secret would eventually be revealed. Secrets didn't stay hidden for long in a town like Ramer. If his fall was inescapable, there was no reason for Ben to suffer as well.

"No," Tom repeated with more conviction. He threw the photo at Cronkite's chest. "Now get the fuck off my property." He turned and walked away.

"You're making a huge mistake," Cronkite hollered. "I will destroy you, and I will see that faggot piece of shit buried beneath my jail."

Tom tromped up the stairs of his porch and grabbed the shotgun he'd left leaning against the doorframe. "I said get off my property," he yelled out. He pumped the shotgun and aimed it at the driver's side of the windshield.

Cronkite obviously realized Tom wasn't throwing out idle threats. He jumped in the car, and the engine roared to life and gravel flew as Cronkite threw the car in reverse, spun around, and stomped on the gas. Tom held the car in the sight of the gun until it disappeared behind a thick cloud of dust. The last of his bravado seeped from him in a rush, and he slumped down on the top step and stared, unseeing.

On one hand, he now had 100 percent proof of who was after him and what they wanted, and with that came some measure of relief. On the other hand, he was scared shitless. Where would he go, what would he do when he lost his home, his family, his job, his community? The only thing that kept the weight of it from crushing him was the fact that Ben wouldn't have to ever deal with Cronkite's sick game.

He took one last deep breath, ejected the shell from the shotgun, worried what he'd do if he thought on it too long, and picked it up. He walked on heavy legs up the steps. He set the gun back against the door and went inside.

Tom found Marna sitting at the kitchen table with a cup of coffee; a second mug sat on the table across from her. He took the seat, wrapped his hands around the hot coffee, and stared down at it. Marna would need an explanation, and he just wasn't sure what to say. The truth seemed like the best route to go, but he had no idea how much to divulge or even where to start.

Marna didn't push, she sat patiently, giving him a chance to collect his thoughts and to calm from the rush of adrenaline Cronkite had caused to spike within him.

"During the night of the storm, I found a stranded motorist by the name of Ben Parker. I was forced to take him into the cellar of the station, and together we rode out the storm. The next morning I turned him loose without running his name. Sheriff Cronkite, who was just here in our drive, called me a week later, and I found myself the alibi for a suspect in a bank robbery. Cronkite is convinced Ben committed the offense, and he's not too happy with me. He thinks I lied."

"Did you?" Marna asked without judgment.

"Yes and no," he admitted and took a sip of his coffee.

When Tom didn't elaborate, let the silence stretch out, Marna finally said, "I need to know what we are up against here, Tom."

"I know," he agreed and took another sip. "Ben was in fact with me, I didn't lie about that, but I wasn't completely honest about the timeframe." Tom looked up from his cup and met Marna's gaze. "Ben didn't rob that bank."

"How do you know this?"

"Because he told me he didn't."

"And you believed him?"

Tom nodded.

Marna went and fetched the coffeepot, refilled her cup, then topped off Tom's. She returned the pot to the counter and took her seat before she spoke again. "Tell me about Ben."

And he did.

While they drank their coffee, he told her how Ben had come to Ramer after getting out of jail. How he helped rebuild the church and their own roof. He even told her about Ben's service in Germany and how he'd been broken when he returned and gotten into some trouble. As Tom talked about Ben, told her what a good man he was and his plans for the future, Marna sat quietly but intently listening.

When he finished, Tom was surprised at how good it had felt to tell someone about Ben, yet remembering caused a heaviness to settle into his chest, and he absently rubbed at the ache that had nestled there.

"And this Sheriff Cronkite is now trying to force you to change your story?"

"Yes, but I refused. I swear to you, Marna, if I thought Ben had committed this crime, I would turn him over, but he didn't do it," he said adamantly. "I know he didn't."

"I believe you," she said gently. "You're an honest man, Tom, and if you believe this Ben is innocent, then that's enough for me."

The belief Marna had in him caused his gut to churn with guilt, and he looked down at his empty cup and spun it slowly. "It's more complicated than that. Cronkite won't stop until he's proven me wrong and has Ben in custody."

"It won't matter, Tom. You have the truth on your side, and you just have to believe that."

"You can't be that naive, Marna. He doesn't care about the truth or what he has to do to get what he wants."

"Then what is the *real* truth, Tom?" Marna asked. "What is it this Cronkite has over you and plans to use against you? And don't say nothing, because I can see it on your face. I saw the look in your eyes when you talked about this Ben Parker. It's the same look you get sometimes, that... that...." She waved a hand. "That same sad look you get sometimes."

Tom looked away. "I don't know—"

"Dammit, Tom, stop hiding behind this façade and be completely honest with me. You owe me that much."

Whether he admitted it or not, the truth, or at least some variation of it, was about to come out. Marna was right: she did deserve his complete honesty. The decision he'd made to not allow Cronkite to blackmail him into giving up Ben was going to irrevocably affect her world.

Time to start paying the price for his decision. "Cronkite is blackmailing me. He demanded I recant my statement, turn Ben over to him, and resign my position." Tom squared his shoulders and looked his wife directly in the eye. "If I don't, he'll make the nature of my association with Ben public."

"Your association?" she asked.

"Cronkite has photos of me and Ben...." Tom took a deep breath and blew it out. "Ben and I had a physical relationship, and Cronkite has proof."

Marna stared at him, both of them scarcely breathing as the silence stretched out between them. Tears filled her eyes, and one rolled down her cheek.

Tom's heart broke. "I'm so sorry, Marna. I truly did try to rid myself of this—" No, he wasn't going to cheapen it nor be ashamed of what he and Ben had done. The only thing he was sorry about was that he'd broken his vows and hurt Marna in the process. "—desire, this part of me, but I couldn't. I never meant to hurt you, Marna. If you believe nothing else, please believe I would never intentionally hurt you or Tommy."

Marna leaned her elbow on the table and covered her mouth as she continued to stare at him. Tears flowed freely down her face.

"Marna, please. I'll step down from my post, I'll disappear—"

"You'd leave your son?"

"I don't want to, but I think it's for the best. Do you know what kind of hell he'll go through growing up as the son of a faggot?" he asked bitterly.

"Do you know what kind of hell he'll go through growing up without a father?" Marna sobbed. "There has to be another way.... We will just prove this Cronkite wrong. We can go on with our lives the way we have been until Tommy is a little older and I can learn a skill.... Typing. Donna has a good job as a secretary. I can learn typing and get a job and...." Marna wiped her tears away, a new look of determination showing in her features, pushed to her feet, and took her cup to the sink. "We just need a little more time is all," she muttered as she began making more coffee.

Tom followed her. "Marna," Tom said gently and laid a hand on her shoulder. "We don't have any more time. Cronkite won't wait." The momentary determination melted away and Marna began crying hard. She turned and buried her face in Tom's chest as she clung to him. "You'll see, you, me, and the rest of Ramer will run him off," she got out between great sobs.

Tom wrapped her in a hug and held her as she cried. She wasn't thinking clearly in her grief. Tom was sure once it all sunk in and she realized he'd sinned, committed adultery not with another woman, but a man, she'd realize Tom wasn't worth the fight. All he could hope for was the chance to say good-bye to Tommy.

Chapter 20

THE SILENCE in the house was stifling, like a heavy weight pressing down on Tom. Marna had barely said more than a few words since they'd awoken beyond asking him what he wanted for breakfast and how he'd slept—he hadn't. So he was relieved when, after sending Tommy out to play, Marna finally met his gaze across the kitchen table.

"I don't want to know the details. I only want to know if you plan on doing it again."

"No," Tom responded.

Marna nodded, then picked up her fork and began poking at her cold and uneaten breakfast without saying another word.

"That's it?" he asked in shock. He'd been waiting all morning for her to begin screaming, pack his clothes, look at him with disgust, pray, something. This quiet acceptance wasn't what he'd expected.

"What else can I say?" she asked without looking up.

"You have the right to ask me anything you want, Marna. I betrayed you, our home, and our son."

"Yes you did, but it doesn't change the facts."

"What facts?"

She sighed heavily and her shoulders slumped. "You're a good man, a good father and…." Her braved front slipped and a tear rolled down her cheek. She wiped it away, her voice cracking with sorrow as she continued. "I'm so sorry this happened to you."

Tom stared wide-eyed at his wife. How could she be apologizing to him after what he'd told her, what he'd admitted to? "You don't have anything to be sorry for, Marna. You did nothing wrong. This is on my shoulders, on my heart, and it's I who should be apologizing to you, but... 'I'm sorry' seems rather inadequate."

"You're right, I didn't do anything wrong," Marna said with conviction and looked up at Tom. "I'm not sorry for what I did or didn't do, or even what you did or didn't do. I only meant it hurts my heart that you have to go through this and for that I'm sorry."

"I...." Tom hung his head. "I should have resisted harder."

"When I was a young girl, I had a friend named Roger. He and I were inseparable until we were sixteen. One Saturday I went to Roger's house as I often did, and his mother answered the door sobbing. She told me Roger wasn't home, that he'd never be home again because he was dead."

"Oh, that's horrible," Tom said sincerely. "How did he die?"

"They said it was an accident, but no one would tell me what kind. I wasn't allowed to attend the funeral, and shortly afterward, his family moved away. I didn't know the truth for a very long time. We don't talk about such things, but there were whispered rumors. Roger had been called nasty names, picked on nearly every day, and although I never had proof, I knew the rumors were true. Roger had been murdered and his family run off because everyone thought Roger was a Nancy boy."

"Was he?" Tom asked cautiously.

"Honestly, I don't know. He was more soft-spoken than most of the other boys, wasn't really into the rough play, more a book lover, but I don't think that makes him a Nancy. He never told me he was nor did I ever ask him," she said with a shrug. "All I know was he was my friend and I loved him. I missed him when they took him away from me. I thought about it a lot over the years, and if he was, I wouldn't have loved him any less."

It struck Tom how little he knew of Marna's upbringing. They rarely talked about the past, hell they rarely talked about anything personal at all. They'd met at a Selmer county barn dance; Tom had noticed her sitting alone and struck up a conversation. They were the same age, unattached, and after only a couple of dates, Tom found himself walking down the aisle. It was a marriage of convenience for both of them, he supposed. The difference being that Marna had dreamed of marriage and children, but Tom never had. He wasn't sure her dreams had come true. Sure, she had gotten a wedding ring and a son, but she hadn't gotten a husband who could love her the way she deserved.

A lump formed in his throat at the compassion in his wife's voice as she spoke of her friend, and he had to force it down with a swallow of coffee. He'd always known Marna was a gentle soul, yet being the devout God-fearing woman that she was, he never expected that she'd accept anyone who was homosexual. The teachings of the church were quite clear on the wickedness of such things.

"Can I get you another cup of coffee?" Tom offered as he took his mug to the kitchen. What he really wanted was a good measure of hard liquor, but he refused to give into the want. He needed to keep his head on straight.

"Yes, please," Marna responded, her voice full of sadness that tugged at Tom's heart even harder.

Tom poured himself a cup, then brought the pot to the table and refilled Marna's mug. He set the pot in the center of the table and returned to his chair. "I'm sorry for what happened to your friend," Tom said gently. "Did you ever wonder if perhaps it was punishment from God?"

Marna shook her head. "I know what you're asking, and I'm quite aware of the teachings of the church on the matter, but you didn't know Roger. He was good and pure and..." Marna met Tom's gaze. A fire burned in her gray eyes and her expression was fierce. "There was nothing evil or wicked about Roger, just like there isn't anything evil or wicked about you."

The unease, worry, and guilt Tom had tried so hard to lock down, deal with on his own, came rushing up, overwhelming him, and he was unable to hold back the sob that passed his lips nor the tears that spilled. So long he'd been strong, denied, hated, loathed, and it all poured out of him in a rush of agony.

"Oh, Tom," Marna cried and rushed to him, wrapped her arms around him. She held him tight as he continued to cry.

Never in a million years had he thought Marna would understand nor accept the secrets he'd worked so hard to hide. All this time, all these years, he'd been living with someone who he could have talked to, and yet he'd kept her at arm's length, a virtual stranger. The thought caused him to sob harder.

Marna continued to hold him until the sobs quieted and the tears ceased. Tom had thought Ben was the first to understand, the only one to understand what lay behind the façade, and yet, he'd been living and sharing a bed with someone for the past seven years who could have been his confidant. The irony of it was painful to bear.

"So what now?" Tom finally asked.

Marna cupped Tom's face in both her hands, tilted his head up and forcing him to meet her gaze. "We fight this Cronkite bastard," she said adamantly.

"But—"

Marna hushed him by covering his mouth with her fingers. "It will work out. You'll see. You're part of this town and the people here love you. They won't stand for an outsider to come in and say such things. They won't believe him."

Tom didn't share Marna's conviction. Yes, he was well respected, maybe even loved, but Cronkite had proof of Tom's misdeeds, and no matter what Marna thought, photographic evidence was hard to refute. He didn't share his concerns with her, nor did he mention someone from Ramer also being involved, too spent at the moment. They needed to talk more, that much was sure, but he needed a moment to get his shit together, let the events of the past hour set in.

"Thank you" was all Tom could think to say. He laid his hand over Marna's and kissed her palm. "I—"

The back door slammed, followed by Tommy's loud and excited voice. "Pa! Pa! There's deer in the field."

Tom pushed to his feet and hugged Marna fiercely. "We'll talk later," he promised.

Marna hugged him back, and he felt her nod against him. He kissed her cheek before rushing to the back door. Although he felt better about things than he had in a very long time, he was still glad for the distraction, a momentary reprieve. Marna was a damn fine woman, but still naive.

Hell was coming to Ramer, and he was its direct target.

Perhaps it was wishful thinking or an unrealistic hope on his part, but as he headed to the station, Tom had the overwhelming urge to reconnect with the members of his community. Maybe if he tried harder, cared more, sacrificed, Tom could withstand Cronkite's planned attack on his character. Sure, he was enough of a realist to know not everyone in town would rally around him, but if enough of the folks of Ramer forgave his transgressions, perhaps he and his family would be spared the pitchfork brigade.

He came to a halt outside Mrs. Simms house and cut the engine. While admittedly he did a lot for the folks in town, he could do more. Without fussing with his hat, Tom stepped out of the cruiser and made his way up the walk. The front door flew open, causing Tom to stumble back in alarm.

"You are no longer welcome here," spat Jenny angrily.

Jenny was Mrs. Simms's niece who came once a week from the next town over to do Mrs. Simms's shopping and help with chores around the house. He'd known her since she was knee-high to a grasshopper. Usually she was quite polite, almost timid.

"I'm sorry?" Tom responded in shock at the venom in Jenny's voice. "Is Mrs. Simms okay?"

"She's fine, but she doesn't need to be bothered by… by… the likes of you," she sputtered, waving her hand around ineffectively in Tom's direction.

Tom stood wide-eyed as the door was slammed shut, and he heard the distinctive sound of the lock engaging. He had no idea what in the hell had just happened or why Jenny was so angry, although the way his belly was knotting up he had a pretty good idea it had nothing to do with a missing cat.

Tom swallowed down his dread and returned to his car. He sat behind the wheel, staring blankly at the house for a moment until the shaking in his hands eased. It had only been twelve hours since Cronkite had made his threat. Surely he hadn't had enough time to put his plan into action.

Tom slowly made his way to the station, the sweat dampening his brow, the sickening churning in his gut and his skin prickling all signs of trepidation that was surging through his system. He knew Cronkite had had plenty of time.

It was the only explanation for Jenny's uncharacteristic behavior.

Chapter 21

THE AIR was so thick within the precinct Tom could cut it with a knife. Frank and Bonnie stared at him wordlessly, with not even so much as a greeting as he hung his hat on the hook by the door.

His first thought was to run back out the door, hop in his cruiser, and run like hell. Instead, he forced himself to turn, to take one step at a time to his desk, although it took great effort. He fought down the urge to flee, but the dread remained. Nothing good was going to happen if he stayed.

Tom took the seat at his desk and sighed internally. "Good morning," he said without looking either of them in the eye.

Bonnie said nothing.

Frank, rather than return the greeting, said, "There is a letter on your desk you might want to read."

Dammit, why hadn't he listened to that little voice and fled? The last thing he wanted to do was read what had caused Bonnie and Frank to behave so coldly, and yet he reached for it, the shaking in his hands more intense than before, and read:

> *Good Folks of Ramer,*
> *It has come to the attention of the Davidson County Sheriff's Department that Officer Thomas Webber did knowingly and with malice lie for a known criminal, one William Parker, "aka" Parker Williams - Willie Parks - Benjamin Williams - Ben Parker, wanted in connection with the armed robbery of the First National bank in Nashville, Tennessee, April 5th, 1952. It has also come to the attention*

of my office that Officer Webber did in fact engage in homosexual activities with the abovementioned criminal.

Rest assured, my office has every intention of bringing these perpetrators to justice. If you have any information regarding this case or the current whereabouts of William Parker, please contact my office. Do not attempt to detain William Parker as he is known to be armed and extremely dangerous.

Thank you for your assistance in this matter.
Sheriff Cronkite
555-7755

Tom stared at the letter long after he finished reading it. Cronkite had won. Tom had been a fool to think he had any chance to weather Cronkite's assault. Perhaps he might have kept a few loyal friends, but that hope was dashed when Cronkite pegged Tom as not only a homo but as a liar and criminal. The sad thing was, he couldn't deny any of it.

"Is it true?" Frank asked.

Tom set the letter down and scrubbed a hand over his face. "Yes," he admitted, resolved to his fate.

He heard Bonnie gasp, but Tom didn't look at her as Frank had jumped from his chair and was storming toward him. Frank's face red, eyes blazing, and Tom steeled himself for the blow he was sure would come.

It didn't come. Instead, Frank came to a halt in front of Tom and slammed his hands down on Tom's desk. "You lied to me! You said this Ben guy wasn't the bank robber."

"He isn't."

"How could you do this? How could you do this to your wife and son?" Frank shouted, ignoring Tom's rebuttal. "You are supposed to uphold the law. I looked up to you! My children look up to you. Fuck, Tom, this whole town looked up to you and you…. You're…." Frank suddenly spun and stomped to the door. "If I have to look at you one more second, I'll do something I know I'll regret."

Tom jumped when the door slammed so hard behind Frank it shook the windows.

It didn't matter that Tom knew Ben wasn't guilty of the crime Cronkite was accusing him of. Tom had no proof. Even if he did, he still couldn't deny that he'd lied for Ben at the time nor could he deny he and Ben had been intimate. The good Sheriff had proof in black and white.

The only question left was what did he do now? Sitting at a desk that was no longer his, listening to Bonnie sob, sure as hell wasn't it. With a heavy sigh, Tom folded the letter, stuffed it into his pocket, and left. He stopped next to the cruiser, key in hand. He briefly thought of removing his badge and leaving it and his service revolver in the car and walking home. His career was effectively and completely over. However, the thought of having to walk through town, to feel the eyes of the community boring down on him as he passed was too much to bear at the moment.

He slid behind the wheel and fired up the engine. He must really be resolved to his fate because he didn't feel anything. No anger, no sadness, nothing. He'd known this was coming, and now that it was all out in the open, he simply felt numb.

"HOW IS this even legal?" Marna fumed as she crumpled the letter in her fist.

"Marna, it doesn't matter."

"How can you say that? Isn't this what they call libel? You can't let this bastard get away with it. He blackmailed you."

"The damage is already done."

"So that's it?" she asked, sounding bitter. "You're just going to take it? You're not going to fight back?"

Tom rested his forearms on the dining table. Thankfully the numbness, the nothingness hadn't dissipated. "I have nothing to fight back with. I did lie about the time Ben was in Ramer. I did have an inappropriate relationship with Ben. Cronkite has proof."

"But—"

"Marna," Tom said gently and reached across the table and laid a hand on hers. "Thank you for wanting to fight for me and for believing in me. Lord knows I sure don't deserve it. I would fight if I could, not for myself, but for you and Tommy, I would."

Marna jerked her hand away and pounded her fist on the table, glaring at Tom. "Then, damn you, fight for us!"

"Pa?" Tommy said meekly from the doorway. His eyes were wide and he looked unsure. Rightly so, Tom and Marna never raised their voices at each other, let alone argue.

"It's okay, Tommy. Mama and I were just talking," he reassured him.

Tommy stared at him for a moment, then tilted his head toward his ma. "Why do you want Pa to fight, Mama? I thought we wasn't s'pposed to fight people?"

"Oh, Tommy," Marna said and went to him. "You're right. We aren't supposed to fight with our fists. We were talking about grown-up stuff."

Tommy glanced back and forth between Tom and Marna several times, then shrugged. "Can I have a cookie?"

God, how Tom wished all his problems could be cured with a reassuring word, a hug, and a cookie.

He and Marna would have to continue their discussion later, since as she went to retrieve Tommy's treat, someone began to knock on the front door.

"I'll get it," Tom called out.

Tom pulled back the curtain to find Pastor John standing on the front porch. Tom instantly knew it was about the letter; Pastor John rarely made social calls.

"Good morning," Tom said, struggling to keep his voice pleasant as he opened the door.

"Morning, Tom. I received some distressing news I'd like to discuss with you."

"Sure, c'mon in," he responded and stood back allowing the pastor entrance.

"Is there somewhere we can talk in private? What we need to discuss isn't proper for womenfolk or youngsters to hear."

"Have a seat and I'll have Marna take Tommy out to play. Can I get you anything to drink?"

Pastor John shook his head. He still hadn't met Tom's gaze, a foretelling of how he felt about what he'd read and had already come to the conclusion was true.

With Marna and Tommy out back, Tom returned with a stiff drink and sat in the chair across from the sofa where Pastor John sat, wringing his hands.

"I see bad news travels quick in Ramer," Tom commented. He swirled the amber fluid around in his glass, not sure if he would need it, but in case the numbness left, he'd be ready.

"I need to know how much of this letter is true," Pastor John said, finally meeting Tom's gaze

"All of it," Tom admitted.

"You invited a known criminal into our midst? Allowed him to work alongside us?"

"Actually, no. I didn't invite him. He showed up, and you were grateful for the help rebuilding the church. And he's not a criminal."

"You just said—"

"I know what I said," Tom interrupted. "It is true that I lied for Ben, but only about the time. This is a personal attack on me because I dared to question Cronkite. He tried to blackmail me into changing my story, but I refused. Ben did *not* commit the offenses the sheriff is accusing him of."

He'd said it a hundred times and he'd keep saying it for as long as he needed to. Ben was innocent and that included the offenses people assumed he had committed against God. Tom no longer felt the devil was tempting him. Ben was a good man, an honorable man, and free of any kind of evil.

"You admit then that you engaged in homosexual activities with this Mr. Parker?"

"Yes," Tom replied without hesitation.

Pastor John's brow dipped into a deep frown as he stared at Tom for a moment. Tom didn't look away nor did he flinch at the obvious disgust on the pastor's face. "The church takes a very firm position on such sins, Tom. You know this. We must pray together and ask God for his forgiveness."

"How long have you known me?" Tom asked instead, ignoring the offer of prayer.

"I blessed your birth, but—"

"And in the thirty-three years you've known me, would you agree that you'd consider me a good man?"

"Yes, but—"

"Have I not spent my life giving to the church, to this community, to God?"

Pastor John tilted his head and studied Tom, a questioning expression on his face before he looked away. "It is why we must pray together."

"I have committed no sin for which I need forgiveness from you or anyone else, including God. I am the same man I was before you read that letter, and if you think less of me for my actions, then I feel sorry for you."

"For me?" the pastor asked, sounding as if he were the one insulted. "You have broken the law, not only man's law, but God's."

Tom set his drink aside and stood. "I'll show you to the door."

Pastor John looked as if he'd been slapped, and he glared at Tom with blazing eyes. It caused Tom's chest to tighten to see someone he'd known and cared for all his life to look at him with such revulsion, but it passed quickly, as there was little he could do about it. He had done what he'd done and was who he was. He no longer hated that part of himself, nor would he even attempt to pray it away.

When Pastor John continued to stare at him without making any movement to rise, Tom said, "I'm the same man you've always known, but now, because of this one thing, you look at me with such hatred. It hurts, but I can't... no, I *won't* change it. I have struggled with my desires my whole life, and for the first time I feel completely at peace, so there really isn't anything further to discuss."

"I too am hurt to see you give in to the ways of the wicked." Pastor John finally stood and headed for the door. "You will no longer be welcome at church until you are ready to ask God for forgiveness. I will pray for you."

Tom didn't respond. He wasn't sure what was going on with his emotions. He should be angry. He'd devoted his entire life to the church and the community of Ramer. He'd worked his ass off, rarely ever telling anyone no and putting the needs of others before his own. And if not angry, then he should at the very least be hurt, shouldn't he? Should he not shed a tear? Grieve the loss of a man who he'd known his whole life?

And yet the numbness lingered.

Tom picked up his drink and headed to the kitchen. He thought briefly of pouring it out, but set the glass down on the counter, sure he'd need it eventually. He went to join his family while he still had the chance.

Chapter 22

TOM, DRESSED in nothing but an old, raggedy pair of pants and a pullover, feet bare, sat on the top step of his porch, staring out over his property, yet seeing nothing. He should have been in his uniform and at the station over an hour ago, but he couldn't seem to get motivated, and it sure didn't take a genius to figure out why.

He'd known Frank and Bonnie his whole life, Pastor John had known Tom even before he knew himself, and to see them look at him as if he were a complete stranger, to have to witness the anger, hurt, and mainly the disgust when they looked at him… well, he simply couldn't muster up the courage to encounter it again.

"Hey," Marna said as she joined him on the porch, sitting next to him. "Shouldn't you be at work?"

"Yeah, I should but…." Tom shook his head. "Where's Tommy?"

"I just sent him out back to feed the chickens. He's getting to be quite the little helper."

"Growing up fast," Tom agreed, his chest constricting. He couldn't help but feel as if he wasn't going to be there to see his son grow into a man. There was also the very real possibility that one day he'd see the same look in his son's eyes that he had witnessed in Frank's and Bonnie's—a look that he no doubt would be seeing a lot in the very near future if he didn't decide to simply hide away here on his piece of land, something that sounded quite appealing at the moment.

The roar of an engine in the distance had Tom jumping to his feet. "Go out back with Tommy."

"What is it?" Marna asked, stammering with confusion as she slowly stood.

The vehicle was getting closer and fast. "Just go and keep him in the barn till I call for you."

"Why? Who is it?"

"Dammit, Marna, go!" He gave her a little shove toward the door as he went for his shotgun. He had no idea who it was, but Tom doubted it was for anything good.

He stood on the top step, shotgun shell chambered and weapon raised, when the car came into view. Tom cautiously lowered the weapon as soon as he recognized the Ramer cruiser and Frank behind the wheel. Still, Tom didn't set the gun away even though he'd known Frank his whole life, but he did hold it in a nonthreatening manner. He questioned his response when Frank stepped out of the cruiser with weapon in hand.

"You best be puttin' that gun down, Tom," Frank called out.

"What the hell is wrong with you? I wouldn't shoot you."

"I said put the goddamn gun down," Frank demanded and raised his weapon, pointing it directly at Tom's head.

Anger bubbled up in Tom, setting him ablaze. How dare Frank threaten him was his first thought, his second to make a grand show of chambering another shell, but he discarded both. As pissed off as he was, he wasn't about to shoot Frank nor did he want a hole blown through him. Grudgingly he propped the shotgun against the railing post.

"Happy now? Again I ask, what the hell is wrong with you?" Tom demanded as he tromped down the stairs, his anger still burning, his footfalls more like jarring stomps.

Frank lowered the gun, but Tom could see his finger still on the trigger. It wasn't the way Frank held the weapon that had Tom wanting to smash his fist into Frank's face, but the expression upon it. He looked at Tom as if he were a vile stranger.

"Thomas Webber, you are under arrest. Please turn around and place your hands behind your back," Frank said dryly.

"What the hell for?"

"You're under arrest for lying to an officer of the law, aiding and abetting a wanted criminal, and lewd and lascivious acts on a child."

Tom had expected the first two charges, but it was the third that felt like a punch to his gut and robbed him of breath, the intensity of which caused him to stumble back. He stared wide-eyed at Frank, too stunned to respond. He couldn't have heard him right.

"Don't make this any more difficult than it has to be. I have a direct order from Sheriff Cronkite."

The son of a bitch's name instantly spun Tom's shock to rage. "He has no authority over you. And tell me I didn't hear you right. Lewd and lascivious acts on a child?"

"Davidson County has issued a warrant for your arrest, and I've been ordered to detain you until they arrive," Frank clarified, his tone cold official.

"Goddammit, Frank! I'll let you take me in, I'm not going to fight you. But Christ, stop fucking looking at me like that. We've known each other our whole damn lives. You can't actually believe that ridiculous charge."

Frank looked away. "I thought I knew you, but apparently I was wrong. Now turn around."

With a heaviness in his chest, Tom complied and allowed Frank you cuff him without another word. He knew Cronkite was hell-bent on bringing in Ben, and he'd stop at nothing to achieve his goal. Hell, he wasn't even surprised the old bastard now viewed Tom as the enemy. But to make something up as hideous as sexual abuse of a child crossed a whole new line.

"Hey, wait!" Tom said when Frank started leading him to the cruiser "I gotta tell Marna where I'm going."

"I'll let her know." Frank opened the back of the cruiser. "Have a seat."

Tom met Frank's gaze with a hard one of his own. "I'll tell you one damn thing. You tell her about that last charge, I won't be so compliant. I won't be having you upset her with a vicious lie like that. Do you understand me?" Tom demanded.

Frank must have realized how serious Tom was, because after a brief pause, he nodded his agreement.

"Fine, she's out back with Tommy." Tom took a seat. He sat there head whirling as Frank went to speak with Marna. *Lewd and lascivious acts on a child.* Tom's gut roiled, and he nearly choked on the bile that rushed up. He wasn't perfect, had done a few things in his day that he wasn't especially proud of, but…. Jesus, the thought was too horrible to even contemplate, and yet here he was accused of it. It made no sense.

"Tom! Tom!"

He looked up to see Marna rushing to the car, Frank following her.

"Everything will be okay," he assured her.

"Oh, Tom, what's happening? This… this…." She spun and faced off against Frank. "You said he was just going to be questioned. Why is he cuffed?"

"I'm sorry, Marna," Frank said calmly. "I'm simply following orders."

"Following orders?" Marna screamed. "He's your friend. How could you do this?"

"Marna, I'll be okay. Please, take care of Tommy and I'll be home soon," Tom lied. He knew neither was true. He damn sure wasn't okay, and he suspected if Cronkite had his way, he'd never be coming home again.

Marna's face was red and tear streaked. Tom could tell by the look in her eyes she was scared, rightly so, and she didn't want him to leave, but when Tom added, "Go take care of Tommy," she did as she always had, put her son's needs before her own and nodded in agreement.

"Okay, but you'll be home for dinner, right?"

"Yes, now go."

She leaned in the window and pressed a kiss to Tom's cheek and whispered, "You better be."

Once again, Tom knew he was hiding the truth from her, but this time it was for her rather than himself.

Neither he nor Frank said a word during the ride to the station. Tom stared out the window, looking out on a town that only the day before felt like home and now seemed foreign. As he passed people he'd thought friends, they either looked away or glared. There were no friends here, nor would there ever be again.

The same cold, unfriendly gaze met him at the station, but Bonnie quickly turned her back on him. The anger and fight drained from him as he sat on the cot and heard the clank of the cell door closing and the lock engaging.

I should have run. Should have run away with Ben. He might have had a fighting chance and been in the company of a friend.

Tom hung his head, not in shame, but in defeat. Because Tom had admitted wrongdoing, it wouldn't matter what lies Cronkite told, the folks of Ramer would believe him.

TOM LINGERED in his cell all day with nothing but his thoughts. Frank hadn't spoken to him beyond asking him what he wanted for lunch, then again for dinner, but Tom declined both. Bonnie still hadn't acknowledged him, but he could hear her muffled voice as she spoke on the phone and knew he was the topic of the rumor mill. It was confirmed by the occasional words he could make out—*homosexual*, *hell-bound*, *disgusting*, *poor Marna*. He did his best to block it out, but he couldn't nor could he stop the sickening churning of his gut or the heaviness in his chest.

When Bonnie finally left for the day, Tom was finally able to doze off, but the peace didn't last long. The sound of the door opening followed by Cronkite's familiar voice had Tom jerking upright.

"Good evening, Mr. Webber," Cronkite greeted, his tone smug.

"What the hell kind of sick joke are you playing," Tom spat as he jumped up, glaring at the bastard through the bars.

"Why it's no joke, I assure you. I'm doing my job and keeping the town of Ramer safe from criminals."

"Hey, now wait a minute," Frank protested. "You have no jurisdiction here, and we're more than capable of taking care of Ramer."

Cronkite removed his hat, his smile broadening. "I meant no disrespect, Officer Compton. I appreciate your assistance in apprehending Mr. Webber."

Tom could tell by the frown and the narrowed eyes Frank didn't like Cronkite much, but it hadn't stopped him from believing the man over Tom. The idea made him ill.

Cronkite pulled a folded piece of paper from the pocket of his shirt and held it out to Frank. "I'll be relieving you of the prisoner."

Frank didn't accept the paper. "He'll be arraigned at 9:00 a.m. tomorrow. You can make your request with Judge Simon."

"The hell I will," Cronkite growled, his face reddening, and he tried to force the letter into Frank's hand. "I have an order from Judge Markum giving me authority to take charge of Mr. Webber and bring him to Davidson County."

Frank didn't flinch. "Selmer County has charged Mr. Webber with police misconduct and he will be arraigned at 9:00 a.m. by Judge Simon. If you have an issue with it, I suggest you take it up with the judge."

Tom rested his forearms on the iron crossbar, hands dangling outside the cell as he watch the drama unfold, enjoying the way Cronkite's face turned a bright red and the visible shaking of his limbs, but not as much as the way Frank stood defiantly against the sheriff.

"I would have thought you'd be happy to be rid of this disgusting piece of shit," Cronkite snarled as he stabbed his finger in Tom's direction.

"And I would have thought a man in your position would respect the chain of command," Frank countered.

Cronkite spit and sputtered, his hands curled into fists as he bristled with apparent rage. Tom had learned the hard way; Cronkite was a man who didn't like to be defied. Frank however, didn't seem to be concerned with what Cronkite wanted. He stood straight, a neutral expression on his face, controlled.

"Fine! But I will be back, and rest assured that when I do, I'm taking Webber with me," he warned. He spun, stomped to the door and yanked it open, then paused. He turned his head, a snarl curling his lip as he met Tom's gaze, but he spoke to Frank. "I hope your boy returned your camera undamaged. It takes such wonderful photos." Cronkite laughed, slamming the door behind him.

Tom wasn't sure who was more shocked by Cronkite's revelation, he or Frank. They stared at each other for a long time as the truth settled in. Gene had taken the damning photos of Tom and Ben. Tom turned away, no longer able to look his friend in the eye. He slumped down on the cot, rested his elbows on his knees, and buried his face in his hands. It wasn't only that he'd been betrayed by his best friend's son, the thought that it would be Gene who would now accuse him of abuse made him sick.

He wanted to puke.

He half expected Frank to put a bullet in him. Tom couldn't imagine ever believing Frank capable of abusing Tommy, but with the doubt Cronkite had planted and Tom's own admission of his lies, he could see how he'd be tempted to do the pull the trigger. Tom had no choice but to wait; his life was over. The only question remaining was if it would be at Cronkite's or Frank's hand.

IT WAS night, the station silent when Tom woke from a fitful sleep. He blinked several times until his eyes adjusted to the darkness enough to focus and realize Frank was standing near the cell. Tom slowly pushed up and placed his feet on the floor, his heart thumping wildly. Would the bullet come now? He tensed when keys jangled in the lock and the cell door squeaked open.

"Time for you to go," Frank said curtly.

"Where?"

"I don't want to know," Frank responded and walked away.

Tom cautiously followed him. Frank grabbed a pile of clothes from his desk and thrust them at Tom. "I don't understand," he said, taking the stack.

"The trumped-up charges I was able to file won't stick. If you stay here, come morning, Cronkite will have you transferred to Davidson, and he'll see you rot in jail."

"But what about Gene? You do realize who the additional charges are more than likely going to come from, don't you?"

Frank pulled out a pack of smokes, lit one up, and sat in his chair. He then tossed the pack across the desk for Tom. "What you did with Ben ain't right, neither was lying. But it's what you did to your family and this town that I can't forgive you for."

"I'm sorry, I never—"

Frank held up a hand. "That being said, I know you didn't, couldn't have hurt my boy. I won't allow Cronkite to use Gene as an excuse to get his revenge on you. Now go."

The relief in Frank not believing the lie was profound but still…. "What about Marna and Tommy? I can't just leave them."

"Goddammit, Tom!" Frank yelled and slammed his hand down on the desk. "You don't have a fucking choice." Frank scrubbed a hand over his face and Tom caught sight of the tears Frank tried to wipe away. "I'll take care of them. My old truck is outside. Keys are in it."

Tom didn't even try to hide his, letting them flow freely. He stared at his friend, his heart breaking. "They will know you let me out. I can't let you get in trouble for me."

"I won't. Everyone knows that damn cell lock has been faulty for years. Now just go, please," Frank said without meeting Tom's gaze.

Frank was right, Tom only had two choices. One really, because he'd be damned if he'd allow Cronkite to win.

Tom slipped the boots on, shoved the pack of smokes into his pocket, and on shaking legs, walked to the door. He placed his hand on the knob and blew out a heavy breath.

"Please tell them I love them." He opened the door, but before stepping out, he added, "You are and will always be my best friend and I'll miss you."

Chapter 23

TOM DROVE slowly down the deserted road. "Road" might have been too generous a name. It was more like a cow trail with overgrown grass between small ruts. The brush and trees scraped along the sides and top of the old truck like hundreds of fingers, the sound as eerie as the thick blackness surrounding him.

The secluded area caused Tom's pulse to race and his belly to flutter. The unsettling feeling was made all the worse by the knowledge that this might not even be the right road. He hadn't dared stop and ask anyone, not even the old man at the gas station. Hell, what would he have asked? *"Do you know a man who might go by Ben who might be in hiding?"* Tom wasn't sure if Ben was using his real name, one of the multiple aliases he'd used in the past, or something else entirely. Another consideration that had kept Tom from asking for directions was that Tom couldn't be 100 percent sure he wasn't being followed. He hoped like hell he wasn't but had the sneaking suspicion he was. The last thing he wanted to do was bring any attention to himself. Strangers in an area this remote were remembered, and witnesses talked.

Tom caught a flash of movement just outside the reach of his headlights a millisecond before something dark, big, and moving fast raced across his path. Tom slammed on the brakes, his hands tightening around the steering wheel, and he locked his arms to keep from being pitched forward.

Eyes wild, he scanned the area as the truck came to a halt. Tom's heart pounded out of his chest as his breath seized within it. "Son of a bitch," he cursed and pried his hands from the wheel, running them over his face. He jumped when another dark flash went across the road, then

another. The tension began to ease as the deer disappeared into the brush
Thankfully he'd been paying attention and going slowly. The job o
pulling a mangled animal from the grill of his truck was averted.

Pulse still racing, Tom eased his foot off the brake and clutch and
got the truck rolling again. He inched his way down the path, intently
watching the edges of the brush. After another twenty minutes—and no
more near misses with the wildlife—the land opened up. The roadway
wasn't much better, but instead of trees crowding it, a wood fence sat six
to eight feet back on either side. Finally a structure came into view in the
beams from the truck's headlights.

Tom brought the truck to a halt outside a small cabin with a covered
wooden porch running along the length of it. From what he could see, no
other vehicles were around, nor were there any lights shining from within
the cabin. No signs of life at all. Tom's first thought was to pull out his
gun—a crazy notion since he was the one trespassing. He was a fucking
fool is what he was. Pulling up to a property, which might or might not
belong to an ex-soldier and bank robber, in the middle of the night? Or
maybe he'd find some crazy mountain-man hermit who shot first and
asked questions later.

Either way, he was about to find out. Tom cut the engine on the
truck and opened the door. Just as he placed one boot on the dirt, the
sound of gunfire had him diving across the bench seat of his truck and
ducking for cover.

"You have all of sixty seconds to cut those lights and step out of tha
truck with your hands up," yelled out a familiar voice that caused Tom to
smile.

Ben.

Tom wasn't so stupid as to rush out and grab the man like he
wanted. Instead he slowly sat up and shoved in the knob, extinguishing the
headlights. As Tom placed his boot once again on the dirt, a beam from a
flashlight lit up the door.

Tom put one hand out the door and, as he slid from the truck, called
out, "I swear, if you shoot me after I came all this way, I'm going to kick
your ass."

"Tom?" Ben shouted. "Tom, is that you?"

"You expecting someone else?" Tom chuckled and slammed the
truck door.

"Well, I'll be a son of a bitch," Ben hooted and tromped down the
porch steps.

They met halfway, and it really shouldn't have come as a surprise when Ben grabbed Tom in a tight embrace and smashed their mouths together without saying another word. The kiss was hard and fast and ended way too soon for Tom's liking.

He licked his lip as Ben pulled back slightly. "I was beginning to wonder if you'd ever show up." Ben kissed him again. "Fuck, I've missed you."

Months had passed since the last time Tom had seen Ben, and it struck him how at ease and comfortable he was in Ben's arms with Ben's flavor on his lips. "I've missed you too," he admitted as the excitement surged through him, heating him from within.

"I don't know if I should be worried you showed up in the middle of the night," Ben said with a shake of his head. "But at this exact moment, I really don't fucking care, I'm just glad to see you."

"Got a lot to tell you, and it ain't all good," Tom admitted dolefully.

"You can tell me the bad news later. C'mon in," Ben responded happily and led Tom toward the cabin with an arm around his waist.

Ben held the screen door and ushered Tom in. It was dark within. Tom could barely make out the furniture, so he stood near the entrance. Ben's footfalls echoed around the room, and a few seconds later, Tom heard the strike of a match. Ben lit an oil lamp and turned the flame up high.

"Don't have any electricity this far out," Ben said, sounding almost apologetic "But you'll be glad to know I got indoor plumbing."

"That's always a bonus."

"Don't get too excited, only got cold water, but I recently found me an old kitchen boiler. Just haven't had the opportunity to fix it and get it installed."

Tom took in the room. There wasn't much for furniture—an old brown couch, a couple of chairs, and a small dining set for two. For an old rustic cabin, however, it was surprisingly clean and smelled of wood, fresh grass, and something almost flowery that Tom couldn't identify.

"It's not much," Ben said with a shrug.

"It's great," Tom complimented, but the place was already forgotten as he took in the man before him.

Ben's dark hair had grown out, as had his beard, giving him a bit of a wild look. Tom liked it. He also liked the deep tan of Ben's muscular arms and the way his belt hung from the loops of his pants. Tom's belly fluttered pleasantly as he looked up and met Ben's dark eyes.

"Been a long time," Tom murmured as he took a step closer to Ben.

"Too long," Ben drawled. The smirk on his face caused a shiver of excitement to race through Tom.

He grabbed Ben's hips in his hands and pulled him in without breaking his gaze. "You got any hounds or hired hands I need to be worryin' about?" he asked, his voice thick with arousal.

Ben gripped Tom's biceps, fingers digging in a little. "Nothing but an ornery ol' feline." Ben tilted his head, the smirk still firmly in place. "Why? What did you have in mind?"

Tom responded by smashing their mouths together and forcing his tongue past Ben's lips. Ben met and matched the urgency of the kiss. They both groaned as they each tried to dominate the other. Ben pushed his knee between Tom's legs, and Tom pressed against it as he rolled his hips, massaging his growing bulge against Ben's thigh.

They really should be talking. He should be warning Ben about Cronkite and the mess back in Ramer, but it had been so long. Memories of Ben were all he'd had to keep him going, his only sliver of happiness the past few months. It felt as if it had been forever since he'd had Ben in his arms, his flavor on his tongue. He no longer cared about anything other than losing himself in the bliss of Ben's body, the pleasure of his flesh.

Ben pulled back from the kiss and looked at Tom with a pair of hungry eyes that glinted in the dim light. The predatory look in them caused Tom's heart to pound, making it hard for him to breathe.

"I can't believe you're here," Ben muttered. He ran a callused fingertip along Tom's jaw and down the side of his neck, making him shudder. "Christ, Tom, I never thought—"

"I know, me neither," Tom admitted and pushed into Ben's touch as he cupped Tom's cheek and kissed him again, gentler this time, yet still with the same effect as the hard kiss. Tom shuddered again as Ben's warm breath and soft lips ghosted against his mouth.

Tom eased his hand between their bodies, thumbing open the button on Ben's pants, and slipped a hand inside the denim. Finding nothing but heated flesh, he shoved his hand inside and grabbed Ben's cock in a firm grip. Ben squirmed and made a low growling sound in the back of his throat.

"Ah fuck," Ben moaned as Tom pulled on his cock and scraped a fingernail lightly over the pulsing organ.

"You really did miss me, didn't you?" Tom muttered as he nuzzled the side of Ben's neck, licking and nipping.

Ben tilted his head to the side, giving Tom more room to work as he thrust against the hand Tom had wrapped around his cock. "The minute I left Ramer," he moaned.

"Yeah. You miss this?" Tom asked as he released Ben's erection and shoved his fingers farther down and captured the delicate sac beneath. Ben nodded and started humping hard as Tom used his free hand to shove Ben's pants down. "And this?" Tom dropped to his knees and wrapped his lips around the flared head of Ben's cock.

"Fuck yeah," Ben grunted, his hand landing on Tom's head, fingers curling in his hair as he continued to thrust and roll his hips.

Tom dug his fingers into Ben's hips, stopping his movements, and took Ben's cock farther into his mouth, sucking hard and humming as Ben's musky flavor filled his mouth. Tom hungrily feasted on Ben's cock, bobbing his head fast as he took Ben deep into his throat before pulling back till just the spongy head was between his lips. He sucked hard, tongue swirling around the head, licking at the small slit, searching out more of Ben's flavor.

"Won't last long," Ben warned on a moan. His hand tightened in Tom's hair as he pulled back. "Wait," he panted.

Tom let Ben's cock slip from his lips and rubbed his stubbled cheek along the sensitive organ. "What am I waiting for?" he asked as he breathed harshly.

Ben tugged on his hair, tipping his head back, and bent to graze his lips across Tom's mouth. "I want you." He nipped at Tom's bottom lip and sucked it into his mouth. "I want you naked and in my bed," he growled. "Need to touch you."

Tom went to his feet, chasing those full, lush lips as Ben straightened. He grabbed the hem of Ben's shirt and pulled it over his head and off. He tossed it aside as he took Ben's mouth in another hungry kiss.

Ben's nimble fingers unbuttoned Tom's shirt as Tom kicked off his shoes. Ben pushed Tom's shirt over his shoulders and down his arms. The second the garment was off, Ben groaned loudly and pressed their heaving chests together, Ben's hardness poking Tom's thigh. As the kiss went on and on, Ben's hands roamed along Tom's back, across his shoulders, down his sides, as if Ben were trying to touch every inch of him.

Tom struggled to get a hand between them, not wanting to lose any connection between their bodies. Ben ended the kiss and chuckled low and throaty. "Let me help you." Ben popped the button on Tom's pants and shoved them down as he rubbed their jaws together, their coarse hair scraping, a sensation Tom hadn't felt in far, far too long. Ben was all male and strength, something Tom would never tire of feeling. The instant Tom's pants hit his ankles, he stepped out of them and grabbed Ben's ass in both hands, dug his fingers in the taut flesh, and yanked hard.

They both hissed when their cocks came in contact. Tom rolled his hips, and Ben bucked against the intimate contact, whimpering as he began to pant. Tom arched into the touch, his eyes fluttering shut as he was overwhelmed with the heat, friction, and the rightness of it. He was torn between humping harder, seeking out more friction and release for his painfully throbbing cock, and going slower, savoring the moment, savoring Ben. Tom's mind raced. He wanted to bury himself deep in Ben's ass, wanted to drop to his knees and suck his cock, wanted to hump and rut and touch. He shook with the overwhelming need and want and.... Fuck, he just wanted it all. All of Ben.

Tom lowered his head as the dizzying sensation overtook him, and he bit into the exposed curve of Ben's neck. Ben yelped at the bite, but pushed against Tom's mouth rather than pull away, his hips snapping hard at the same time. Tom moaned as he released Ben's ass and licked a path up his neck. Tom sucked on the sensitive flesh beneath Ben's ear, sucking in time to the slow rock of their hips. He slid his hands up the sinew of Ben's back and back down to squeeze the meaty flesh of his ass.

The rhythm of Ben's thrusts increased, and he grasped Tom's hips tightly, encouraging him to thrust harder. "I can't.... You drive me out of my fucking mind," he panted.

Tom's lust spiraled and the need to come became too urgent to deny. "Better.... Ah fuck... better slow down. Gonna...."

"Do it!" Ben snapped his hips brutally against Tom's and held Tom close as he kept rolling his hips. "Need to...."

Whatever Ben was going to say next was lost in a guttural shout as he threw his head back and came all over Tom's cock and stomach. It was the nudge Tom needed, and he lost the hold he had on his control. He jerked, moaned, cursed, and shook as he came so hard his toes curled. When the last drop pulsed from his body, he slumped against Ben, and they held each other, breathing harshly as they both began to chuckle.

"Holy shit," Ben laughed as he curled one of his hands in the hair at the back of Tom's neck, pulling him close.

Tom nudged Ben's cheek with his nose, encouraging him to turn his head, then captured Ben's lips in a soft kiss. "My sentiments exactly," he chuckled.

Neither of them seemed to be willing to release the other. Tom was more than content to stand in the middle of the room under the low light of the oil lamp and hold Ben, listening to his breathing and feeling the steady beat of his heart, even if Tom's legs were shaking and threatening to give out.

Ben was the first to pull away, and Tom grumbled at the loss of Ben's heat. "C'mon so I can give you a proper welcome."

"Proper welcome?" Tom asked sheepishly and allowed Ben to pull him along by the hand.

"Yup." Ben winked at Tom over his shoulder.

Ben pushed open a door without slowing his strides, and once within the room, Tom flailed as he was jerked forward and spun before his ass landed on a soft mattress. "Make yourself comfortable," Ben instructed and lit a match. The grin on his handsome face caused Tom's flesh to tingle in anticipation. Tom didn't say a word as he pushed to the center of the bed, spread his legs a little, and folded his hands beneath his head, doing as he'd been told.

Ben lit an oil lamp and turned the flame down low. He started to set it on the bedside table but stopped and ran a leisurely gaze down Tom's nakedness. Tom felt the gaze as a kiss to his exposed skin and another shudder threatened.

"Might not be such a good idea," Ben surmised and instead turned and set the lamp on the dresser across the room.

"Why is that?"

Ben stopped next to the door and looked back over his shoulder. "I'm going to put out the lamp in the other room and lock the door, then I aim to show you just how much I really did miss you."

Ben stepped out of the room, but the hint of danger in Ben's tone caused Tom's breath to hitch and his cock to twitch.

Chapter 24

MONTHS OF isolation with only the occasional contact with anothe human had left Ben with plenty of time to think and daydream, and 9(percent of the time his thoughts had centered on Tom. And oh man, wha thoughts he'd had. Still, nothing could compare to actually having Ton there.

He'd been having one of his regular nighttime fantasies, one of hi favorite recurring ones. He and Tom would cool off in the pond at th back of his property, then heat up as they rolled around in the soft grass a the water's edge. Most days he really hated waking to the reality of a col(bed and another day of loneliness, so he'd been pissed when he'd bee) jerked awake—denied his dreamtime with Tom—by the sound of a truc) engine. Now, he felt absolutely giddy as he padded across the floor with big goofy grin on his face.

"He's really here," Ben mumbled in disbelief as he cut the flame o) the lamp.

And you're standing in your kitchen while Tom's lying naked in you bed. Ben chuckled quietly and shook his head. He scratched at the dryin(mess on his belly and rushed back to his room, stopping short in th(doorway as he caught sight of Tom.

Tom was lying in the center of the bed in the same position he'd lef him: legs spread, arms folded behind his head. Ben ran his gaze leisurel) down Tom's body. The glow of the lamp highlighted each ridge an(valley of his muscular body and glinted off the damp head of Tom' semihard cock, causing Ben's mouth to water and his body to thrum. Be) was riveted by the amazing vision before him.

"I like the way you look in my bed. Although, you look a littl(tense," Ben commented, his voice husky. "At least parts of you do."

Tom met Ben's gaze and licked his lips as he slid one hand out from under his head and reached down to brush his palm over his dick. "It was a long drive." Tom moaned and thrust his hips up off the bed, pushing his impressive cock against his hand. "Even longer few months."

Ben had the sudden urge to pinch himself. He had to still be dreaming. No fucking way was Tom lying in his bed stroking his cock for him. Ben squeezed his eyes shut and shook his head. When he reopened his eyes, Tom was still there. Ben trailed a finger across the soft hairs on Tom's thigh. He felt real.

Ben sat on the edge of the bed, his heart thumping. He leaned down and pressed his lips against Tom's. "Been too long," he whispered.

Tom reached up and ran his hand along Ben's cheek. He didn't say anything for a long moment. There seemed to be so many different emotions shining in Tom's eyes. He sucked in a breath as his eyes fluttered closed. Ben grazed his lips over Tom's again, then kissed his cheeks, nose, forehead, and even his eyelids, breathing in Tom's unique scent as he tasted the musk of his skin. Now that they had taken the edge off, the urgency less acute, Ben wanted to explore each and every inch of the man.

Ben shifted and lay on his side, propped his head up on his elbow, and ran his free hand down Tom's neck, over his collarbone, and down to the soft hairs on his chest. Tom opened his eyes and silently watched Ben as he explored. As much as he wanted to lose himself in Tom again, he needed to know they were safe and why Tom was here after all this time.

"Tell me what happened," Ben asked as he met Tom's gaze. He drew random patterns with his fingertip along Tom's chest.

"Do we have to talk about it right now?"

"I think we should. I at least need to know if we're safe."

Tom stared at him for a few seconds, the relaxed expression on his face tightening and regret glinting in his eyes. "Honestly, I don't know," he finally admitted.

Suddenly the needs of his lust didn't seem all that important as Ben felt Tom tense next to him and heard the solemn tone of his voice. Ben's physical need to touch didn't wane, only now it was his need to comfort and protect that drove him.

"Who's after you?"

Tom drew in a long breath through his nose and let it out slowly. "Pretty much the entire town of Ramer," Tom admitted, sounding dejected, and looked away.

Alarm skittered along Ben's spine. On some level when he'd first realized Tom was in his driveway, Ben had hoped Tom had come to his senses and snuck out of Ramer to be with Ben. But he should have known better. One of the things he liked most about the man was his loyalty. Even with everything Tom had been through, the self-loathing and the doubt, he was still a good and caring man, trying to do right by his town and his family even above and beyond his own needs.

"What the hell happened after I left, Tom?" Ben asked gently.

Tom met Ben's gaze, a flare of anger burning in his narrowed eyes. "Cronkite came to town," he spat.

"What?" Ben asked in alarm and jerked to an upright position. "Sheriff Cronkite came looking for you?"

"No," Tom said, shaking his head vigorously. "He came looking for you."

All the good things he'd been feeling rushed out of Ben, and he leaped from the bed. "What the fuck did that son of a bitch do?"

Tom pushed up, sat on the edge of the bed, and ran his hands through his hair. "If you want to go through this now, I'm going to need a drink." He looked down at himself, then back up at Ben. "And pants."

Ben was too full of rage to respond to Tom's attempt at humor. He'd known Cronkite was a prick. Hell, Ben had enjoyed pressing the bastard's buttons just to see the veins bulge in his neck and the ugly red color heat up his fat face. But he hadn't considered for a second that he'd go after Tom.

"Motherfucker," Ben growled and stomped out of the room.

For months he'd been watching out the corner of his eye, looking over his shoulder, waiting. He'd been waiting and watching, as he knew Cronkite would eventually track him down. Dammit, how could he have been so goddamn stupid? Of course Cronkite would use Tom. *Stupid. Stupid. Stupid.* Tom had been Ben's alibi, so of course he'd go after Tom.

Ben snatched his pants from the floor and pulled them on as he headed to the kitchen. He grabbed a bottle of whiskey from the cupboard and a couple of glasses from the counter. As he poured out two healthy portions, Tom walked out of the bedroom looking wary and grabbed his pants.

"I was hoping we wouldn't have to get into this conversation yet," Tom muttered as he slipped on his pants and buttoned them up. "But I guess we need to talk about it. I wouldn't put it past Cronkite to show up and ruin my fuckin'. He's ruined everything else in my life."

Tom took one of the glasses, threw back the whiskey in one gulp, and slammed the glass down on the counter. "Better pour me another."

Ben rolled his shoulders, gulped down his drink, and poured them each another. He handed one to Tom and nodded toward the front door. "Let's go sit on the porch. I'm thinking the cool night air might keep my anger from incinerating the house."

On his way out the door, Ben picked up his gun. He shoved open the door and took a deep breath of the cool night air as he plopped his ass down in one of the old rocking chairs. Tom, right behind him, took the other rocker.

"Just a minute," Ben said suddenly and set his gun and drink on the small table between them.

He stomped back into the house, snatched the bottle of whiskey off the counter, and tromped back out. He set the bottle on the table and picked up his glass. "Alright, now you can tell me what the hell has been going on."

Tom eyed the half-empty bottle, then looked up at Ben. "You got another bottle in there?"

"Yup."

"Good," Tom grumbled. "Gonna need it."

Tom was right. Over the next couple of hours, as he recounted what had happened since Ben left Ramer, they polished off the first bottle. The sun came up, and they were well into the second bottle by the time Tom finished. Even with the alcohol coursing through his system, Ben's muscles were tense; his anger burned off any calming effect the booze might have had on him.

For the first time since his days on the battlefield, Ben had an all-consuming need to kill. He was going to fucking kill Cronkite with his bare hands. God how he wanted to wrap his hands around that fat son of a bitch's neck and squeeze. Ben wanted nothing more than to watch Cronkite's eyes bulge from his head, see the life seep from him, and know that the last face the sheriff ever saw was his. He'd love to send that fucking memory to hell with him.

"By the look on your face, I'm pretty sure I'm not going to be liking what you're plotting over there," Tom slurred, the alcohol obviously affecting him more than it was Ben.

"I'm going to kill him," Ben growled and slammed back another shot.

"The hell you are," Tom responded and stabbed a warning finger at Ben. "You're going to do the same fucking thing I am. Nothing."

"The hell I am," Ben spat. He shoved out of his chair and began pacing, each footfall angry and jarring. "I'm going to give that fat fucker exactly what he deserves."

Tom leaped up, grabbed Ben by the arm, and slammed him against the porch railing. "You're not," Tom growled with only an inch between their noses. "You are going to let it go, continue the quiet life you got here, and put all this bullshit in the past."

"I can't," Ben said adamantly as he shook his head. "I can't let this go. What he did to you because of me…."

"That's right. What he did to me. Not you, me! It's over, Ben. He won, and I have to take my licks like a man and accept defeat."

"Goddammit, Tom," Ben muttered angrily and wrapped his arms around the man. Ben laid his forehead on Tom's shoulder and took a deep shuddering breath as he struggled to push the rage down into his churning gut. "It's not fair, and he shouldn't be allowed to get away with what he did."

Tom hugged him back, one hand rubbing Ben's back soothingly, the other threaded in Ben's hair. "It's not about fair, or even right and wrong. I should have left Ramer when you asked me to. I only have myself to blame for that."

Ben started to comment, to protest, but he snapped his mouth shut and held Tom tighter. Tom was wrong. This wasn't his fault, and he damn sure didn't deserve to lose his job, his home, and his family all because Cronkite was hell-bent on getting back at Ben. Tom also didn't deserve to have his entire town turn on him, not after all he had given up for them.

"You want to know what burns my ass the most?" Ben asked against the side of Tom's neck.

"It doesn't matter," Tom murmured. "Just let it go."

Ben jerked his head back and met Tom's weary gaze. "How can you just let it go? After all you did for that town, all you sacrificed, and they just turned on you like that."

Tom's eyes filled with a sadness that stole Ben's breath, and he let out a heavy sigh. "Because I need to let it go, Ben. If I think about it too much, it will crush me. You don't know how hard it was to live through that. To see the look of disgust and scorn on the faces of people I'd thought were friends." Tom pulled out of Ben's arms and turned his back, no doubt trying to hide the tears that had welled up in his eyes. "Just let it go, please."

Ben tipped his head back and closed his eyes. There was no way he could let it go. Tom might not be able to see it now, but if he let Cronkite win, what was stopping him from doing this to someone else? Cronkite had looked down his arrogant nose at Ben, thought himself better than Tom, and he'd destroyed a good man, stole his life, and worse, his son. No, he couldn't let it go. However, he would for the moment.

"Alright," he offered as he stepped up behind Tom and wrapped his arms around Tom's waist. "I'll let it go for now. You need some sleep."

Tom leaned his head back on Ben's shoulder. "I can't remember the last time I actually slept," he laughed, the sound bitter and full of sadness.

"I'll make sure you get some." He kissed Tom's temple and nuzzled the side of his face briefly. "C'mon."

He released Tom long enough to grab his gun from the table, then led him inside and into the bedroom. Ben set his gun on the bedside table and turned, silently helping Tom out of his pants and into bed. He quickly shucked his own pants and slid into the bed next to Tom, pulling the covers up over them. Ben encouraged Tom to lay his head on Ben's chest.

"I can't imagine what you must have gone through, but I'm glad you're here now," Ben murmured softly and kissed the top of Tom's head as he wrapped him in a tight embrace.

"I don't…." Tom let out a heavy huff of breath, then was quiet for a long time. Ben thought he'd fallen asleep when Tom murmured, "I'm glad I'm here now too."

Ben smiled as he held Tom, listening as his breath took on a slow, even rhythm. Eventually he began to make small snoring sounds. Ben was beyond thankful to have the man back who'd consumed so much of his heart and mind since meeting him. He had begun to think he'd never get to experience Tom's touch again. However, as thankful as he was, and regardless of what he told Tom, Ben would make Cronkite pay.

He lay in bed as long as he could, watching over Tom as he slept. Regretfully, he slipped from the bed, careful not to wake the sleeping man. He left his gun on the table where Tom could reach it if he needed it and made his way out to the main room.

After dressing and donning his boots, Ben grabbed his shotgun from where it hung over the fireplace and headed out to care for the critters. As usual, Tom was never far from his thoughts as he started on his morning chores, but Cronkite was nestled there as well. His mind plotted and planned while he worked.

Chapter 25

BEN CUT the engine and slumped down in the seat, hiding behind his dark shades as he waited for his prey to make a move. He'd been following Cronkite for three days, waiting and watching for his opportunity to strike. He was running out of time, the lie he'd told Tom only afforded him two more days. Tom expected him back from the "cattle auction" on Friday.

Today was the first day the arrogant bastard had deviated from his routine. Normally he left for work at eight in the morning, spent his entire day inside the sheriff's office, then drove his squad car home where he stayed until he left for work the next morning. Ben hoped he'd finally get his chance today, as Cronkite had elected to take a dark sedan rather than the cruiser and had left the office in a pair of dark slacks and tan shirt rather than his uniform.

Ben's interest piqued all the more when Cronkite stepped out of his car with the collar of his shirt up and his dark fedora pulled down low over his eyes. Ben slumped down farther in his seat as Cronkite looked back and forth down the street before hunching his shoulders and trotting across the road and up the steps of an old Victorian at the end of the block. Without knocking, Cronkite pushed the door open and disappeared inside.

"Well, that wasn't suspicious as hell." Ben smirked as he sat up and pushed his shades up on his head.

Ben scanned the neighborhood. It was quiet, with turn-of-the-century homes and well-manicured lawns. He'd almost bet Cronkite had been visiting an elderly family member, perhaps his mother, except his strange behavior just didn't fit. Ben waited a few more minutes before lowering his sunglasses, grabbing his old Stetson, and setting it low on his head. He stepped out of the car and, acting much as Cronkite had, checked his surroundings before heading to the house. The only difference was that Ben walked with slow, measured steps, as if he belonged there, and didn't try to conceal his face. With his longish beard and hat, he doubted anyone would recognize him even if old wanted posters still existed. He looked nothing as he once had, his scar camouflaged by facial hair. A car pulled up in front of the house opposite Cronkite's car. Ben slowed his steps further still, suddenly interested in the wrought iron work of the fence two houses down from his target. Out of the corner of his eye, Ben watched as two young men, smartly dressed, stepped out of the car, laughing and joking as they made their way up the steps and entered the Victorian house without knocking.

"What the hell is that place?" Ben wondered under his breath.

Another young man came out seconds later, tucking in his shirt, and Ben had his first clue. Was it possible the upstanding Sheriff Cronkite was visiting a house of ill repute? Ben had seen Cronkite's wife while staking out their home, and he wouldn't blame the bastard for straying. Then again, that probably wasn't fair since Ben couldn't imagine being with any woman.

Figuring enough time had passed since Cronkite had entered, Ben made his way up the steps and strained to look in through the windows discreetly. Unfortunately, they were blocked with heavy window coverings.

"Now or never," he muttered under his breath and pushed open the door.

The two young men he'd spotted going in were standing near what appeared to be a hotel desk. A man dressed in a fashionable jacket and bow tie was smiling and chatting with them. Then he reached back, grabbed two keys from the wall, and handed them to the men.

In the parlor to his right, Ben got his next clue as to the nature of the home, and he had to bite down on his tongue to keep from laughing out loud. *Well, I'll be a monkey's uncle. You sly dog, you.* Ben shook his head and stepped up to the desk as the two men headed up the stairs.

"Good afternoon, sir," the clerk greeted with a wary smile.

Ben removed his glasses and slid them into his shirt pocket, then removed his hat. "Afternoon, my good man," Ben said cheerfully. "May I inquire as to whether you're the owner of this fine establishment?"

"Who wants to know?" the young man asked, his tone hesitant and suspicion in his bright blue eyes.

"A friend of mine—" He pretended to check to make sure no one was within earshot, then leaned in a little closer to the clerk. "—a Mr. Cronkite said I would enjoy very much my time here. After witnessing the beautiful creatures in the parlor, I'd have to say he was quite right."

The man's lips curled into a smug grin. "I do pride myself on having the best. I'm Ian, and you are?"

"Name's Ben," he said and held out his hand.

Ian shook the offered hand, his smile growing. "And what can I do for you this fine day, Ben?"

"Mind if we discuss this in your office? What I'm in the mood for is a little, shall we say, unique."

Ian held Ben's gaze for a moment, his eyes hard and his expression one Ben would describe as disgust, which made no sense at all. Still, Ben did his best to keep his smile easy and not to shift nervously, although it was difficult with the way his heart raced with excitement. He must have done better than he thought, because Ian nodded.

"Johnny, can you cover the desk for a moment?" Ian called out.

A young man dressed in a suit similar to Ian's popped out of the parlor with a wide smile. "Sure, boss."

"Right this way," Ian said coldly and held out his arm.

Ben winked at Johnny in passing and stepped past the counter. Then he followed Ian down the hall.

ONCE IAN learned who Ben really was and the nature of his visit, Ian's demeanor changed from cold to cheerful, and he turned out to be quite a wealth of information as to the comings and goings of Sheriff Cronkite. Ian, as it turned out, had quite a wicked side and had laughed quite evilly as Ben had given Ian a quick rundown of events. Ian had little love for the man or his practices and agreed to allow Ben to carry out his plan as long as Ben agreed to tell him all the sordid details later, to which Ben readily agreed.

"First things first," Ben mumbled under his breath and placed his ear to the door.

At first Ben didn't hear anything, the room eerily silent, but then there was a small noise that sounded suspiciously like a grunt. Ben pulled his gun from his waistband as he strained to listen.

Another grunt followed by Cronkite's muffled voice. *"That's it, suck it, you nasty little cocksucker."* Ben stepped back with a wicked grin. With his gun at his side and as quietly as possible, Ben slid the key Ian had given him into the lock and turned it. He heard the distinct sound of the mechanism disengaging and, with one deep breath, opened the door and rushed into the room, gun drawn.

Cronkite was sitting in the middle of the room in a straight-back chair facing the door, pants around his ankles and hands fisted in a young man's blond hair. His eyes widened in shock, then narrowed as they settled on the gun. He shoved the young man on his knees away.

"Hands over your head. You so much as flinch and I'll turn you from a boar to a sow with the first shot," Ben warned, gun trained on Cronkite's spit-slick cock.

Cronkite raised his hands slowly. "You are making a very big mistake, you little piece of shit," he spat.

Without taking his gaze from Cronkite, Ben said, "Alvin, Ian would like to see you in his office."

"Yes, sir," Alvin squeaked and scrambled to his feet.

"And shut the door on your way out," Ben instructed the young man.

"Ye-yes, sir," Alvin sputtered as he did as he was told.

Once the door clicked shut, Ben took a step toward Cronkite and smiled. "Well, well, well, Sheriff. It appears I've caught you with your pants down." Ben chuckled.

Cronkite started to reach for his pants. "Ah, ah, ah," Ben said warningly and pulled the hammer back. "I suggest you keep your hands right where they are. In fact, I must insist you lock your fingers behind your head."

When Cronkite didn't move, Ben smirked and trained his gun on the space directly between the man's eyes. Cronkite wasn't a complete idiot; he moved his hands slowly and laced them behind his head as he'd been instructed.

"What the fuck do you want?" Cronkite snarled, but the look in his eyes betrayed his angry tone. He was scared. The thought made Ben's smile grow.

"Well now, you see. Originally I had planned to come and have a little chitchat with you about the way you treated Officer Webber. Put a little hurting on your arrogant ass and make sure you never even so much as uttered his good name again. But now…."

Ben tilted his head and studied the man before him. Cronkite's face was bright red and beads of sweat covered his forehead and rolled down his temples. His mouth was twisted in an ugly sneer, but oh, the sweet look of terror in Cronkite's eyes made Ben nearly giddy with pleasure. He forced himself to rein in the good feelings and focus on the real reason he was here.

"Just fucking tell me already. Now what?" Cronkite barked.

"You're not really in much of a position to be making demands."

Ben inched around the sheriff and with his free hand pulled the cuffs from his pocket. He slapped one cuff on Cronkite's right wrist and locked it in place. Ben wasn't stupid enough to lower his weapon, nor did he trust the bastard to unlace his fingers when he was this close. He was prepared. He pulled a second set of cuffs out and attached one to Cronkite's left wrist, then connected the two sets of cuffs together.

"Now, keeping your fingers locked, stand up."

Cronkite didn't move. The stupid bastard was no doubt testing him. Ben grabbed the joined cuffs in one hand, twisting them as he pressed the barrel of the gun against Cronkite's temple.

Ben leaned in closer. "I can always take the easy way out and put a fucking bullet in your brain and feed your guts to the buzzards. Now either stand up or say your fucking prayers. It's the last decision I'll allow you to make today."

Cronkite rose slowly. Ben didn't release the hold he had on the cuffs, but he eased the gun around to the back of the man's head. "Wise choice," Ben grunted. "Now taking it real slow like, move on over to the bed."

This time Cronkite didn't hesitate. He shuffled to the bed and stopped next to it. Ben released his hold on him and took a full step back.

"Sit," he commanded. Once Cronkite complied, Ben added, "Keeping your hands where they are, I'm going to need to you scooch on up in that bed and lay in the center of it on your back."

It took him a minute, hindered by the cuffs on his wrists and the pants bunched around his ankles, but once Cronkite was in the desired position, Ben rolled his neck and relaxed a little. However, he didn't ease off on the hold he had on the weapon.

Ben scooted the chair Cronkite had been in until it was facing the bed, and sat down. He had to give the sheriff credit: he didn't ask any questions or plead for his life. He no doubt realized it wouldn't do any good.

"I've come across a lot of assholes in my time," Ben drawled. "But I gotta say you take the cake. You go after a man, turn his town against him, cause him to lose his job, his home, his family, and his friends all because you find out he's had a relationship with another man." Ben shook his head and scrunched his face up in disgust. "And you, you nasty fat fuck, come in here once a week demanding the owner supply you with the youngest men he can find. And yet, men like me and Tom disgust you?" Ben said in disbelief.

"I'm nothing like you two nasty faggots," Cronkite growled. "I don't allow thieves and murderers to go free so I can fuck them."

"You're right about one thing, you're nothing like Tom and I," Ben said with a sneer. "You're a bully, a bigoted asshole, and worse, you're a sick bastard who gets his jollies fucking young boys. And I'm goddamn proud to be a *disgusting faggot*, as you so eloquently put it. Unlike you, my relationships are between two consenting adults. I don't intimidate, strong-arm, or threaten." Ben leaned in closer, stabbing the gun at Cronkite as Ben's rage burned bright, his voice dropping dangerously low. "You're a disgusting pedophile who should be castrated for the good of the world."

Cronkite stared at him with wide eyes, and for the first time, the arrogant expression on his face drained away right along with all his color. Ben shook with the restraint it took not to shoot the man where he lay. He moved his finger from where it ghosted near the trigger as he took in harsh breaths in an attempt to calm himself. Christ, he wanted to put a bullet in the man's head, protect the world from the filth lying before him, but he didn't dare, reminding himself death was too easy for this bastard.

Cronkite seemed to get control of himself, and although he was breathing heavy and visibly shaking, the contemptuous expression returned. "You obviously don't have the balls to shoot me or you would have already. What do you want? Money?"

There was a knock at the door followed by a meek voice calling out, "Mr. Parker, it's Jeffrey. Ian sent me."

Cronkite jerked his gaze to the door, but Ben didn't look away from him. "Come in." The lock clicked and the door squeaked opened. "Please lock the door behind you."

"Yes, sir."

"What the fuck are you looking at, boy?" Cronkite growled.

Ben leaped from his chair and, in a heartbeat, had flipped the gun in his hand and slammed the butt of it against Cronkite's head.

Before the sheriff could respond, Ben pressed down on Cronkite's throat with his other hand. "I don't think you understand the gravity o your situation. Today is the day you change your nasty ways, and tha includes learning to treat your betters with respect," Ben informed him with deadly seriousness.

Stunned, with blood seeping from his hairline, Cronkite began to struggle weakly, his eyes bulging, but Ben pushed down harder on his throat, not only robbing him of breath but effectively pinning his bound hands beneath him. *So easy.* Ben's fingers curled, his nails digging into delicate flesh. So easy to rid the world of this parasite, eradicate any threat to himself and Tom. Justice for the victims.

Just let it go, please.

The sound of Tom's pleading voice in Ben's head caused him to ease his grip. Cronkite began coughing, trying to take in air as Ben eased back and stood at the side of the bed staring down at him. He felt nothing for the man as he struggled to get air into his oxygen-deprived lungs. Bu Tom's voice, the goodness in him, and the desire Ben had to be a better man for him were enough to bring Ben back from the edge, although his soul still screamed for vengeance.

Ben glanced at Jeffrey, who was standing, staring wide-eyed at the scene before him, his lean limbs visibly trembling.

"It's okay, Jeffrey," Ben said soothingly. "Did you bring what asked for?"

"Yes, sir," Jeffrey murmured without taking his gaze from Cronkite He held up the camera.

Ben took it and studied it briefly, then realized his dilemma. He wouldn't be able to protect Jeffrey sufficiently while taking the picture "Jeffrey, could you please ask Alvin to come back up and join us?"

"Yes, sir. Right away, sir."

"Kind of fitting, wouldn't you say?" Ben asked as he held the camera up.

Cronkite grunted and turned his head toward the wall. Ben laughed heartily.

It only took a moment before Jeffrey ran back into the room with Alvin in tow. Jeffrey shut and locked the door behind them. "Jeffrey, I'm assuming Ian explained what was required of you," Ben inquired as he stepped up to the end of the bed.

"Yes, sir."

"And are you okay with it?"

Jeffrey stared at Cronkite, his expression no longer one of fear and horror but one of contempt. "Yes, sir. I'm going to enjoy making him pay for what he's done," Jeffrey said accusingly.

Ben didn't ask him to explain. Considering Cronkite's history with the younger men, Ben was inclined to think Jeffrey was one of Cronkite's victims. *Sweet vengeance.*

Ben checked the camera and held it out to Alvin. "You know how to use one of these?"

"Yes, sir."

It took some... *persuasion*, but Cronkite finally took to his new role as model and provided Ben with some scandalous photos for his portfolio. His humiliation was complete, as evidenced by the cum drying on his belly.

Alvin seemed to relish his role behind the lens, snickering and giggling, and he clicked away. However, Jeffrey was the true star. Had it been asked of Ben, there would have been no way he'd have been able to touch the disgusting piece of shit, let alone pretend he was enjoying himself.

"Will that be all, sir?" Jeffrey asked as he tucked the money he'd taken from Cronkite's pocket into his own and buttoned up his shirt.

"You've more than earned your money." Ben smirked. "You really should pursue a career in theater."

"Broadway or bust, baby." Jeffrey chuckled. His demeanor turned serious, and he glanced over at Cronkite, who was completely subdued, his head turned away toward the far wall. "Thank you," Jeffrey said sincerely as he met Ben's gaze.

Ben clenched his jaw and gave a curt nod as emotion welled up in him.

Camera tucked safely away in his pocket, Ben waited for the younger men to leave before he addressed Cronkite. "Get up."

The sheriff complied immediately. Gone was the arrogant bully, and in his place stood a limp-dicked, browbeaten man. He grimaced and groaned pitifully when Ben had him lower his hands, but still Ben couldn't muster up the least bit of pity for him. Cronkite was sorry all right, appearing regretful, but Ben knew his type well. Men like Cronkite were incapable of remorse for their victims. He was only sorry he got caught.

Ben removed one handcuff, returning it to his pocket, and ordered Cronkite to dress. Once he had his shoes on, he stood as Ben instructed, and muttered under his breath, "This means war."

Ben highly doubted Cronkite intended him to hear it, but he had, and he wrenched the bastard's arm up his back, causing him to cry out, then shoved his head down on the small table.

Ben leaned down over the man, his mouth a hairsbreadth from Cronkite's ear. "Let me tell you something about war. I was given a gun and dropped right down into the middle of one. I was ordered to kill men, hundreds of men, and do you know what I discovered?" When Cronkite didn't move or say a word, Ben lowered his voice to a deadly whisper. "I fucking liked the way it tastes." He licked Cronkite's ear to make his point and manhandled him back to his feet. "Now let's go."

Keeping one hand on the cuff and the other discreetly gripping his gun, Ben led Cronkite out to his car. Once the bastard slid into the driver's seat, Ben attached the cuff to the steering wheel.

He laid his arm over the open door and leaned down till he was eye level with Cronkite. "You will continue to protect this place as if your life depends on it, because it does. You will never again torment one of these young men or any other, because I will fucking know and I'll hunt you down. And you will never, ever, so much as utter Tom's name again."

Ben righted himself and brushed the front of his jacket. "Now you have a nice afternoon, Sheriff," he drawled coolly. "Give my regards to your daughter and tell her I truly enjoyed our visit."

From the wide eyes and even paler skin, Cronkite wasn't as stupid as he looked, interpreting Ben's message easily. *Fuck with me or what's mine, and I will return the favor tenfold.* Ben smiled a satisfied grin and waved as Cronkite pulled away from the curb. He patted his pocket and chuckled as he bounded up the stairs of the old Victorian. He had a promise to keep to Ian and he'd have a little conversation with the gentlemen in the parlor to ensure the promise he made Cronkite was kept. Most satisfying was the fact that he was sure neither he nor Tom would ever be bothered by the likes of Sheriff Cronkite again.

Chapter 26

TOM LOOKED up from where he was sitting on the porch to see Ben's car coming down the drive. As soon as Ben stepped out of the car and shouldered his bag, Tom called out, "How was the auction?"

"It was promising. Didn't buy anything, but I made some great contacts. There's another one in Trident weekend after next. Maybe you and I can go together."

"What about the critters?" Tom asked.

"It's only a half-day's drive. We could go after the chores are done and be back by dinner time." Ben dropped his bag near the door, a broad smile lighting up his handsome face as he made his way over to Tom.

Tom couldn't help but smile back as his pulse sped up. Fuck, he'd missed his man. *His man.* Damn, he liked the way that sounded. "I think that sounds fun."

"You think so, huh," Ben murmured as he leaned down and brushed his lips against Tom's. "Want to know what I think sounds like more fun?"

Tom nipped at Ben's bottom lip, then swiped his tongue along it. "Do tell," he responded huskily as his arousal began to ignite.

"Taking you inside and showing you how much I missed you," Ben whispered against Tom's lips. Then he kissed him breathless.

Tom threaded his fingers in Ben's hair, moaning as Ben explored his mouth with tongue, lips, and teeth. Without breaking the kiss, Ben grabbed Tom's hands and encouraged him to stand. He slid his arms around Tom, holding him close as the kiss went on and on. Tom began to chuckle as they stumbled blindly toward the door, Ben nearly landing on his ass when he tripped over his bag.

"This isn't working quite the way I planned," Ben snorted.

"You've been planning this?"

"Since the minute I left. After you," Ben said regally and bowed as he held the door open.

"Don't you want a report of the goings-on since you left?"

"We obviously have a house. Do we have critters?"

Tom nodded, smiling broadly.

"Any immediate dangers I should be concerned about?" Ben inquired as he stalked Tom.

"Nope."

"Then everything else can wait." He rushed at Tom and started pawing at his clothes.

"Well, isn't this déjà vu? No immediate dangers and all you want to do is fuck." Tom laughed. "Works for me."

He slapped Ben's hands away before he could rip his shirt to shreds and pulled it off himself, tossing it haphazardly to the floor as he walked backward toward the bed.

"Don't wanna fuck," Ben murmured as he removed his shirt and bent to pull of his boots.

"No?" Tom removed his own boots, then shoved his pants down and off.

Ben looked up, the boot falling from his hand with a loud thud as his gaze settled on Tom's groin. "Well, maybe later." He smirked.

Tom's hard cock twitched and his pulse sped up as he took in Ben's magnificent body, all hard planes and firm muscle. Tom's body sure as hell didn't want to wait till later. Every last inch of him was beyond ready and was screaming now, now, now.

He cocked his head and met Ben's gaze as he continued to stand there staring at Tom with dark eyes. "Later?"

Ben slid an arm around Tom's waist and pressed a gentle kiss to his lips. "Yeah, later," he replied and eased Tom down onto the bed. He covered Tom's body with his own, propping himself up on his elbows. He placed soft kisses over Tom's face. "I've been thinking about you a lot. In fact the whole time I was gone, you were on my mind."

"Yeah," Tom murmured, chasing those soft lips. He ran his hands down Ben's back and over his ass. "And what were you thinking?"

"I was thinking, I've essentially been alone most of my adult life. I don't want to be alone anymore, Tom."

"Me neither." Tom shifted a bit, rocking his hips a little and enjoying the friction of their bodies.

Ben situated himself between Tom's legs, spreading Tom's knees wider apart so he could kneel between them. "I'm glad you're here." He started kissing his way down Tom's chest, stopping to give each nipple a little attention.

"I'm glad I'm here too," Tom moaned as Ben teased the hard nubs with sharp teeth, easing the sting with a nimble tongue.

Ben moved down farther still, brushing his lips across the flesh of Tom's belly. Ben ran his hands up and down Tom's sides as he rubbed his cheek and chin over Tom's heart, tickling him with the soft beard.

"Hey, that tickles," he chuckled and tried to squirm away.

Tom expected Ben to keep tormenting him or keep moving down Tom's body. Ben was an aggressive lover. They both liked sex that was rough and dirty, and if they both had a few aches and pains and sported a few bruises, they considered it successful. What Ben actually did shocked him and caused his breath to hitch.

Ben pressed his lips over Tom's heart and whispered, "I love you." Ben lifted his head, his eyes shining and an expression on his face Tom had never seen before. Ben took a shuddering breath and kissed Tom's chin, then his lips. "I've never said that to another human being. I thought for a long time I never would, that I would live and die a lonely old man. But—" Ben took another shuddering breath and brushed his lips against Tom's. "—I love you and I want you and me to spend the rest of our lives right here on this little patch of land. Just us. There is nothing I wouldn't do for you. Nothing I wouldn't give to make you happy."

Tom had heard those three words countless times in his life, but never had they rocked him so hard. He'd never been one for sentiments or crazy notions of love and romance, so Tom was stunned to find his heart skipping a beat and tears burning at the back of his eyes. The feeling was so foreign and unexpected he had no idea how to respond around the lump in his throat. *He loves me?* Tom was struggling to wrap his mind around the notion, but he did like the way warmth was spreading through him, the way his stomach was fluttering. He especially liked the way a strange feeling he could only describe as rightness seemed to settle into his soul.

Tom stared unblinking at Ben. *He loves me.*

"Well, that's not quite the response I was hoping for." Ben chuckled nervously. "You look downright sick."

"I…." Tom swallowed hard and reached up and cupped the side o Ben's face, loving the way Ben pushed into his touch. "You love me?"

Ben looked a little anxious, but he nodded. "Yeah, I do, and I don' expect you to say—"

"I don't think I've ever heard anything more beautiful in all my life," Tom interrupted. He slid his hand back to grasp the back of Ben's neck and held him close, their lips touching. "Say it again."

"I love you," he whispered.

"I love you too," Tom whispered just before he took Ben's mouth ir a deep kiss. "Fuck, you make me happy," he growled and tightened his grip, curling his fingers in Ben's hair.

"Say it again," he demanded and kissed Ben again.

"I love you," he said again, or at least Tom was pretty sure that' what he was trying to say as Tom shoved his tongue deep and kissed the man breathless.

"Now that that's settled, can we fuck?" Tom growled and thrust his hips.

Ben held his gaze for a long, drawn-out moment, breathing heavily Ben's lip curled a second before he clutched Tom's shoulder hard and rolled them. "No, but you can show me how much you love me," he said with a smirk.

"That I can do," Tom assured him. He kissed his way along Ben's jaw, sucking briefly on the sensitive skin below his ear and smiling agains the side of Ben's neck as he shivered. "You taste good," Tom murmured as he licked and nipped his way down to Ben's shoulder, worrying the thick muscle with his teeth and lips until Ben cried out and bucked "Wanna taste every inch of you."

"God, yes," Ben moaned when Tom took his right nipple into his mouth, teasing it until it was erect, then giving the other the same treatment.

Tom moved down Ben's body, licking, kissing, and tasting every inch of delectable flesh as he'd promised. As he bathed Ben's balls and the sensitive skin on the inside of his legs with his tongue, Tom's cock throbbed, but he ignored his own need, instead concentrating on Ben's pleasure. He took his time, moving from one patch of skin to the next ir no particular order and in no particular hurry. When he finally settled down on Ben's cock, he was hungry and he devoured Ben single-mindedly, his fingers tight around the base of Ben's cock.

"Oh… oh, damn," Ben gasped. His grabbed the headboard and thrus his hips up.

Tom hummed his response, the vibration causing Ben to gasp again. Tom dragged his tongue over the soft skin, swirled it over the head of his dick.

"Damn," Ben panted. He planted his feet on the bed and let his legs splay open, offering himself to Tom wantonly.

Tom released Ben's cock, swiped his tongue down the shaft, and bathed his balls before pushing himself flat and ducking his head lower. He spread Ben's ass even wider and teased around Ben's hole with the tip of his tongue.

"Jesus! Where the hell did you learn to do that?"

Tom looked up and grinned wickedly. "I told you I was going to taste every last inch of you."

Ben licked his lips and released his hold on the headboard. He grabbed his legs behind his knees and pulled them back. "Well, then, by all means," he chuckled and shook his ass.

Tom accepted the invitation but, instead of teasing Ben's hole, went instantly to full-on fucking it. He rubbed along the sides, pressing a finger in, stretching him.

Ben cried out as a violent shudder went through him. He arched his back off the bed and panted harshly. Tom knew Ben wouldn't be able to hold back much longer, but it was too soon for it to end. Tom pushed up to his knees and scrambled for the drawer, nearly pulling it from its casing in his haste.

"God, Tom, hurry. Please," Ben begged as he lowered his legs and grabbed the headboard once again.

Tom pulled out the oil they kept there and poured some on his palm. He ran his slick hand along his cock as he moved back into place between Ben's knees. "Guess I'll have to taste the rest of you later," he uttered as he guided his cock to Ben's opening.

Ben mumbled something quietly that Tom couldn't make out as he pressed gingerly against his hole. Then inch by agonizing inch, Tom pushed into him past the tight muscles until he was balls deep. Ben's ass spasmed around Tom's cock as his body adjusted to the invasion.

The room was silent except for their rapid breaths and the rush of blood in Tom's ears as his pulse raced. In that moment, deep inside Ben with their lips pressed together, everything changed. The last piece of the puzzle settled into place, and Tom felt whole. It was no longer about racing to the end, reaching orgasm, or satisfying anything as basic as a physical need, an itch. It was deeper. The true measure was beyond his grasp, yet wholly simple. "I love you," he whispered again.

"Love you too."

Tom stared into Ben's eyes, seeing the truth in them, and began to move. They touched and kissed and rocked at a leisurely pace, exploring each other, learning each other, loving each other. Tom wanted to shout his joy at the top of his lungs, and yet the feeling was so consuming, he wanted to weep. The two conflicting emotions made him feel intoxicated. It was something he could easily become addicted to.

No matter how Tom wished it could last forever, it couldn't. The demands of his body began to overpower those of his heart, and he began to move faster, rolling his hips.

Ben moved with him in perfect sync, licking and lapping at Tom's mouth. "Ah… damn, you feel so good," he moaned between hard, biting kisses. "C'mon, baby, fuck me."

Tom trembled with the effort it took to hold back, but Ben's pleas shredded his hold. Tom pulled back till just the head of his cock was breaching Ben, then thrust in hard and deep.

"Fuck yeah, again," Ben growled.

The soft, sweet lovemaking was over, and Tom slammed into Ben over and over and over again. Tom groaned deep in his chest, the sound a deep rumble that rolled through him. His cock throbbed and twitched within Ben, aching.

"Yes! Fuck me harder," Ben urged, wrapping his legs around Tom's waist and locking his ankles.

Ben grunted with each thrust. It was a damn good thing Ben was holding on to the headboard, or Tom might well have fucked him through the wall. He grasped Ben's thighs, pushing them up and out, using them as leverage as he slammed into Ben's heat with brutal force. Still Ben begged for more.

"Oh God," Tom groaned, his movements becoming erratic. "Close. God, so close."

"Do it," Ben said, his voice husky, and clenched around him. "Make me come."

Tom growled, the sound turning into a roar as he slammed into Ben again, passion and love overtaking him and rushing him to climax. He couldn't even speak as he came, the roar filling the room, growing in intensity as Ben's shouts mingled with Tom's, echoing off the walls. The silence that fell as his dick twitched and throbbed in Ben's ass was ringing and sustained, broken only by their panting breaths and whispered "I love yous." Tom released Ben's legs, shifted to the side, then collapsed, melting into the mattress, his face against Ben's sweaty, rapidly rising and falling chest. Tom savored the moment, content as he listened to Ben's heart beneath his ear.

Epilogue

THE MARE danced sideways and threw her head as Tom slid the saddle from her back. "Whoa, girl," Tom murmured softly and patted the horse's neck. He hung the saddle on the stall and grabbed an apple from the barrel.

"Here ya go, Mabel. Now don't you go—" Tom wrinkled his nose and shook the slobber from his hand. "You're lucky you ride well, or I'd turn you into glue."

He wiped his hand on his thigh and grabbed a brush from the tack box. Steam rose from the mare's heated flesh as he ran the brush over her sweat-dampened coat. Content, he began humming a tune.

He loved the isolation of the farm, especially in the winter, but Christ, did it have to be so damn cold? He pulled his gloves from his pocket, slipped them on, then returned to brushing down the mare.

He'd spent the morning wearing the poor horse out chasing after cows who'd decided the grass must be greener on the other side of the fence and crashed through it. Stupid critters found the snow just as deep and the ground just as frozen on the other side. They probably did it simply to irritate him.

"What do you think, Mabel? Those damn cows bust my fence just to piss me off?"

"I thought that was my job."

Tom looked over to find Ben leaning against the stall with a slight grin and two steaming mugs. "Figures you'd be influencing those damn cows." He chuckled and set the brush aside.

"You know," Ben said slyly as he handed Tom his coffee, "people're gonna start thinking you're crazy if you keep talking to the animals."

"You hear that, Mabel? Ol' Ben here thinks I'm crazy for talking to you."

Mabel stomped her foot and whinnied like she understood him, causing Tom to chuckle.

"I rest my case. Even the old hag thinks you're crazy," Ben snickered. "Put your friend in her stall and let's go in. Breakfast is just about ready."

"Give me five," Tom said and took a large gulp of his coffee, moaning as the warm liquid heated him within. He took another one.

Tom set his coffee mug down and finished brushing down the mare, then gave her hooves a quick cleaning. He could feel Ben's eyes on him the entire time. The thought of Ben watching him heated Tom better than any pair of gloves or warm cup of coffee. Even after more than a year together, Ben never failed to get Tom's engines roaring. He couldn't get enough of the man, doubted he ever would. After all, he had a lifetime of bitter denial to make up for.

Mabel happily followed Tom and the bucket of oats into the stall. He patted her one last time and closed the stall door. He retrieved his cup of coffee, wrinkled his nose at the cool temperature, and poured it out.

"I hope you got more coffee in there too," Tom said as he stepped up next to Ben and bumped shoulders.

Ben wrapped his arm around Tom's waist and led him out of the barn. "I got anything you want," he said wryly.

"Anything?" Tom asked with one brow arched.

"Anything," Ben responded without hesitation.

"Well, then, I'll be having me a big heap of you for breakfast," Tom said huskily and waggled his brows.

"You may need a few more calories than I can provide." Ben chuckled.

Tom curled his fingers into Ben's hip and pulled him closer, nearly making him fall over. "You can feed me after you feed me."

Ben cocked his head and blinked at Tom. "You make absolutely no sense. You do realize that, don't you?"

"Sure I do. A little calorie-free protein to help stimulate my appetite, then I'll be as ravenous for your biscuits and gravy as I am for you. See? Plenty of calories to be had."

Ben shook his head. The sound of Ben's laughter caused a large smile to spread across Tom's face. Damn, he couldn't remember ever being as happy as he'd been since coming here. The worst day here on the ranch was still better than the best day during his previous life. Ben made everything better.

They tromped up the stairs, both laughing like loons as they tried to fit through the door without turning the other loose. Ben finally gave up and shoved Tom through the doorway, but then instantly wrapped his arms around Tom and pulled him close. He took Tom's mouth in a hard kiss, knocking his hat from his head.

"So, you wanting a little lovin'?" Ben growled into the kiss.

Tom hissed when Ben bit his bottom lip, but the sound turned into a husky moan as Ben sucked on the abused flesh. "Yeah, I do," Tom murmured around kisses and nips. "Need a shower first."

Ben brushed his lips along Tom's cheek, then licked up the side of Tom's neck to just below his ear, causing him to shudder. "Nope, want you just like this." Ben ground his groin against Tom's. "Like it when you smell like sweat, horses, sunshine, ranch, and—" He ran his tongue back down Tom's neck. "—man."

Tom grabbed Ben's hips, rolling their groins together, the friction delicious against his hard cock. "You can have all the man you want."

Ben ran his tongue around the shell of Tom's ear, causing him to shudder again. "You're the only man I want. Only man I need."

Tom's chest tightened, and his eyes fluttered closed. Damn, he didn't know what he'd done right, but it must have been something pretty fucking spectacular to deserve someone like Ben. Every day Tom spent with him was better than the last. Sure they had their bumps, the occasional disagreement, but the majority of their time was spent laughing and loving. Just the two of them and the critters, and that was exactly the way Tom wanted it. Hell, if he never had to see another human being again, he'd be just fine with that.

Ben shoved Tom's heavy barn coat off his shoulders, and it made a thud against the hardwood floors. Ben then reached for the button on Tom's pants. A loud crash caused them both to jump.

"What the hell!" Ben growled.

Prissy, their old mama cat, screamed and rushed out of the room in a blur of white, brown, and black fur. The glass pitcher was shattered into a hundred little pieces; milk covered the floor and cabinets.

"Goddamn feline," Ben cursed and stomped over to the sink. "Leave it to the pussy to interrupt my good time."

Tom laughed and snatched a towel from a hook. "I told you to keep that damn thing in the barn," he chastised lightly and started sopping up the spilled milk while Ben carefully picked up the shards of glass.

"I keep putting her out, but she keeps finding her way back in," Ben grumbled.

"Yeah, through your big ol' softy heart."

Ben glared at him for a moment, then rolled his eyes. "She just had babies," he muttered.

"Uh-huh."

The kittens were now six months old and running after mice in the barn. Prissy hadn't joined them; rather, she had become a permanent fixture in their small house, curling up to Ben on the couch after each workday and at his feet each night in the bed. Ben tried to act like a hardass, but beneath the gruff exterior was a heart of pure gold. A heart that belonged solely to Tom... and Prissy, not to mention the rest of the critters and the land. Tom smiled and pressed a kiss to Ben's cheek before taking the wet towel to the sink to wring it out.

"What was that for?"

"For being you," Tom replied with a wink.

Ben didn't respond, but the big grin on his face and the pink in his cheeks caused Tom's smile to grow.

The hot and heavy passion that had been sparking between them cooled just a bit as they cleaned up the mess the cat had made. Tom was pretty used to his hard-on rubbing in his trousers, Ben taking every chance, day and night, to get him going. Hell, it rarely took more than a look from the sexy fucker and Tom was popping wood. He kind of liked the feel of wanting, the anticipation.

"So where were we?" Ben murmured, his tone husky.

"You were about to feed me," Tom reminded him. His belly growled loudly.

"Oh, right." Ben laughed. He opened the oven and bent down to retrieve a pan of bacon.

Ben's ass was perfectly displayed, and Tom couldn't help but press his cock against the tempting flesh. "Not that kind of food."

"Your belly is sayin' otherwise." Ben wriggled out of Tom's grasp.

"Ignore it," Tom said, stalking after the man. "I am."

Continuing to chuckle, Ben picked up another pan from the counter, spinning out of Tom's reach. "I made your favorite."

Tom got a glimpse of the breakfast pie as Ben set it on the table, and his belly growled again. "Well, maybe just one slice," he said, licking his lips. "You know, to ensure I've got plenty of energy and stamina."

Tom swatted Ben's ass before he could spin away again, and sat down at the table. The dishes, silverware, and glasses of juice were already set out. "Damn, this looks good! Feed me, baby," he said happily and shook out his napkin before stuffing it in the neck of his shirt.

"I take damn good care of my man," Ben said wryly.

"Yes, you do," Tom agreed wholeheartedly.

The aroma of fried bacon, buttered biscuits, and vegetable, ham, and cheese breakfast pie mingled in the air pleasantly. If Tom wasn't careful, he was going to end up as big as a barn; his man was an amazing cook. Tom popped a piece of bacon in his mouth and hummed at the saltiness. He tilted his head and studied Ben as he dished out the pie and smiled while he chewed. He didn't have to worry about gaining too much weight, not with Ben as his dessert.

"So did you find all the missing cows?" Ben asked as he took the seat next to Tom.

"Yup. Stupid critters were standing a hundred yards down waiting for me to open the gate. I only had to chase down two wayward calves and that mean bull. Fence is fixed too."

"Weather is supposed to break a bit tomorrow. We probably should take a ride around the pasture and check the rest of the fence."

"Good idea," Tom said around a big mouthful of pie.

They finished their breakfast, making plans for their ride the next day as well as dreaming and planning for what they wanted to accomplish when spring finally arrived in their little slice of country solitude. The farm took up most of their energy. There was always something needing to be fixed, critters to feed, roofs to patch, wood to cut, and a hundred other little things it took to run a farm. It was both the most exhausting job Tom had ever had as well as the most ewarding. He was actually looking forward to the extra work spring would bring.

Tom was happiest when riding the open fields of alfalfa, especially when the small clusters of small purple flowers were in bloom. Christ, he'd never seen anything so beautiful. The mountains in the backdrop never failed to take his breath away. Planting and caring for their large vegetable garden was another favorite. Ben wasn't keen on the idea; he didn't share Tom's love of hoeing and weeding, but Tom planned to double the size of the garden come spring.

However, no matter how spectacular the landscape, no matter how much he loved using his hands, building, and gardening, none of it could compare to the love he had for Ben. There would always be a hole in his heart, a place only his son, and yes, Marna, could fill, but perhaps one day…. Perhaps in time attitudes would change, and the integrity and generosity of a man's heart would be more important than who he shared that heart with.

It was a dream, just as seeing his son again was. Maybe one day. He could hope—what he couldn't do was dwell on it.

Tom sat back in his chair, groaning happily and patting his belly. "Thank you. That was an amazing breakfast. I'm stuffed."

"Too stuffed for dessert?" Ben asked with a sly grin. He grabbed his empty plate and cup, taking them to the sink.

Tom quickly gathered up his own dirty dishes and followed. "Hell no!" he said adamantly. "I'm never too stuffed for that."

Ben took the dishes from Tom and set them in the sink with the rest. "So where were we before Prissy and your belly so rudely interrupted us?" Ben asked as he curled his fingers in the belt loops of Tom's pants and jerked him closer.

"I think you were saying something about feeding me." Tom cocked his head and met Ben's gaze. "But you know what? I think I may have come up with a better idea."

"Oh, do tell," Ben encouraged, then released his hold on Tom and began to slowly move back.

"Well," Tom murmured, following Ben, Ben countering by taking another step back. "I figure since you stuffed me so well…." Another step.

"Uh-huh," Ben hummed around his grin. Another step back.

"It's my turn to stuff you," he shouted and lunged.

Ben spun out of his reach, laughing as he raced toward the bedroom, Tom right on his heels. Tom laughed too. He knew exactly where Ben was heading and where he'd land. The winds were calm and the sun was high, but the storm that had brought Ben into his life still raged, only now, it spun wildly within them. Their passion was as powerful as any tornado, and their love was strong enough to rival any storm.